Chosen Ones

Chosen Ones

the lost souls
book one

tiffany truitt

Entangled Publishing, LLC
2614 South Timberline Road
Suite 109
Fort Collins, CO 80525
Visit our website at www.entangledpublishing.com.

Edited by Stacy Abrams
Cover design by Heather Howland

Print ISBN   978-1-62061-000-8
ePub ISBN   978-1-62061-001-5

First Edition June 2012

Manufactured in the United States of America

To my nephew:
May you always be brave enough to speak your mind and
reckless enough to love fully.

They taught us all the wrong things growing up.

They didn't teach us what it meant to want.

Or that there was a certain kind of purity in feeling.

They taught us about lust but not love.

About losing power but not gaining it.

They didn't teach us girls what we needed to know.

Instead, they damned us.

Chapter 1

I didn't expect him to be so rough with me. It wasn't what the chosen ones were made for. They were meant to protect and guide us.

My arm throbbed where his hand had latched onto it, dragging me from my hiding place. The thought of being touched by anyone, especially a chosen one, would be enough to make any girl flush with embarrassment, but I only felt confused. It was strange to feel anything at all.

He was good. The chosen one didn't betray the desperate fierceness of his grip to the crowd that had gathered to watch my branding. He remained as we were meant to see him: beautiful salvation. No flaw marred his face. Perfectly symmetrical. He looked human. Only the mismatched colors of his eyes—one green and one blue—signaled his artificial status, despite all the genetic work done to make us feel comforted by his appearance. And he *was* human. He was humanity's only hope for a future.

"You do understand why you're here?" asked the chosen one. I wanted to smirk at the dryness that issued from his voice, but I didn't think it would do me any favors.

Instead, I simply nodded. I wouldn't speak until he forced me.

"Can someone silence him?" the chosen one said. It was the third time he had asked for the sobs coming from Robert to be quieted. The moment the chosen one had brought out the branding iron, Robert had fallen apart. I refused to look at him.

Louisa, my younger sister, moved to him. His sobs ceased for a moment, just long enough to listen to whatever she whispered to him, but he soon started up again. I couldn't help but think of her then—Emma. She was the reason I was being branded.

She had died only hours before, and I could still hear her screams echoing inside the dark place I kept all the other memories.

Anyone else would have run to her, but I wasn't so keen on watching blood ooze from her as that *thing* tried, granted pointlessly, to crawl its way out. I had remained rooted to the lopsided chair in the hallway outside the compound's infirmary.

That broken chair, discarded and forgotten, clung to me as much as I clung to it. The chair was simply another reminder of the state of my people. It still existed, but no one seemed willing to notice it was damaged.

I had known my sister was dying. I would watch her go not in the comfort of a happy home, but in the compound, a place we were forced to live in during the war, when our women's inability to breed started the creation of the chosen ones.

She'd screamed. I could hear it stick in her throat, caught in a mixture of saliva and blood. I didn't know what I was supposed to do. Cry? Run around frantically? Beg God for her deliverance? These were the actions of the girls in the videos we were commanded to watch over and over in the compound—countless examples of weakness. There was nothing to be done. No cure. I couldn't fight this battle for Emma. To feel was beyond dangerous.

I'd glanced down the hallway outside the infirmary and saw them waiting—the crowd. It was small, but I knew every scream, every outcry, every warning that the end was near would bring them closer. They needed to watch her death. They *wanted* to watch. Sometimes I thought the only way we could remind ourselves we were alive was to experience these moments of death.

What happened to Emma was a consequence of her breaking the rules. She'd heard the same lessons I had. She knew them by heart. Emotional entanglements only led to physical trespasses. We, humans, were weak. We couldn't be trusted with our emotions. Unlike many of the naturals, she seemed to understand. But she fell in love. She gave in. When she was with Robert, she was crazed.

I wouldn't be like her. I planned on surviving this place. After she was gone, I would be free of all connections, all parasitic relationships that threatened to make me care in a world where caring about anything was a waste of time. There was still Louisa, but I never knew how to be there for her. Robert would have to pull himself together for both of them.

I couldn't care about anything or anyone.

I'd kicked over the chair before heading inside the infirmary. The outburst was all I would allow myself. Emma had been lying on the cot, soaking herself into the fabric.

Sweat covered every inch of her body, and I noticed her blood seeped beyond the white sheets onto the cement floor. I looked to Robert. Her husband. What fools they had been. Didn't they know this sort of thing was pointless? I couldn't understand why anyone got married anymore. It wasn't commitment. It was murder.

She reached out her hand to me. I hesitated. It would make her feel better, but was this small bit of comfort worth the risk of feeling something?

I glared at the midwife who was vainly trying to keep my sister breathing. I wondered what it would feel like knowing no matter how hard you tried, you would always fail.

Death was expected.

There were no exceptions.

The midwife looked to me and I could read the emotion in her eyes: she was asking my forgiveness. I gritted my teeth and moved my gaze away. Emma had decided some uncomfortable meeting of two bodies in hopes of creating life was more important than her family and her own existence. It wasn't the midwife's fault, but I couldn't give her any comfort.

I knelt down beside my sister, hoping the action would quiet her unnerving, unceasing cries for me. Her bright, feverish eyes bore into mine. "Did she live?"

"She?" I asked skeptically.

Emma repeated her question. Her longing for an answer was evident in her voice.

"No. It didn't live." I knew my words sounded harsh, but what was she expecting to hear?

Her gaze had flickered onto Robert then. She was done with me. She had only needed me for the truth he was too weak to give her.

. . .

"We have brought you together today to witness the branding of natural 258915. Do the naturals accept this transfer?" asked the chosen one. His words jarred me from my thoughts, and I reminded myself that thinking about Emma's death would do me no good. I should remember my new responsibilities. As the oldest female in my family, Emma had been branded and forced to work at Templeton. Now that she could no longer carry out the term of servitude, I would take her place.

The crowd nodded together. They accepted this without question.

"Very well. Natural 258915, do you understand why you are being sentenced to work at Templeton?"

I nodded. I covered my wrist where my identification number could be found. Strangely, my leg twitched. I took a deep breath, steadying myself for what was next. The questions I would answer. The only time I would let them own my voice.

"We do these things to continue the education that can only save your people," the chosen one said. "Why is the female so dangerous?"

I cleared my throat, wishing I didn't have to do it before talking. I wanted to sound strong.

"Natural 258915?"

I blinked. How easy it was to fall away from this place, settle in my own mind.

"The female is dangerous because of her natural tendency to embrace humans' emotional side and her ability to elicit and encourage sexual activity," I responded. "Sex equates full and utter dependence on someone else both physically and emotionally. There is a brutal war going on right outside our home; we can't afford to be distracted."

I was happy with how confident my voice sounded. Sure, it was almost a word-for-word imitation of the videos we were compelled to watch growing up, but I had always excelled at playing the part assigned to me.

"How does the council offer you salvation?"

"The council created the chosen ones. These beings are meant to protect us, created to be superior to naturals in every way. They fight our wars. They offer hope that our species will go on."

"And your payment?" he asked.

"Nothing but our aid in the chosen ones' training center at Templeton. Every family will offer their eldest daughter as servant for a period of three years starting at the age of sixteen. We supply the female because it is her wantonness that has allowed our men to become weak. It is her body that will no longer bear children."

"And what of the women unable to turn from their own feelings of lust? What do we offer them on top of our many gifts?"

"The council will sterilize any woman who chooses to have the procedure done. It's a choice, not a mandate," I answered.

Many women took the council up on the offer. Young girls at the first sign of menstruation would be rushed into surgery. Yet often this sterilization process was seen as a sign of weakness—no one wanted to appear ruled by her own desires.

I knew there was no point in physical relationships at all. I would never be stupid enough to enter into one.

"Do you see, naturals, how we offer you protection?" the chosen one asked the crowd.

Yes.

"What would make someone ignore our warnings? What would cause someone to quicken the end of her people?" he asked me.

At this moment, I looked straight toward Robert. I wanted to watch him as I said these words. "Not all women listen. Some are able to turn a deaf ear to the videos, choosing to ignore the connection between sexuality and betrayal."

Many naturals claimed the council could fix us, rid us of whatever genetic coding caused us to want. Hell, they created life in a lab; surely they could end our suffering. Naturals for years begged the council to rewire us girls. But the council refused to force this on anyone.

The illusion of choice was all-important. Some people just didn't realize that choice doesn't necessarily mean freedom.

"Please, step forward, natural 258915."

I didn't blame the chosen one who would burn the mark into my skin. My eyes didn't waver from Robert's. I hoped he remembered the promise he failed to keep.

This was a small sacrifice to be protected. I would serve my time. I would do my duty.

As I stepped forward, the hair on the back of my neck stood up. Someone else was watching me, as he always watched me. Henry. He was a boy who had once been a childhood friend. Somehow he had turned into a man without my noticing but, then again, it was hard to follow all the changes in a person when that person didn't want anything to do with you. He was no longer my childhood friend; we were no longer children.

I felt my face go red. I could still always find him in a crowd. I was ashamed.

A second chosen one entered to assist in the procedure. I

found myself unable to look on him for long, afraid he would notice the redness of my cheeks. I quickly glanced at his face and saw the most peculiar thing: he had a scar. A chosen one with an imperfection. Right on his chin. Strangely, I wanted to laugh. It was there I stared. Right at that scar as the iron burned the slash mark into the back of my neck.

My skin was enflamed.

It was bliss.

I felt safe.

Chapter 2

I stared at myself in the mirror in the compound's communal bathroom. If I turned my head just the right way, I could see the edge of my bright red scar creeping out from the collar of my shirt. I would be marked forever. There was no erasing the slash mark from my body.

It tingled, like skin after ripping off a bandage. The only difference was this sensation didn't seem to be going away. I thought about the young chosen one who assisted in my branding, about the imperfection that marked his chin. Was his scar like mine? A punishment for something he had no control over? Payment for some act he wished he didn't need to perform?

I wanted to know more about the chosen one. The mark on my neck felt like the final line in some story no one bothered to read. I wasn't the author of my own history. And no one cared how it ended.

I tugged on the sleeves of my uniform. Perfectly fitted white cotton shirt with a ruffled collar. Ankle-length gray skirt that didn't dare show any leg. My hair covered the wound on the back of my head. I looked exactly as if I had been pulled from some nineteenth-century painting of a little servant girl.

The uniform was like a second skin.

Footsteps sounded from the hallway. I left the bathroom to see Robert staring at me. He looked sickly, like any minute he could join Emma in death. This was what love did to you.

He opened his mouth to speak, but I held up my hand to stop him. "Don't bother. I'll be fine," I said.

I didn't wait for a reply. I pushed past him and headed toward whatever future had been decided for me.

The smell hit me first. It was unfamiliar and seemed out of place in the chosen ones' posh training center. It burned my nostrils. I tried to push my nose under the top of my cotton shirt, but still the odor invaded my space.

The light of the room was blinding and so different from the natural light that streamed from the windows of the upper levels of Templeton. Here in the basement, the darkness felt like it was hiding Templeton's secrets. But of course, this place didn't have any secrets to hide.

A continuous beeping noise drew me away from the doorway and deeper into the room. I was not prepared for what I saw.

They were everywhere. Young chosen ones, not older than ten or eleven.

I clutched the bucket my supervisor had given me earlier.

They lay perfectly still in medical beds, tubes protruding from their seemingly innocent-looking shells. I could barely contain the need to touch one. They couldn't speak, couldn't move, and despite their eyes being open, I knew it would be years before they were truly awakened. So many chosen ones waiting for their moment to seize control.

This was not how I expected my first day at Templeton to go.

Built in the mixed styles of Jacobson and Victorian architecture, Templeton was a monument to what the council sought for our war-torn country—a return to supremacy. The large estate was built of brick and stone, the inside filled with works of art and period furniture ravaged from museums left penniless when funds were redirected to war programs. Everything in the mansion was a statement of purity, including the glaringly white walls and floors. Combined with the pastel-colored adornments, it was a reminder to all naturals, who themselves lived in glorified prisons, of what we once were. Nothing could appear too modern in the home of the very things that defined our modern age.

It was the picture of deception.

I would have to pretend I didn't notice the imbalance of it all. The council watched my people lose their homes, move to shanty towns and tent cities, before finally being rounded up to live in barely hospitable compounds that were mostly renovated abandoned buildings—somehow having survived through the bombings.

But nothing came free. We would have to pay dearly to feel so protected.

The war started before my grandparents. My father's generation was the first to live in shantytowns, and my generation the first to die inside the walls of the compound. The next generation would be filled with only chosen ones. Places like Templeton would be their homes.

We were supposed to be thankful to have a training center located in our sector. There were only three total in the whole of the Western lands, and because our sector lay close to the borders that separated us from the Middlelands, we were honored with a whole young army of genetically engineered superhumans.

My time at Templeton would be spent making sure the training chosen ones had everything they needed. I would stand silent as I watched them learn physical combat. I would clean out the trash from classrooms where the teacher preached on about the evils and wantonness of the naturals. I would scrub floors as the chosen ones wandered aimlessly among the bountiful grounds of Templeton, while my people were confined in the compound. I would wash dishes as the chosen ones wished for the day when they would no longer have to keep watch over the naturals. I would fold laundry as those above us lavished in their life of decadence, while my people struggled to mend our hand-me-down uniforms.

At least that's how I expected to spend my days.

Instead, I met with something a little different. I was directed down to the basement while the other girls were given the menial jobs I expected to receive. And there I found nearly thirty of them. Thirty incubating chosen ones.

Perhaps this was some sort of initiation? Most new girls at Templeton started in the spring, but because of my family's special circumstances, I started in the fall. No one bothered to spend much time welcoming me or boring me with all the rules. I couldn't help but feel slighted and wondered if it was because of the way in which my sister had died. I was marked, and not just by the branding that graced my neck.

As I stared wide-eyed at the young boys, I wondered

how many would make it through the incubation period. The first thirteen years of their lives were spent in this fashion. The creators had to make sure they were flawless, with no sign of deformities or illness. From ages thirteen to seventeen, they trained.

Should I have felt sorry for these things? They had no knowledge of the world. They had no parents. They had no God. They were soulless.

"Through the next door," a voice called out, startling me from my observations.

An older natural looked at me over the chart he was holding. A creator. The chosen ones may have been wielding the power, but the naturals created them. We gave away everything. I wondered how I didn't notice him when I first entered the room.

"You're in for a treat," he said with a chuckle. His laugh sounded odd as it echoed off the walls. He worked directly with the chosen ones. How did he have time to laugh? His job was so important.

I said nothing as I pushed past him and headed through the second door. For reasons I couldn't explain, I dreaded going inside this room. I actually feared it. And I didn't embrace fear—it was a harmful emotion. Yet some part of me had awakened, now screaming to turn away.

The bucket I was holding fell out of my hand.

I had entered hell.

There was blood everywhere. It was spilled onto the floor and splattered against the walls. I vaguely heard a low cough somewhere in the room, and it reminded me of my sister—the way the blood had gurgled up from her throat. The beating of my heart inside my ears made it difficult to determine where the nagging, wet sound was coming from.

I could see the outline of a man hunched over a table, could make out what appeared to be red-stained handprints on his white coat. He didn't stop whatever he was doing to instruct me. He merely called out, "I'm almost done here."

I couldn't move. I drew breath in ragged increments, hoping to force air inside my quickly closing lungs.

"There. Finished."

It was as if these words suddenly wiped out the mysterious sound of coughing.

The man turned to me. A smile graced his face.

"Sorry for the mess, darling. But that's how these things go sometimes. It must be your first day. They always send me the newbies."

As he moved away from the table to come and shake my hand, I saw it.

The body was so small, so lonely. So pathetic. I could see in the structure of its face that someone had wanted this thing to be perfect. I could see the attempt. But it was a monster.

One arm, obviously longer than the other, was covered in cuts and bruises. It hung halfway off the medical table. The legs, which appeared to be broken, lay at such jarring angles that it seemed geometrically impossible they should exist. There were fresh scars and stitches covering the small thing's abdomen.

And the blood. It was everywhere. A memory whispered to me. I had seen something like this before. Something to do with my father.

I couldn't turn away, unable to deny what I saw. I noticed the dirt and blood that lingered under its fingernails. This thing had tried to fight back. There was no way it had been allowed to be awakened, not fully, but somehow it knew to fight.

"If you could just clean up the mess, please. Someone will be down for the body."

He didn't wait for me to shake his hand.

I wanted to scream at the man, beg him not to leave me in this room, but he was gone before I could produce the words. I hadn't been alone in years. Living in a compound with hundreds, I was never able. Here, just me and the body, I couldn't fight the growing sense of panic, no matter how hard I tried. If fear were going to devour me, it would be in this place.

I stumbled to the floor, pulling my bucket closer to me. I didn't reach for the rag, but placed my hand directly into a puddle of blood. I let it ooze through my fingers. It looked and felt just like our blood. It was nothing to be afraid of. You must face your fears in order to conquer them. My father had always told me that. It was only blood.

But I couldn't stop the images.

I thought of her, my sister. I thought of the dead thing they ripped from inside her.

I wondered, was this what life was?

Blood.

I let it drip from my fingers.

Nothing to be afraid of.

With a shaking hand, I grabbed the rag and began to scrub.

After I was done, I somehow made it back to the main floor of Templeton, where my supervisor was waiting. She was a natural just like me; I vaguely remembered her saying her name was Gwen. Everything about her was perfectly tailored, from her starched skirt to the gray hair she had tightly pulled back.

I wondered how long she had spent at Templeton. What sin had been committed for her to work here long enough to be promoted? Not that it was really a promotion.

A slave's still a slave no matter what you call her.

"You are probably thinking I sent you down there as some cruel joke," she said, leaning against the wall. It was the first time I noticed how tired she seemed. When she'd met me earlier in the day, she'd snapped out her commands, barely looking at me. Now, it was as if she was too exhausted to even put on an act of disdain.

I said nothing, just looked at my hand. There was still blood there. I began to furiously wipe it against my skirt.

Gwen sighed. "Down this hall and to the left. That's where you must go. The room needs dusting."

I continued to rub my hand against the fabric.

She shook her head and started to walk away. "Welcome to Templeton," she called out. As she moved down the hallway, I noticed there were two slash marks burned onto the back of her neck.

I wondered if the old saying held true: three strikes and you're out.

Chapter 3

As my hand met with the doorknob, my heart beat faster than normal inside my fragile body. My blouse stuck to my sweaty back. I gripped the doorknob harder to stop the shaking of my hands.

God. Please let me be able to breathe.

The moment I shut the door behind me, the feeling ended, done as suddenly as it had began. I'd read about these symptoms in the pamphlets they used to pass out to us girls. I just didn't expect to ever feel them after an event that had nothing to do with me. What did I care if a chosen one died? They were making new ones every day.

It was then I noticed how dark the room was—the curtains had been pulled closed. No wonder my job was to dust the place. I bet the moment I turned on a light, I'd notice piles of the stuff draping itself over the room. I ran my hands against the smooth walls in search of a light switch. I knew I could simply pull the curtains open, but somehow the thought of the sun shining into this room felt wrong.

In my attempt to find the switch, I bumped into a small end table. I could barely glimpse the outline of a lamp. I was sort of impressed I knew what a lamp was. I must have come across a picture of one in a book when I'd still been allowed to read. Not something you would ever see in the compound— only fluorescent lights for us. As I clicked on the lamp, I could barely contain the gasp that threatened to escape my lips.

I never wanted anything more in my life than to stay in this space forever.

The room was a mixture of browns and greens, marble floors and wood. Rows and rows of books covered the walls. A leather couch with giant olive green pillows sat next to the end table. And then I saw it. I went still.

A piano.

It had been years since music and books were outlawed. But there stood a piano against the oversize windows that protected us from the outside world.

I wanted it.

Was this another lesson? I knew my supervisor had sent me below to show me that beneath the façade, Templeton held many secrets. But what did she mean by sending me here? Unless she wanted me to understand the chosen ones made the rules, but did not have to follow them?

I had already known this truth a long time.

The thought of them having music so readily available was oddly worse than what I'd seen below, and my heart began to pound again. I couldn't stop myself from taking a step toward the instrument. I sat down on the bench, my toe slithering its way onto the pedal, somehow securing myself to the piano.

A brief and shadowy memory swept before me—my

father, his hands guiding mine along white keys. I inhaled sharply.

"Why does Mom always sing that song?" I remembered asking him.

"Because it means something to her, Tessie," he'd replied with a heavy sigh, glancing toward the door to their bedroom. Mother was having another bad night. I could hear her humming the song most days, but when she got to drinking, she sang it full out.

I'd rolled my eyes and turned my attention back to the piano. My father took one of my hands in his and gave it a squeeze. "Don't be mad when she sings, Tessie. We all want something we can pretend is ours. You'll understand some day. When you're older, you'll want your own song, too." Emma had sung my mother's song at her funeral. I found out it was an old one from some place named England. The song was called "The Snow They Melt the Soonest." I never really knew my mother, so I never really knew what the song meant.

No kid likes to imagine getting older, but with the war changing life for us every day, it was hard not to think of the future. "Will they take the music?" I'd asked my father. Somehow, even at five, I knew things were ending.

"Of course not," he replied. These were the early days, before I saw my father defeated. He placed my hands back on the keys. "But why don't we start with your song now?" The first one I ever learned to play was "Moonlight Sonata."

I couldn't hold onto the memory for too long. It wouldn't be healthy. Besides, thoughts of my father didn't belong in the home of the chosen ones.

It was madness. Sitting there in that room, so close to music. If this was a test, I was going to fail. I couldn't help it. I would rather receive another slash mark than give up touching the keys. I would volunteer to work below for every minute of my sentence if I could play just one song.

My aching fingers grazed the keys, and then I quickly pulled my hands back from the slick coldness. I considered touching it again. It might help to block out thoughts of the many things I had lost. It would be like medicine.

I gently, hesitantly, pushed down a key. It quivered slightly under my touch. The hair on the back of my neck shot up, and my skin tingled. I imagined this was what it felt like to fall in love. In that moment, I was ready to fall.

I plunged recklessly into my newfound freedom, pushing and caressing the keys. The council had gotten rid of music along with the books. My mind, and my fingers, never forgot either.

It was a freedom the darkest part of my soul sought out. How long had it been since I'd experienced anything close to that? I felt deep down I was allowing the emotions that simmered to dance freely, but somehow I knew I could both have this and remain in control. I found it easy to ignore the shame I should be feeling, as long as I continued playing. I began to put more force into my fingers.

I repeated the same movements over and over again; it was the only song I could recall. The song my father had taught me. How long had I been playing? I couldn't tell. Somewhere in the middle of my dark euphoria, I heard it, a quiet, intruding noise that stirred my senses from their hypnotized state and made me freeze in place. I had trained my instincts to be sharp. Never as sharp as a chosen one's, but useful all the same.

Someone, or something, had cleared his throat.

I was aware of him behind me. I could hear him breathing.

From that noise, I tried to determine my fate. Did it sound angry? Disgusted? I couldn't move as I heard the noise of steps getting closer. I knew I wouldn't be able to escape—not because my body wouldn't work. Not because I wasn't brave enough to make a run for it. I couldn't leave the piano.

That was when I saw him. It was the chosen one from my branding. Not the one who held me down as the iron burned into my skin. This was the one who was beautiful. While I knew it was wrong to admit, even if only to myself, some part of me liked seeing him.

As I looked to the chosen one beside me, I saw past the perfection the creators intended when constructing him. Behind his alluring appearance laid danger. His artfully sculpted cheekbones, curly black hair, and dazzling mismatched eyes didn't impress me. Those weren't the things that stirred something inside me the way playing the piano did. It was the flaw. The small scar on his chin. It was glorious.

Sometimes it felt too difficult to look on the chosen ones; they were so far superior to us naturals in every conceivable way. It was as if that scar allowed me to see him, begged me to see him.

How silent it was. I was so used to the hustle and bustle of the compound that it startled me. I could almost hear the air weave itself around everything in the room. He was silence itself. And in that stillness I was more aware of myself than I had ever been. I could feel the way a few stray strands of my red hair were brushing against the branding on the back of my neck. I could sense my pulse beating quickly against my wrist, my body craving to touch the keys again. Or maybe to touch the boy. I could even taste my breath sticking inside my throat. But for one brief moment, I couldn't feel fear. It was only a second. I saw his hand twitch and suddenly the moment was lost forever.

Without wasting another minute, he was sitting beside me as if it were normal to do so. His hands took the place of mine, which now sat clutched in fists on my lap. He glanced quickly out of the corner of his eye, and I tried to stop the curiously delightful tremble that surged through me. Still no expression crossed his face as he began to play. It was the same tune, but I noticed he played it with greater ease and skill. I wondered if he heard the same stifled emotion, the same story behind the notes. And yet, how could he possibly know this song? How could he know any song at all? His kind took away the music.

I could feel my body react against my will. My heart skipped a beat, then started to pound. My breathing became ragged. This wasn't possible. How could he know this song, of all songs? Could he read the thoughts inside my head? Surely he must be able to see the notes dance inside my mind, because there was no way he would bother to learn to play music when his purpose was only to serve and protect.

The newer versions of the chosen ones were said to be gifted. Rumors swirled concerning everything from mind control to levitation. The ability to play music could not have come to him naturally, and I wondered briefly if the rumors were true.

I couldn't move from my spot. I didn't dare look at him again. It was going to happen, an attack. I hadn't had a panic attack in years, but now I'd had two in only a matter of days—I thought I'd gotten so good at maintaining control. I tried to concentrate on breathing. As I did, my hands somehow moved to the piano of their own accord. They didn't hesitate before they graced the keys and began to dance with his. Never touching, but corresponding all the same.

My eyes searched the keys, blindly following his hands as they moved with a graceful force, never attempting to entrap mine. They almost seemed mindful of the space in which my fingers glided along. I focused on his hands to keep myself from the rising, unknown emotion that was surging through me.

God, this would be my downfall. He would report this. Was he merely teasing me? Allowing me a brief second to lavish in the illusion of freedom, the frail dream of equality, before he ripped it from my clutching hands?

I realized the music had ended. My hands froze accordingly. I stared forward, never thinking to look at him, almost forgetting to blink. The silence seemed to envelop us both. I didn't even hear him breathing. Was he breathing? Yes. Why didn't he say something? This was too much to bear.

"Name?"

He was going to report me. I couldn't find my voice.

He cleared his throat. "Name?"

"Tess," I replied. Though I was sure it was so low he couldn't possibly have heard it.

Not only had I been caught near a piano, but I had played it in front of a chosen one. This was an act that could only be read in one way: defiance.

"Tess. Number 258915," I said, louder. I hoped by complying, I would somehow get myself out of this mess. The flash of bravery I'd felt while playing the piano had vanished.

"Tess," he repeated. The tone of his voice was unsettling. It was not what I had expected. His voice was soft, contemplative, and I didn't understand it. I didn't like how inviting it sounded in my ears. This wasn't how things were supposed to be. He was playing with me, and I was allowing myself to be played with. No doubt he saw me as some stupid, mischievous natural who was dumb enough to get caught playing music that was forbidden. And while that might be true, why the game? I was not a field mouse to be pawed at.

I felt him turn to me, and I couldn't help but look back. I shuddered and forced my gaze down. The chosen ones didn't look at us much and never in the eyes. We weren't worth the acknowledgement. And yet, I couldn't help but peer back up again. His eyes narrowed as if he were confused. We stayed like that for a long, agonizing moment. "You should leave," he whispered.

I could go? He was letting me leave? Just to report me later? I wouldn't be able to take the waiting. If I was to appear before the council, I'd rather I was taken now, from this place. I inhaled a deep breath. "No."

It was right then that my heart calmed. Why at the moment of my greatest danger did my heart cease to thrash about my chest? Was I scared? Yes. But maybe there was something worse than fear.

His eyes reflected his shock, his anger, and his regret. All this passed across his face seamlessly and quickly, and then he did something else that I did not expect: he laughed.

This made me angrier than I had allowed myself to be in a long time. My heart once again began its tirade. Irrationally, my hands found their way back to the keys. As I continued the melody, my heart slowed down once more.

"How do you know this song?" he asked roughly. Good, he was angry. This was to be expected. I needed the world to work in such clear ways.

"My father."

He seemed to doubt my answer. I felt him look behind him as I continued to play.

"You do understand that I should report this?"

"Yes."

"You do know the council won't just ignore it? There are rules to be followed."

"I didn't realize I wasn't allowed." I did; of course I did. What was I saying? What was I doing?

"With that kind of attitude, you won't make it long here."

He reprimanded me like a child.

"You should leave," the chosen one repeated. He placed his hands on mine, and I swear my heart stopped altogether. He moved them slowly, gently, away from the keys, and held onto my fingers a second longer than needed. It was only a second, but it unnerved me. It appeared to unnerve him as well. In an instant he was standing, backing away from the bench.

"I won't tell anyone, if that's what you're worried about." He seemed uncomfortable, as if he wanted to crawl away.

I had to ask. "Why won't you report me?" I kept my eyes on the keys, not daring to look at him. I didn't want to see that he was lying. I had begun to hope that somehow I would actually get out of this.

"I don't know." He sighed, seemingly troubled by his own answer. "Isn't it near time for the transport to take you back?"

"I suppose so. Yes."

"Very well."

I had been dismissed. I could feel his gaze on my neck. Then I heard him retreat.

I closed my eyes; my heart stuttered for a brief moment but then regained its normal, monotonous rhythm. How I loved it at that moment. After a deep breath, I began to head to the door.

And stopped deathly still in my tracks. He had not left. He was standing in the doorway. I found myself unable to look away, intrigued. I couldn't remember how long it had been since I had felt curious about anything in my world.

"Tess, you are not to do anything like this again."

I shivered at the sound of my name.

"Not under any circumstances," he continued.

I found my voice. "Yes, sir."

"And Tess? You play beautifully." And then he actually smiled.

Chapter 4

After dinner, I spent the hours that supposedly belonged to me shifting through paperwork in order to claim my sister's remains. Idiotic. As if everyone in the compound didn't know she belonged to me. Or at least she used to. While Robert was Emma's husband in the eyes of the naturals in the compound, the council didn't recognize the marriage. As a result, all legal and family matters now fell to me.

As I signed my name to the document that gave me ownership of her body, I felt more repugnance for the compound, for the formality and audacious ceremony of it all, than anything I had seen at Templeton. The chosen ones had the right idea. They didn't put on costumes and acts of sorrow. A dead body was a dead body.

That night I dreamed of everything I was afraid of. I was alone with the boy from the piano room. But we weren't playing the piano. He reached for my hand, and I let him. I just allowed myself to feel his skin against mine.

It was a nightmare.

The next day's assignment was less colorful than the previous one. My task was to clean up around the grounds after the Introduction Ceremony. During the ceremony, the young chosen ones were required to perform an array of tasks before the higher-ranked members of the council. These activities, rumored to be focused on the chosen ones' physical abilities, combined with a series of interviews, were the official start of the bidding. Each subcommittee within the council would review their notes and lobby for their desired candidate. Then chosen ones would report at the end of their training at Templeton to the council member who paid the highest price. They had no choice but to comply. From what the naturals were told, though, they had no other desire than to fight for our country. They wanted nothing more.

That was part of what made them so different from us naturals: at some point we had stopped fighting the enemy. We grew tired of a war that seemed eternal, and we became more content with destroying ourselves. At least then we wouldn't have to wait around for the Easterners to do it. We could control our own end.

The Miles Incident.

We began to terrorize our own people.

Miles was a small town, one ravaged by the effects of the fall of our country. Most of the town's males had joined the army because it was a way to provide for their families, not because they believed in the cause. Out of the seventy-five fathers and sons who went to war, only four came back. Those four came up with a plan. A message.

They strapped explosives onto their children, their blood. They turned on a video camera. They placed the triggers into the hands of their wives and let the world see their demise.

They would rather destroy what was left of the world than live in it.

The naturals gave up our power then. We gave it all away. We wanted to save our world.

The council convinced us to embrace the creation of artificial life. Let the soulless die in our foreign war. Let those without souls bring our country back to greatness. And when we the naturals died, our women no longer able to give birth, the chosen ones would inherit the earth they fought so hard to save.

I would spend the next couple hours at Templeton cleaning up after a party celebrating the chosen ones' eagerness to defend the naturals. The Introduction Ceremony was the first step in their lives of service. There was a variety of subcommittees a chosen one could be selected for during his time at Templeton. Since most of them were particularly good fighters, they would join the militia's subcommittee to fight hand and foot against the Easterners. Guns and other weapons of mass destruction had been outlawed during the Treaty of Modernization a couple years back—no Eastern or Western army could use them in battle any longer. It was rumored the Easterners created a chosen-one army of their own, but none of us naturals had ever seen it. Some even whispered the reason behind the treaty was that these artificially created humans had been, for lack of a better word, upgraded. Like superpowers or something. Moving crap with their minds.

Not all of us were gullible enough to believe those rumors.

But there were other subcommittees, too. I didn't know all

of them, and our council didn't seem too keen anymore to keep us informed. I knew we had a committee of explorers who went out into the Middlelands and searched for survivors or usable resources in the places where the bombs first fell. There were also chosen ones selected to be bodyguards for members of the council.

A natural had never been allowed to witness an Introduction Ceremony; I was only allowed to clean up after one. My supervisor had given my orders without so much as a whisper of the previous day's incident. Apparently I had passed my first day's test. The chosen one from the piano room had kept his promise.

I realized some part of me secretly hoped that he had told. I didn't want to owe him anything. Just thinking about the scarred chosen one made my skin explode in red blotches like a flare in the dark of night, warning of some attacking army.

I glanced at the girls walking ahead of me toward the lawn of Templeton. They looked rather silly. I noticed how their hair hung low down their backs, hiding their slash marks. I never bothered, always choosing to wear my hair up. I wouldn't be ashamed. It wasn't a part of me. It was my duty.

The girls linked arms and giggled as they separated from me. I never shared these types of moments with girls from the compound. I wasn't sure if this was because they kept their distance from me, or because I pushed them away.

It didn't matter. Not really.

They wasted their free time flirting with boys from the compound. While they knew, as we all did, that nothing could come from it, they seemed just the sort of pretty girls who lavished in the attention of others. I was above such acts of stupidity. My sister's body was proof enough where that sort of feeling, that attachment, could lead you.

I slung a bag over my shoulder and headed out on my own. I wandered the grounds for hours, picking up trash, stuffing my bag till it was full. My plan of throwing myself into work was such a success that I still had two hours left of my shift when I had completed the task. No clues remained to shed any light on what had actually occurred at the ceremony.

Instead, I was reduced to a glorified maid. I picked up barely stained silk tablecloths that would no doubt never be used again. The amount of food wasted by members of the council was astounding; piles of plates half covered with leftovers littered the lawn. Some of the food I didn't even recognize. I watched as a few of the other girls snuck bites, but I wasn't so brave.

Gwen thought me too slow to fill my bag in such a short amount of time, and she wouldn't expect me back so soon. If I had been like the other girls, I would have attempted to work in pairs, spending more time talking than working. But that just wasn't me.

I debated for a short while the idea of going back for more work. But I feared my next assignment would be in Templeton, and I didn't desire running into any of the Templeton boys. Especially mine.

Mine?

I remembered how the chosen one's hands had caressed the keys, and my stomach tightened at the image. There was so much passion to the way he played. Could someone, something, like that really only desire war?

Whatever he was, I didn't want to see him again.

I decided to wander instead of returning to the mansion for more work. I knew what awaited me when I got back to the compound—more pointless arrangements for Emma's burial. I sought solace in the open air. It took a while, but eventually I came across a bit of woods toward the end of the property. I thought briefly back to the days when I would have found comfort in such a place. But even nature had been tainted. Nothing was sacred. Nothing was above corruption.

The heat was unbearable for the peak of fall. It was as if nature didn't know how to behave, either. I decided to rest under the shade of a large tree. I undid the top two buttons of my shirt, the loose strands of my hair stuck to my sweating face. My breathing slowed. If I didn't move an inch, maybe it would cool down. I would become stone.

Something jarred me from my moment of peace. It was quiet and low at first, but suddenly it got louder and very close to me. I felt an insurmountable sense of disorientation; the sounds were so alien to me. It was only as the moments crept on that I realized I was hearing a mixture of laughing and yelling. Why did it take me so long to recognize it as noise coming from humans?

They were the sounds of people, and I was quite sure they were not my people. Maybe if I kept still enough they would not see me, would not hear me.

Templeton boys. Chosen ones—five of them. I had never seen this many in one location at one time outside of a wrangling or deportation.

Most of the chosen ones would soon be shipped off to command posts throughout the Western sector, working alongside the council to devise and implement ways to fortify the boundaries against attack. Only those who had been found wanting, lacking, receiving no bids after the Introduction

Ceremony, were left to monitor one of the thirty compounds in the Western district. They would be stuck babysitting the naturals. Even my people understood it to be a mark of shame.

But these men—boys—appeared to have no concerns that such a fate awaited them. They looked as if they had been playing a game of some sort. Their faces were flushed from running around and they held their shirts in their hands. I noticed how their bare chests and backs were covered in a variety of bruises. Was this a result of the Introduction Ceremony?

Of course the bruises were nothing a good creator couldn't fix in a matter of moments. Their whole physical being was a testament to the power of science and illusion. I reached up and trailed my fingers across my slash mark.

It was as if this movement somehow alerted the group to my presence. Their eyes bore into me like I was a science experiment, and I felt a growing sense of mortification as they continued to stare down at me. Why did they linger?

He was there, too, the boy from the piano room, and I felt my heart beat a little faster at the sight of him. His face didn't show any sign of recognizing me, though I noticed how his fingers tapped furiously against his side. So much emotion seemed trapped within those fingers. I remembered how his hands had moved across the keys of the piano and I shivered.

From disgust or something else?

"What is this thing?" a boy asked, sizing me up.

"It is what it is," another one of them said. His words snapped me from my dizzy recollections. His eyes lingered on my shirt, focusing on the undone buttons. This seemed to be rather amusing to the others, as they all laughed.

"Are you lost?" one of them asked with a sloppy grin. It

was weird to see them so…so unrefined. My knowledge of the chosen ones was very little, scripted in the sense that we only saw them as they wanted to be seen, but in the time I had spent around them, they seemed to be so emotionless, so controlled. The two chosen ones assigned to our compound barely raised their voices when a fight broke out over missing laundry or the volume of someone's snores. They would coldly look over the culprits, demand they stop, and the incident was soon forgotten.

My mind wandered to the sight of the mangled reject bleeding onto the floor. What sort of training changed these boys into the humans I was taught to revere above all things?

"It's lost, all right," another laughed.

I hated myself for my inability to speak at that moment. I wish I could claim it was out of defiance, but I knew it was from fear—not fear of these monsters, but fear of something more instinctual, fear of revealing how unnatural I was. I stood up weakly and made a move to leave.

Why did it have to be so hot? I felt dizzy.

"Look, it's embarrassed!"

Their laughing was becoming unbearable. One of the boys stepped in front of me. I tried to move around him but he was faster.

"She must be new."

Another one took a step toward me, and I instinctively took a step back. The action caused the boy to grin, like this was another game for him and his friends to play. He was just as stunningly perfect as the others, but there was something in his eyes that left me feeling naked, like he could see right through me if he chose to and I would be unable to stop him. He wore his power proudly. "Are we sure she's a she? I know she's a natural, but damn, she's ugly."

It wasn't like I'd never heard the word, but it had been a while since anyone had bothered to describe me at all. I had worked so hard at disappearing that to be acknowledged at all still felt wrong. Besides, I hadn't invited this boy to judge me. Before I could make sense of why my appearance mattered to a chosen one, the boy yanked me to him by the wrist. The suddenness of the movement and the closeness of another person, chosen one or not, caused my breath to burn inside my throat.

"I guess we should check and make sure?" he asked his friends as he winked at me. Before I could protest, the boy leaned down and grabbed the hem of my skirt.

This wasn't right. This wasn't right.

The chosen ones were supposed to protect.

"George, stop this. You're scaring her," the boy from the piano room called out. He didn't sound angry. More like bored.

George dropped my skirt and sighed. "Who does she belong to? Any of you?" he asked.

"She's not new," the boy from the piano room spoke up. Then, in a sudden succession of movements, he pulled his shirt back on and grabbed my wrist, pulling me away from the group. His hand gently held onto mine, and I wondered if it took all of his concentration to hold back the strength I knew coursed through him. The chosen ones weren't created to play nice.

"I guess we can count you out of the game?" yelled George, his voice no longer holding the amusement he'd showcased only moments before. I heard it between the notes—suspicion.

The boy holding onto me shrugged as he continued to move us away from the crowd. "I guess so."

"Slow down," I begged as I stumbled.

"No."

I could still hear the boys behind us laughing—that damn laughing. They were calling out words I didn't understand.

Slut.

Whore.

"Ignorant," he uttered under his breath. "They're still looking. I need you to keep it under control."

Sights blurred before my eyes. I tried not to look at anything too closely, instead choosing to focus on not letting my fear completely dominate me. After an interminable distance, he stopped abruptly and forced me down onto a stone bench. Not saying anything, he began to pace frantically. Occasionally, he would mutter some curse word to himself, stop to look in my direction, and then proceed to pace again.

"What time does your shift end?" His tone continued to sound reckless, as if he were also struggling to keep it together. But what did he have to fear?

I had to remain focused, alert. Yet how could I focus on details? I shook my head, trying to make sense of my cluttered thoughts. "Not long. Maybe an hour."

The chosen one sighed, obviously frustrated. Why did he drag me from those boys? What could they have possibly wanted from me? Why did his demeanor alter so suddenly once we were away from them? The only thing I knew was that I was scared. There was something familiar about the way he looked at me; it reminded me of Henry. And I could never think of Henry without feeling weak and vulnerable in a way that made me want to crawl someplace where no one could look at me, someplace where I would never want someone to look at me.

"I can go back, tell them I finished up early. I'm sure my supervisor will find something for me to do."

All I knew was what I felt: the need to escape.

"That won't work." He must have sensed my confusion. "Because those boys back there will find out I wasn't with you. Don't let the grandeur fool you; they see everything."

"And that's a problem?" I asked.

"It's a great problem," he said softly. For some wild reason outside my realm of understanding, I suddenly wanted to be back in the piano room. With him. I found my eyes moving down his face, resting on his chin. The scar. I wondered where it came from. Why did he keep it?

Why did I care?

I closed my eyes. "I…I don't understand."

"No, I guess you wouldn't, would you?"

I cringed. He thought I was simple-minded. And yet, he almost seemed relieved, calmed by my lack of understanding. The chosen one was staring at me. I didn't like it one bit, yet didn't dare tear my eyes from his. How did we possibly have so many moments like this in our short time together?

Together.

His eyes moved once to my shirt. I inhaled sharply and quickly re-clasped the buttons. He looked away, turning his back to me, and I thought for a moment I saw embarrassment on his face. But he owned the world. He didn't have to make any explanations for his actions.

"We'll have to go somewhere." He seemed to be talking more to himself than to me. I stood up, preparing to receive my orders.

"Follow me."

Had I done something wrong?

The slash mark on my neck tingled.

Chapter 5

How was this happening? My goal, ever-constant and more important to me than the luxury of having friends or relying on loved ones, had always been to keep my feelings in check. This chosen one had already witnessed an incident where I failed, and I couldn't help but fear the more time I spent around him, the more likely it was that I would commit another transgression. Was I a total failure?

He didn't say another word. The chosen ones were known for being agile, completely at ease with their bodies, their movements, but he seemed tense. I could see, almost feel, the anxiety he was holding within him. This worried me more than anything. What would a chosen one have to be nervous about?

I followed as quickly as I could behind him as we entered the building, keeping my head down when I noticed several of the other girls slyly looking us over. One of them snickered. I avoided the eyes of Jacobson, my father's old friend, who stood on a ladder changing a light fixture. Somehow I felt closer to danger as I moved past him than I had ever felt before, like I was doing something terribly wrong by walking with this chosen one. I had to remind myself that I had no choice. Perhaps it was only guilt I felt, because it was Jacobson's involvement with my father that had led him to being placed at Templeton. The only natural men here were serving out punishments, prison sentences. Funny that we should both be left here while the true culprits were dead and gone.

Everywhere we walked there seemed to be people, both naturals and chosen ones. Surely, wherever we were going there was a less populated route available. If I didn't know better, I would have thought this boy wanted us to be seen together.

He stopped abruptly when we reached a room on the third floor that appeared unmarked. The chosen one stood facing the door, his back toward me, not saying a word. I took a moment to try and catch my breath. It was only when another chosen one walked by that his hand reached for the door and pushed it open.

Nothing could have prepared me for what was within. Obviously, it was his living area, but what was surprising was how different it looked to what I'd expected. The chosen ones were the makers of the rules, the enforcers of decorum and order. Yet, in this room, order didn't exist.

The space was cluttered and so oddly personal. It contained sheets of paper with various writing samples crossed out here and there, a record player on the desk. It felt warm, and the natural light that slithered in through the window was almost blinding in its purity. I wondered if he liked the light, desired something so natural when he was so…artificial. But what surprised me most were the rows of books stacked haphazardly around his room.

After my father had been taken by the council, my mother

held my mouth open and forced burning vodka down my throat until I told her where he kept his books. She called my father a traitor, said she wouldn't be one like him. I remembered Louisa clutching onto my leg the whole time. Emma couldn't bear to watch, or to stop my mother. She was helpless.

I told my mother.

And then the books were gone.

"How?" I whispered. I had no right to, but I couldn't help myself. He seemed perplexed by my question.

"All of this…it's outlawed. I haven't seen books in so long."

How I craved to reach out and cradle one in my hands.

"It's easy enough to get them. The council doesn't mind so much. It's a small bribe for the work we are to do. The minute we step out of this place, poof, there go our lives."

I stared longingly at the books. I could feel something working its way through me that I couldn't identify. Whatever I was feeling, it was seductive, willing me to surrender.

I licked my dry lips and glanced away from the books to see the chosen one was staring at me. His eyes roamed everywhere. I could feel them pause over certain places, spaces of imperfection: my slightly too long neck; my much too thin arms; my general lack of torso; my long, disproportioned legs; my thick reddish hair.

Yet somehow I could tell he wasn't judging me or reeling in distaste over the physicality that exists as a result of random genetics. Instead he looked at me in what felt like approval.

Was this the first time he had been alone with a girl?

Emma used to joke that the chosen ones had to sit through a seminar on female anatomy—countless hours on reproduction and menstruation. The council did such a good job expounding on the female's natural wantonness, weakness, and our general pits of disgustingness, they actually thanked the council for not creating any female chosen ones.

But this chosen one didn't seem disgusted.

With a heavy sigh, he walked to his closet and reached in to retrieve something. I tried not to look too closely at the room while he was busy, but in another world, another time, this could have been my room. The council told us we were lucky to have a home at all, blessed to have a safe one. So much of our sector had been destroyed in the Civil War with the Easterners. The council used what we had left. They could only protect us if we lived in a central location. Soon each sector built a compound. They all looked the same and held the same story. Individuality was a trend of the past.

Of course, Templeton didn't look quite so shabby.

This boy's room could pass for a home, or what I imagined a home would look like.

The boy returned from his closet holding a bottle of tanish liquid and a shot glass. My stomach tightened at the sight of these objects, and I could detect the beating of my heart quicken. The boy poured himself a glass and threw it back without a second thought to me. As the contents of the bottle slid down his throat, he closed his eyes. I knew the routine well. My mom was the one who'd first taught it to me. Maybe if he had been a natural I would have told him drinking doesn't let you forget anything; it just prolongs the pain. But everything I had seen today reminded me he wasn't a natural.

He looked to me again and stilled as if suddenly remembering this was something I wasn't supposed to see. He shook his head slightly and moved to return the bottle back to the closet. It was almost as if he were embarrassed. Nervous. Around me.

When the chosen ones were first presented to us, flashed across our television screens in a haze of stylized infomercials, there was a lot of rumbling and joking around—we were going to let these pretty boys fight our wars? Some of our more artistically inclined naturals protested that it would be a sin to mess up such stunning faces, proof of the ability of science to create art. That was until we saw what they could do.

It only took a single chosen one to destroy, demolish, annihilate five POWs from the Eastern sector. They had been caught attempting to thrust a suicide bomber into the midst of Supplies Day in an improvised tent town called Disputania. The Western sector was horrified and disgusted that these men had been willing to kill people as they attempted to receive food and medical supplies from our council. These people weren't soldiers; they were mothers and children who were starving and sick. Their husbands and fathers were away fighting to keep the Eastern sector at bay.

We all wanted revenge for the mere thought that they could terrorize these innocents.

The council made a point of playing video of the POWs as they awaited their confrontation with the chosen one, to ensure us they'd been well-fed and taken care of. The council wanted to show us that these pieces of scum were in their best physical condition when they faced off with the chosen one.

It took him less than ten minutes to kill them all. As my people watched the creature snap bones in a dizzy dance of brutality, we didn't feel horror. We felt hope.

The boy in front of me didn't seem frightening. It was as if he didn't know what to do with me.

"What would you like from me, sir?" I asked, staring at the scar on his chin. It was easier to focus there while I spoke; it helped to calm the feeling that this endearingly nervous chosen one could snap my neck if he so chose—and that no one would care. He could say I committed some crime and the world would believe it. I had already been marked.

Of course, he *had* taken me away from the other chosen ones, whose grabs and laughs made me feel beyond uncomfortable. I was intrigued.

"Some rules they overlook," he spoke, answering a question I had not asked. He cleared his throat again; I was beginning to think this was a nervous habit. This was a boy who felt uncertainty. What else did he feel? I thought they would have made him stronger, without these impediments.

It was one of the promises made to the naturals during the "informational" phases of the initial creation of the chosen ones. The naturals were sick and tired of seeing their husbands, brothers, and sons returning from war forever damaged by the things they had seen and done. Women weren't trusted in battle—it was believed our emotions would get in the way. But maybe that's just part of being human, a natural. Many of the men who fought were left crippled not by some battle wound they received while fighting the Easterners, but rather were left immobilized by the truths they learned about humanity that seeped between the blood and dirt of the battlefields.

And when they returned from combat, they were no longer of any worth to their towns. Many were unable to work or help their families. These men simply became another mouth to feed during a time when the naturals already felt so helpless.

The absence of hope was the worst plague that ever ravaged my people.

As a result, the council swore the chosen ones would feel no sympathy for their enemies. They would be hardened by their training, prepared for what had to be done in order to keep the infidels of the Eastern Sector where they belonged. It was in our makeup as naturals to shy away from the gruesome things that had to be done to survive in this world. Something in us humans shied away from the idea of "kill or be killed." The council called it selfishness. It was a dirty word.

The chosen ones would devote their lives to the cause. They would live in the estate houses built in every sector— mansions that were immersed in the grandeur and luxuries of the Victorian style. They would live like gods before fighting like gladiators.

Would this boy kill? Was that the only thing he would ever be good for? Could those hands I so admired cause death without contemplating the ideology behind the action?

"Why did you bring me here?" I asked, again unwilling to admit that I felt a need to construct meaning from the person who stood before me. I felt jittery the more time I spent inside his room. It was the same way I'd started to feel around Henry before he no longer could be around me. Yet I didn't understand how Henry and the boy in front of me could ever possibly be connected.

He didn't reply. He just looked at me. What the hell did he find so damn interesting? He knew the story of my people. What kept those eyes searching? He sat down slowly, gracefully, on the chair in front of his desk. Everywhere I felt his eyes travel across me, I couldn't stop my eyes from following along his body. Before I could convince myself to stop looking, he was standing behind me.

"May I see your mark?" he asked, his breath tickling the

back of my skin.

I shuddered—I couldn't refuse if I wanted to. I slowly moved my ponytail over the front of my shoulder. I could somehow feel his eyes take in the new, raw mark on my skin, and my face flushed at the mere thought that he was looking at it. I never before cared who saw it, but something about a person who could produce such music, someone I could maybe respect in another world, examining the mark caused my throat to dry. When I could stand it no longer I turned to face him, my hand sliding up my neck to cover the branding.

He cleared his throat.

The silence trapped us together; the only noise I could detect was our breathing. The more I listened to the pattern our breaths created, the more I realized they had become in sync. In. Out. In. Out. I caught a glimpse of us in a lone mirror leaning against the corner of his room. His cheeks reflected the warmth of mine. When his chest rose, so did mine. His eyes followed me to the mirror.

I shook my head. "We don't have glass at the compound, sir," I blurted out, embarrassed.

Not since my mother had smashed her fist against the mirror in the communal bathroom and was found slicing her hands, screaming that if someone didn't get her a drink she would kill herself. But now both her and glass were only memories.

He swallowed. "Are you the eldest girl in your family or do you suffer for someone else?" he asked, choosing to ignore my random comment about the glass.

"Suffer, sir?"

"Don't call me sir. Let's not pretend there is anything civil about all of this," he replied, running a hand over his eyes.

"Whatever you say, sir…I mean, well, thank you."

"For what?"

"For…the boys…taking me from them," I mumbled, looking away from him.

"Don't be so fast to thank me. Out of the frying pan and into the fire. That is how the saying goes, right? I missed the signup for idioms 101."

I didn't know how to respond. He failed to fit into my definition of what a chosen one should be. He played the piano and read. He wrote. He even attempted humor. Though it was becoming more and more obvious humor wasn't something they taught in his classes.

And he felt things. He didn't know how to deal with what he was feeling, obviously. But he felt all the same. I didn't understand why, but it was sort of beautiful to watch.

"Why did I bring you here?" He sounded dejected, lost, and exhausted by his earlier performance. I certainly had no answers for him.

"What shall be shall be," he said to himself. He moved and picked up several novels that were scattered around the floor near his bed. He placed them in my arms.

"When you check in with your supervisor, bring her a note detailing my schedule and that you are to come here. You work for me now."

I nodded. More rules I didn't understand. Did I want to come back here?

"I am sorry, Tess."

"For what?"

"Mostly I feel sorry for myself," he admitted with a small, empty laugh as he ran his hand over his face, which still burned bright.

I shifted as I waited for him to continue, clutching the books against my chest. But he didn't answer, merely sat back at his desk and placed his face into his hands. The silence was uncomfortable. There was a small part of me that felt responsible for this boy's state. He had lost something the moment he took me by the wrist and led me away from the others.

On the whole, this knowledge didn't bother me. I shouldn't care what he felt—it was wrong he felt anything at all. But deep inside, waiting in the place where weakness still struggled to live, I did feel bad. It was the same part of me that longed to see my sister again. The part of me I worked so hard to destroy.

I began to pick up the other books around the room, placing them nicely and neatly onto the bookshelf. I tried to make as little noise as possible. I'm not sure if I did this for his sake or for mine. As I reached for a novel that lay on his bed, the boy snatched it from my hands with a quickness that left me startled.

"Don't touch this. Do you hear?" he whispered.

I nodded.

I glimpsed the title as he shoved it in a drawer inside his desk: Mary Shelley's *Frankenstein*.

He cleared his throat, offering a small smile.

"Music? I mean, if we're going to do this, we might as well do it right. So how about it?" he asked suddenly. It was an obvious attempt at concealing the man he had briefly flashed before me—a chosen one, a boy, someone who felt fear.

I should have told him no. The council may not have cared that he listened to music; I knew they would care that I did. But I didn't say a word. He quickly moved around his room bringing out what I recognized as records. Of course I had never owned any, but growing up my father had described them to me so vividly. He was a lover of music.

The council had been convinced these things, treasures of knowledge and expression, aided in our natural need to weaken ourselves. We were slaves to our emotions, our sensitivity. The council and its chosen ones would only protect us if we gave them something in return. We gave them everything. Music, books, our personal sense of style, our houses—these were only the material things. Most of what we gave them could not be quantified.

As I watched the chosen one flip through his collection of records, I felt the tiniest bit of guilt. There was a part of me that had always agreed with every word the council had told us.

But there was another part of me, the quieter side of myself, that experienced a sense of sublime ecstasy at the sight of them. I felt my legs go weak and didn't wait for permission to sit down, instead taking the chair across the room. I felt safer the farther away I was from him. But if a chosen one allowed me to listen to music, could it be so bad?

"What shall we listen to?" he asked, more to himself than to me. It was odd. While his hands held onto the records, he seemed calmer. At ease. Normal.

"Oh, anything." When had my voice ever sounded so eager?

He chuckled and flashed me a genuine smile, and I couldn't help but smile back. I felt something drop in my stomach. Did I just smile? It had been an unconscious response.

It was then I heard the song, the same song we had played on the piano. My hands shook slightly as if they ached to play it themselves, awakening in them the freedom I had tasted in the piano room. I leaned my head against the back of the chair and closed my eyes. This was heaven. I heard the crackle of the record player as the song ended.

"Again," I whispered, still keeping my eyes closed.

He didn't reply. I barely heard him move, but the song started up again.

I let the music seep through me, taking me over—I didn't care if he was watching. The notes ran up my spine; I could feel goose bumps rise across my hands. I suppressed the chattering of my teeth. It was rebellious, and I craved it so. But it was more than that. It was love—pure, uncomplicated love. It was my father. It was Emma. Everything I had to repress on a daily basis. It was Henry. It was the boy sitting in the room with me.

My eyes flashed open at the thought of him. He was looking away, though I saw how the blush moved down his cheeks to his neck. He looked as if he had stumbled upon something he wasn't supposed to see. The music came to a stop. The sound of my heavy breathing filled the room; it was almost deafening. I could feel my heart happily fluttering.

He cleared his throat.

"Beautiful," I said softly.

"Yes," he replied, staring down at his hands, still avoiding my gaze.

How could I explain what the song meant to me? There were no words.

"Don't worry; we will listen to it again next time," he said.

When the song ended, I couldn't fully believe that I would ever get to hear the music again. I wondered if he read the disappointment I felt, because in that instant he reached out to touch my face, and I slammed myself against the wall as fast as I could. He would not touch me like that. I wouldn't let him. He had tried to touch my cheek. That was unacceptable, a world of danger I was not willing to enter.

And worst of all, I actually wondered what it would feel like to be touched again.

He placed his hands out, palms facing mine, a stance of surrender. "I'm not going to touch you. I promise. I'm sorry."

I wanted to run, but I had to remember who and where I was. I still answered to him and his people, and overreacting would only make things worse. After a few moments, I moved a step closer to him.

"I'm sorry. I overreacted."

I hadn't, of course. My reaction was justified, right, and acceptable.

"No, your reaction at least made sense. You must always remind me of my place, Tess."

"Isn't it your job to remind me of mine?" I blurted without thinking.

He laughed. His laugh was almost becoming familiar to me.

"I think it is probably all right for you to return now."

"Oh, yes, right," I mumbled.

"Well, I guess I will see you next time. We'll move on to books. I was thinking maybe a bit of Shakespeare or the Brontës. You seem like you would be a fan."

My mind was whirling with the thought. Part of me never wanted to see him again, and part of me shuddered at the possibility of passing up the opportunity he was offering. The more realistic side of me knew it did not matter what I felt—I had no choice, of course. I shook my head slightly, trying to clear it. Then I stopped abruptly before exiting the room.

"I don't even know your name."

I'm not sure why this mattered.

"James."

I could feel the change even on the transport home. The other girls kept looking at me in such strange ways. Some girls giggled and whispered, pinching me with their eyes. A few avoided my gaze so forcefully it was bluntly and painfully obvious. One girl in particular just stared. She looked at me with what could only be described as sadness.

I couldn't shake the feeling that the next chapter of my story was already known to everyone on the transport. Everyone except me.

Chapter 6

I remember the day Emma told me she was getting married.

"Please try and understand, Tess," my sister begged.

Of course I understood. If I were honest, I would have told her I understood perfectly. I knew what everyone thought of me—they thought I had no heart. I did. It beat the same as everyone else's. I was just better at controlling it.

But I didn't know how to put a smile on my face and pretend it didn't destroy me a little more every time I admitted I wished for something or someone just to stay with me. And so I avoided wishing for anything at all.

"You like Robert. You told me you liked him," she said.

She was begging me now. I sat on my cot with my knees pulled to my chest. Emma sat next to me and placed her forehead against the side of my head. I could feel her tears fall onto my shoulder.

"You don't need my permission," I snapped.

"Yes, yes I do."

I couldn't help but laugh. "So, if I said right now that I

didn't want you to marry him, you wouldn't?"

She fell silent. My sister, who had always put everyone first, finally had done something for herself. I didn't mind that. I just wished she wasn't showing her independence by choosing death.

"What if you get pregnant?" I whispered.

She hesitated before answering. "I won't."

"You can't just say it won't happen and hope it doesn't. That's not how it works."

She let out a sigh.

She was going to leave me.

I grabbed for her hand and clutched onto it with all my might. "Please. Don't. This is dangerous. I like Robert, but he messes you up. You don't think around him."

"Tess…"

"You have a family. Why can't we be enough?" I asked, my voice cracking.

"I love you and Louisa, but there's more to this life than what you have settled for. You've crawled so deep inside yourself I wonder if you even know you have a self to save. Trust me. There's so much more to this life. I love him, Tess. I love him."

I shook my head.

"One day you'll know what I'm talking about."

"No. I won't ever be dumb enough to fall in love!" I yelled. I pushed myself off the cot and stormed out of the room, colliding with Louisa on my way. No doubt she was eavesdropping.

"You're not being very fair."

"Leave me alone," I muttered.

She grabbed me by the arm to stop me. "I'm scared, too." Her eyes filled with tears, and I wondered if she was freaking out. When our sister died, she would be stuck with only me. The girl who sought approval would never be able to win mine.

We were too different from each other to ever have that happen.

"Come on. She's really excited about this. Can't you be happy for her?"

I wished I could. I wished my sister would be happy. But I turned on Louisa. "Do you want to see her dead?"

Her face went pale. "She promised she would be careful. And I believe her. She won't let us down. Rob's a good guy, Tess. He wouldn't let anything happen to Emma. You should know that."

I rolled my eyes. Delusional.

"You're just jealous," Louisa replied.

"What?"

"You think you're better than all of us, but I see the way you look at Henry. You think he's cute. You're always so quiet when he's around and you used to laugh at his weird, dark jokes. You like him, but you figure you're not brave enough to let him in, so no one else can have anyone."

I wanted to yell at her, tell her she was ridiculous, but suddenly found it impossible to speak.

Out of nowhere, I was struck by how much Louisa resembled my mother. She looked less and less like a little girl and more like a woman every day. Her reckless nature and uncontrolled emotions left her vulnerable. And she was growing prettier and prettier.

"If you think I'm a girl who cares more about some boy than the safety of her sister, then you don't know me at all," I said.

"How can anyone know you? Me least of all. You think I'm just some kid, an annoying little brat. Emma's all I have too, you know. But I love her enough to be happy for her!"

Without another word, Louisa left me standing in the hallway.

I pushed through the crowds that were heading into the mess hall. I just wanted to be alone. No. I didn't want to be alone. I wanted to be with Emma, but she had chosen someone else.

Robert.

Was I jealous?

I walked back and forth in the little dirt courtyard behind the compound. It wasn't much, but at least it was away from the constant noise. There's nothing like being surrounded by a bunch of people to really make you feel alone.

I grabbed a piece of coal and threw it into the air. There was a ton of the stuff lying around—relics from the compound's past. I noticed how the coal left black smudges against my hand. I liked the feel of it on my fingers, a silky yet gritty coating over my skin.

Contradictory. Different. Always.

With a ragged grunt, I sat down on the ground. I took the piece of coal I held in my hand and began to sketch out a set of piano keys. I just needed the music again. If I could only have the music, I would be able to save my family.

As I pressed my fingers into the dirt I began to hum. I hummed the only song I could remember.

I kept playing it over and over until a shadow fell across me.

"I didn't know you were planning a concert tonight," Robert remarked.

I didn't turn to look at him. I worried his face would undo me. He was hard to hate.

"Please. Go away," I whispered.

Instead, Robert crouched down beside me. I could see him out of the corner of my eye, and I fought against the strange need to turn my body toward him. I was filled with the same feeling that always consumed me when I was around him— like I knew him. Like he had existed in my life before this place.

But that wasn't possible.

"I'd love to let you sit here and mope, but that wouldn't be very nice of someone who's going to call you family soon."

"Family," I repeated.

"Yes, Tess. Family. Can't you see what you're gaining here? I can help protect your sisters. I know you feel like you've got to do it all on your own, but I can help," he said.

"By getting Emma pregnant," I charged.

"I won't let that happen. I'll make her do the sterilization."

"Good luck. She refuses it, Robert, you know that. Please stop talking to me like we both don't know what this is about."

"What's this about then?" he asked quietly.

It was about everything changing. Robert had been a good friend to us all. Now he wouldn't be that anymore. He would belong to her, and she would belong to him.

Robert reached out and grabbed my hand. "Please, talk to her. She's really upset. I'll protect her, Tess, I swear."

I could feel the coal residue slip between our hands. I was unable to stop myself from turning to face him. He loved my sister. I couldn't blame him.

I couldn't.

"Swear, Robert. Swear again," I urged.

"I swear."

I swallowed the lump that had risen in my throat.

"Now will you go talk to her?" he asked.

I shook my head. "No. I can't. I just needed to hear you promise to take care of her."

I ripped my hand from Robert's and walked away.

Chapter 7

Emma's funeral was a joke. If the naturals from the compound expected me to wither under their need to see me mourn, they only found disappointment. I wasn't going to pretend to feel something just to give others hope there would be someone to cry over their deaths. I was better than the rest of them when it came to dealing with loss. I'd had years of practice.

Whatever I felt was for me alone.

I was able to drown out the noise of crying from the fellow inhabitants of the compound. I was even able to force out her smell, the heat trying in vain quite forcefully to drown me in her decay. I glanced toward Robert, his promise from back then echoing in my ears. He wasn't hiding his tears, but it was something else that locked me to him: the way he clenched his fists. A need for violence.

Was he angry with me? I'd never approved of their relationship. I refused to go to their wedding. When she told me she was pregnant, I didn't talk to her for weeks. And Robert, I loathed him and made no secret of it. It was the most powerful emotion I had ever felt.

As our eyes met, it was as if we were in a soundproof cell, just me, him, and an unspeakable anger. When the clergy finished, we both reached for a handful of dirt, waiting to see who would drop it onto her grave first. Who would bury her? I refused. He had killed her, not me. You can wrap it up in a pretty package and call it love, but it was still murder.

Robert's hand released the dirt. Then, without warning, he grabbed my wrist, pulling me close to him. I ignored the gasps of the others. No one seemed to move, and I never once flinched. I could feel his fingers digging into my skin. But then, as soon as it happened, he released me, staggering back. Lost. I kept my eyes on him even as his back turned to me. I continued to stare as my hand reluctantly released the dirt onto her grave. I seriously began to wonder why women had been labeled the weaker sex.

Gwen told me I didn't have to attend work that afternoon. Maybe she thought she was doing me a favor; she wasn't. The compound was the last place I wanted to be. Everywhere I went people sought me out to ask how I was coping, or if I needed anything.

The funny thing about death is how much people want to take from you. I was the one who had lost a sister, but everyone looked to me to ease their own fears, their pain. Her death was cathartic for them—a release, a space in which to mourn the lives they had lost.

Death was also an opportunity for some to spout their religious views. The whole "this life sucks but the next one would be better" crap. I didn't believe that. Maybe there was a God. It didn't matter either way. Did we need to pray to Him anymore? We had allowed the council to put our faith in the chosen ones. They were God, and we had made it that way. I couldn't answer to someone I didn't see, someone who didn't feed and protect me.

Believing in Him had done nothing for my grandparents, who watched as millions and millions of people died from the bomb that was dropped, and thousands of others who died from the effects of radiation. It did nothing for my parents, who tried to build a life in the ruins of a war that started before they were even born. It did nothing for my sisters and me, who spent our childhoods feeling the pangs of hunger because our country had split in two, unable to agree on the best way to rebuild, reorganize, and regroup after the devastation.

The crazy thing was, the council supported freedom of religion with an indescribable passion. One of my people's greatest fears concerning the creation of the chosen ones surrounded the belief that they had no souls. Scientists had played God, and the naturals warned that our government was trying to convince us we didn't need one. The council maintained that it was God who had given them the intelligence and technology to create beings that would protect us. The council's abilities to analyze and create, the gifts of intellect and innovation, were no different than the chameleon that could hide itself from a predator. Their ability to create life in a lab, an endless army of soldiers, forever strong and dedicated to the cause, was a gift from God—our own Moses. Except now we had an army of prophets. And to prove the council's support of religion, their dedication to all things holy, they allowed copies of all religious texts inside the compound. The only books allowed.

Some naturals clung reverently onto their religion. I always thought it allowed them to convince themselves they still had a purpose. We had no jobs, no need to be educated, and no reason to get married. No sense of importance at all; we just existed.

As I made my way toward my sleeping quarters, I noticed I was being followed. Jacobson, my father's friend. The only one I remember my father having. Could I even call them friends? Or were they merely partners in some deception?

I was sure something about his connection to my father had led him to be assigned to Templeton. What had he done? It must have been something bad—not bad enough to disappear, but bad enough to be sentenced to that place for so long.

Was there any relationship I was familiar with that wasn't about taking something from someone? My mom used people to score booze. My little sister used people to make herself feel worthy. Robert used my sister for sex.

Right?

No. He loved her. He loved her so much.

Jacobson looked nervous, and I wondered if it was merely a manifestation of the uncomfortable nature of talking to someone who'd just watched her sister die. Perhaps it had something to do with the strange look he'd given me when I was walking with James.

For some reason, I was willing to talk to him. Jacobson had been very kind to my mother and sisters after we first entered the compound. I wasn't naive enough to ignore the fact he did it out of guilt. The council had taken him with my father for questioning, and he was the only one who returned. But I never blamed him. I blamed my father.

Besides, I kind of had to respect the man for surviving. That's all I was trying to do.

"Hello, Tessa," Jacobson half mumbled.

Tessa. I hadn't heard him call me that in almost a decade. I used to think he was loopy and couldn't remember my name. He looked so old, so broken now. Would my father look like this if he still lived? I nodded, suddenly unable to produce any words. Jacobson took a deep breath and pulled something from inside his coat. Paper. Letters, tied together by a black ribbon.

"These are for you," he whispered.

I looked up at him in confusion. What the hell did they have to do with me?

He sighed, pulling me into the darkness of the hallway, away from the masses of people who were settling in for bed. "I think I did you a great wrong, Tessa. These belonged to your father. I…he…well, we had a deal. Before the council took us, well, we may have sensed it was coming to that. So we agreed to keep letters for each other's families. This way if one of us made it back, we could offer the other's loved ones some comfort."

"Why didn't you give them to my mother?" I managed. It was suddenly stifling in the hallway.

"Because they weren't for your mother. Every single letter in here is addressed to you."

My hands began to shake.

"I held onto them because I couldn't convince myself to bring you any more pain. What good would his words do? I thought you were young enough to move past it and start a new life. Find some comfort in this place. Or maybe I just hoped that by protecting you, you wouldn't be so angry about your life here."

He was right. I could understand his reasoning. My father was a traitor, an outspoken citizen killed for his distrust and mutinous tendencies. If I had spent my childhood reading his letters, I wouldn't have survived. I would have died because I would have been unable to strangle the emotions inside me. I was too young back then. Too weak. Too innocent.

"Why are you giving them to me now?" Why tempt me with my father's legacy now?

"I thought you needed something of your family to hold onto. And I realized, maybe anger isn't such a bad thing. Your sister and the other women—I know the council can stop this. It isn't right," he replied softly, staring past me. He moved his fist and pushed it against the wall, all without an ounce of bitterness crossing his face. His body was unsure how to handle the feelings that had lay dormant in him for so long.

I recognized this look—a need to fight back. Every so often I would see it cross the face of some natural, and every so often they would find a way to ask for their own death.

I shook my head, not wanting to touch the letters and desperately needing to clutch them to me at the same time. "How did you even get those in here? Weren't you searched?"

"Considering the things your father and I were doing, it should be no surprise I could hold onto some letters. I have my ways."

I laughed. "Right. If you two were so good at keeping secrets, then how come you got caught?"

Jacobson smiled. "Your dad always said you had one hell of a sense of humor."

I wanted to smile back. I'd been called a lot of things, but funny usually didn't make the list.

"Maybe I'm making a mistake here. I can't be sure reading these will do you any good, but the truth is I don't think I've got much time left in this body, and I can't go knowing I made a decision that was not mine to make."

It would be my choice to read the letters or not. *My choice.*

That night, I didn't sleep, just lay on my cot, staring at the ceiling. I shared a room with Louisa and a girl named Grace who had lost her mother to suicide some time back. I guess the council figured that, since we had been through something similar, we could help her out. The thought of talking about our dead mothers didn't seem helpful for anyone. Louisa liked Grace because she let her prattle on and on without interrupting.

It was only when I heard their snoring and off-key breathing that I found a moment for myself. I sat up, stretching my muscles. I held my body tight, tense from the day. It was hard keeping my emotions in check. I was a natural, after all. I curled my fingers under the rail of my cot and leaned forward, resting my head on my knees.

I could feel the weight of my father's presence crushing down upon me. I had never been a big crier, but my first night in the compound I'd cried myself to sleep. The night they took my father I'd felt only anger. I hadn't shed a tear. Somehow, almost two years after he was gone, surrounded by so many other people, I cried for my father. I whispered out his name, begging him to take me from this place. Eventually, I stopped calling for him.

What would happen now if I read one of his letters? Would I find it ridiculous? Pathetic, senseless ramblings from a man foolish enough to get himself killed? Would I find a clue as to why he chose some mission, some useless political statement, over me? Would I find a way to embrace the memories of the man without opening up the pain I knew could consume me?

Suddenly, the letters were in my hands. I couldn't stop myself. I cursed Emma silently. This was her fault. If she were still here, I wouldn't be like this. I would be strong. I would be invincible. But even I couldn't convince myself of my own strength. In the darkness of the night, the hours where I was unable to sleep, I felt the pain hum inside of me.

With a shaky breath, I began to read.

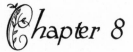hapter 8

TESS,

I NEVER REALLY WANTED TO BE A FATHER. MAYBE THIS ISN'T SOMETHING ONE SHOULD TELL ONE'S DAUGHTER, BUT IT'S NEVER BEEN MY WAY TO MUCH WORRY ABOUT THINGS YOU SHOULD AND SHOULD NOT SAY. GUESS YOU SORT OF TAKE AFTER ME IN THAT REGARD.

DO YOU REMEMBER WHEN YOU WERE THREE AND YOUR MOTHER ASKED YOU IF YOU WANTED TO HAVE A NEW BABY BROTHER OR SISTER? YOU LOOKED HER DEAD IN THE FACE, STUCK OUT YOUR TONGUE, AND PROCEEDED TO GROWL. YES, YOU ACTUALLY GROWLED. AND WHEN YOUR MOTHER LET YOU SEE LOUISA FOR THE FIRST TIME, YOU TOLD HER SHE LOOKED LIKE A TURTLE.

I KNOW YOU DON'T REMEMBER GRANDMA AND GRANDPA, BUT I CAN'T SAY I WAS EVER MUCH LIKE THEM. IT'S A WEIRD THING HOW CHILDREN TURN OUT. I CAN SEE

SO MUCH OF YOUR MOTHER WHEN I LOOK AT LOUISA, EVEN IN THE WAY SHE COVERS HER MOUTH WITH HER HAND AS SHE EATS. SHE'S THREE FOR CHRIST SAKES, AND YET SHE MIMICS YOUR MOTHER SO WELL. WITH EMMA, IT'S LIKE SHE GOT THE BEST QUALITIES OF YOUR MOTHER AND ME. BUT THERE'S THIS STRANGE STRAIN OF COMPASSION THAT RUNS THROUGH HER. YOUR MOTHER AND I AREN'T EVEN ABLE TO FAKE THAT AMOUNT OF SYMPATHY FOR OTHERS. WHERE DOES SHE GET IT?

YOU, YOU'RE ALL ME. I USED TO SORT OF LIKE THAT. NOW, IT MAKES ME SCARED FOR YOU. EVERY DAY I WAKE UP TO A WORLD THAT'S GETTING DARKER AND DARKER, AND IT'S SUFFOCATING ME, KID. I TRY TO PRETEND, LIKE THE OTHERS, THAT IT ISN'T HAPPENING. BUT I JUST CAN'T.

TONIGHT, AS WE WATCHED THE COUNCIL'S FIRST DEMONSTRATION OF THE CHOSEN ONES, I KEPT MY EYES ON YOU.

IT'S PRETTY SICK, REALLY, THE WAY THE COUNCIL ARRANGED IT ALL. JUST IN TIME FOR DINNER. COME, COLLECT YOUR FAMILIES AROUND THE TELEVISION, WATCH OUR GREATNESS. IGNORE THE FACT THERE ARE COUNTLESS FAMILIES WHO CAN NO LONGER AFFORD ROOFS OVER THEIR HEADS, LET ALONE A TELEVISION. BUT, OF COURSE, THE COUNCIL HAD THAT COVERED. THEY SET UP BIG SCREENS IN EVERY SHANTYTOWN IN THE WESTERN SECTOR. NO DOUBT THEY WILL BE TAKEN DOWN BY TOMORROW MORNING.

WERE WE SUPPOSED TO CHEER AS THAT CHOSEN ONE KILLED THOSE MEN? I HAVE NO DOUBT THAT MANY FATHERS LOOKED TO THEIR CHILDREN AND FELT COMFORTED,

SOMEHOW CONVINCING THEMSELVES THEY WOULD BE PROTECTED NOW. WE WOULD NO LONGER HAVE TO WORRY ABOUT TERRORISTS OR WARS. WE COULD SIMPLY WHIP UP AN ARMY IN A LAB, AN ARMY THAT NO ONE COULD MATCH. FORGETTING THAT WHEN ONE COUNTRY SHOWS THEIR BIG GUNS, ANOTHER COUNTRY GOES OUT AND CREATES BIGGER ONES.

I SHUDDER TO THINK WHERE OUR GENETIC MEDDLING WILL LEAD US IN FIFTY YEARS. WILL THEY EVEN LOOK HUMAN THEN? WILL THERE EVEN BE ANY OF US NATURALS LEFT TO NOTICE?

LOUISA CLAPPED HER HANDS IN DELIGHT. I COULD HEAR YOUR MOTHER'S WORDS OF ENCOURAGEMENT AS THE CHOSEN ONE PERFORMED HIS DUTY WITH EASE. EMMA, BLESS HER SOUL, COULDN'T BEAR TO WATCH. BUT YOU, YOU JUST STARED AT THE SCREEN. YOU NEVER FLINCHED. YOUR LITTLE FOREHEAD SCRUNCHED UP AS IF YOU WERE TRYING TO COMMIT EVERY MOVE TO MEMORY, AND YOUR LITTLE HAND CURLED INTO A FIST. DO YOU KNOW THAT? WERE YOU AWARE OF YOUR OWN MOVEMENTS? WHO DID YOU WANT TO FIGHT?

I FEEL IT, TOO, THE URGE TO FIGHT THIS. I JUST DON'T KNOW WHOM TO FIGHT ANYMORE. THE COUNCIL? THEY'RE SUPPOSED TO BE THE ONES PROTECTING US.

MY MOM AND DAD HAD IT ROUGH, BUT AT LEAST THEY KNEW WHO THEY WERE FIGHTING. DAD ALWAYS SAID IT WAS IMPOSSIBLE TO SUM UP THE CAUSES FOR THE WAR IN SIMPLE, CONCISE SENTENCES. HOW CAN ONE DEFINE HATRED? I ASKED HIM TO TRY. HE TOLD ME OUR COUNTRY, OR THE COUNTRY THAT ONCE BONDED ALL PARTS OF THIS

LAND, LOST ITSELF. WE HAD FALLEN ONTO HARD TIMES AND ENTERED INTO A DEPRESSION. SOMETHING OUR PEOPLE HADN'T SEEN IN A HUNDRED YEARS. THERE'S NOT MUCH LEFT OF THE MIDWEST NOW. ALL OF THE SURVIVORS MOVED TO THE WEST COAST.

WE FOUGHT WITH OTHER LANDS ACROSS THE SEA. FARAWAY LANDS THAT HATED US FOR REASONS THAT SEEMED ANCIENT AND EVER PESTERING. BUT AS WE SQUANDERED AWAY OUR MONEY, WE FOUND IT DIFFICULT TO FIGHT THE ENEMY, AND PEOPLE BECAME DISILLUSIONED. WHY SIGN UP TO FIGHT A WAR ACROSS THE SEA WHEN ONE'S OWN FAMILY WAS STARVING? WHY FIGHT FOR A COUNTRY THAT COULD NOT TAKE CARE OF ITS OWN PEOPLE?

WHEN I LOOK TO MY NEIGHBORS WHO HAVE LOST EVERYTHING, I CAN UNDERSTAND THESE FEELINGS.

WITH ONE BOMB DROPPED, THE MEN FROM OVERSEAS KILLED MILLIONS AND DESTROYED THE MAJORITY OF OUR MILITARY. THE MAJORITY DIED FROM THE BOMB ITSELF. OTHERS FROM RADIATION POISONING. OTHERS FROM STARVATION. OUR GOVERNMENT TOOK TOO LONG TO BRING SUPPLIES AND RELIEF TO THOSE LIVING IN THE HEARTLAND. OUR COUNTRY FELL APART.

FEARING COMPLETE ANARCHY, PEOPLE BEGAN TO BAND TOGETHER. TEMPORARY, MAKESHIFT GOVERNMENTS CAME INTO POWER. WE WERE NO LONGER A UNIFIED COUNTRY, BUT RATHER A SERIES OF COLONIES FIGHTING FOR A SENSE OF SAFETY. SOME MEN THOUGHT IT WOULD BE BEST TO REBUILD, FORM A NEWER, STRONGER GOVERNMENT. THERE WERE COUNTLESS MEETINGS AMONG THE COLONIES, WHICH

NEVER AMOUNTED TO MUCH. SOME WANTED TO REBUILD THE GOVERNMENT ACCORDING TO THE DOCTRINES THAT THE UNITED STATES WAS FOUNDED ON. OTHERS SAID THE PREVIOUS SYSTEM WAS CORRUPTED AND WE NEEDED A NEW FORM OF GOVERNMENT. THERE WAS A LOT OF IN-FIGHTING AND MORE VIOLENCE.

I WONDER SOMETIMES WHY MY PARENTS DECIDED TO BRING ME INTO SUCH A WORLD OF CHAOS. AND YET, I DID THE SAME TO YOU.

THE ONLY THING ANYONE COULD AGREE ON WAS A NEED FOR STABILITY. AFTER YEARS OF TALKS AND A FEW VIOLENT FLARE-UPS BETWEEN THE WARRING FACTIONS OF OUR COUNTRY, A TREATY WAS CREATED. OUR COUNTRY WOULD NO LONGER PRETEND IT COULD COME TOGETHER. EASTERNERS. WESTERNERS. THE MIDDLELANDS WERE LEFT TO THEMSELVES. NO ONE CHOSE TO SETTLE THERE EXCEPT THOSE WHO WANTED NO GOVERNMENT AT ALL.

WESTERNERS LIKE MY PARENTS UNDERSTOOD THE NEED FOR SOME SORT OF GOVERNMENT, AN AGENCY MEANT TO SERVE THE PEOPLE'S INTERESTS AND BAND US TOGETHER BEHIND A COMMON BELIEF SYSTEM. EXCEPT OUR GOVERNMENT REFUSED TO BE CALLED A GOVERNMENT. INSTEAD, WE WERE A COUNCIL. SOMEHOW THE TERM MADE IT SEEM LESS INTRUSIVE.

IRONIC, HUH?

MY PARENTS HELD STRONGLY ONTO THEIR FAITH IN THIS NEW SYSTEM. I WASN'T ALLOWED TO QUESTION. WHEN THE COUNCIL TOOK CONTROL OVER THE MEDIA I REMEMBER ASKING WHY, AND MY FATHER SLAPPED ME

HARD ACROSS THE FACE. HE GOT ALL RED AND MUMBLED SOMETHING ABOUT ME NOT KNOWING A DAMN THING ABOUT FREEDOM OR WHAT HAPPENS WHEN SOMEONE TRIES TO TAKE IT FROM YOU.

I CAN'T TRUST THE COUNCIL. SOMETHING INSIDE WON'T LET ME. WHO AM I SUPPOSED TO DESPISE MORE? THE EASTERNERS WHO ATTACK OUR LAND? THE MIDDLELANDERS WHO SEEK OUT THE WILD? OR MY OWN GOVERNMENT? I JUST FEEL A FIGHT COMING ON. I THINK YOU FEEL IT, TOO, TESS. AND THAT SCARES THE LIVING HELL OUT OF ME. PART OF ME WISHES YOU WERE NOTHING LIKE ME.

I DID SOMETHING STUPID TODAY. I VOLUNTEERED TO WORK AT ONE OF THE NEW TRAINING CENTERS FOR THE CHOSEN ONES. IT'S DECENT MONEY, AND THE BEST JOB I COULD HOPE TO GET. ALSO, I WANT TO KNOW MORE ABOUT THEM, AND WHAT BETTER WAY THAN TO WORK THERE?

WHO KNOWS IF YOU WILL EVER READ THIS. I HOPE YOU NEVER HAVE A REASON, BUT YOU PROBABLY WILL.

I NEVER WANTED TO BE A FATHER. MOSTLY BECAUSE I SOMEHOW KNEW I WOULDN'T BE AROUND FOR YOU. I'VE BEEN WAITING MY WHOLE LIFE FOR A FIGHT.

~DAD

Chapter 9

I was shaking. Somehow I could hear my father's voice as I read his letter. Ten years later, I could still hear him. It was yet another reminder of all the things I kept locked away. I knew my people's history, but sometimes it was easier to let the council rewrite it all.

I couldn't change the council or this life. My father was wrong—I wasn't strong enough to be the kind of fighter he thought I was. The only thing I wanted to defeat was my own weak self. And I couldn't even do that lately.

I closed my eyes and took a deep breath. And then I waited for whatever was going to come next.

When I sensed it was near morning, I crept out of the room and headed toward the showers. I hoped the rest of the compound would still be asleep. I needed just a little more time to myself.

I turned the water as hot as I could get it. It burned, and I found comfort in the pain. It was strange that sitting in the shower, the blazing heat causing my naked skin to erupt in blotches of red, I thought of Emma. My sister. The girl my father said was filled with compassion. What were those last moments like for her? Did she cry out? Did she ask for me at all? Or was it all about him? Did her eyes simply close or did her body lurch, fighting against the darkness that was attempting to claim it?

My heart began to speed up, and I leaned against the wall of the shower. Breathing in and out. In and out. In and out. The letter made me weaker, not stronger like my father had hoped. It would be so easy to just cry, to give in. In frustration I slammed my head against the cement wall. The pain vibrated from my head down to my toes. And I liked it. My heart stopped beating so wildly. I could focus on this new pain. I threw my head back again into the wall. And again. And again. Again. Again. Again. My head was throbbing. I reached my fingers to the back of my scalp and found blood.

Always blood.

When I arrived at work, my head still throbbing from the morning, Gwen was waiting. She looked me up and down. Whatever she saw, she was not impressed. I knew she could find no fault with my appearance; I'd made a point of ensuring my uniform was perfect. No wrinkles. No dirt. No sign of the laziness that consumed the people of the compound.

I was perfect.

With a heavy sigh, my supervisor turned and began to walk down the hallway. When I didn't follow, she snapped her fingers at me without stopping to make sure I understood her directions. She knew I would follow. She knew I would have to.

We didn't speak to each other as we climbed the marble staircase to the upper levels of the Templeton mansion—the servants' quarters. Women, girls, who had received two slash marks were forced to live at Templeton. While I could go home to my family, or lack thereof, every night, the double-slash girls had to serve out their sentence twenty-four hours a day, six days a week. One day for rest, of course—that is what the Bible demanded.

I was still unsure what happened when one received the third mark.

When we stopped, my supervisor pulled a skeleton key from the pocket of her skirt. It struck me as odd that the doors of the servants' quarters were locked from the outside, as if one of them would try to escape. No one would be that stupid. If a girl ran from her punishment and life at the compound, the next oldest female in her family would not only have to finish the remainder of her sentence, but would be punished for the new transgression as well.

Besides, the minute someone left, the council's promise of protection was null and void. In the early days of my life at the compound, back when my mother was still alive, a group of women and Henry ran off. It was before I knew him. The women were unhappy with the council's system of punishment—why should the females be forced to serve for the sins of all? Why must we be responsible for the morality of a people who just didn't give a damn anymore? At the time, I remember asking my mother why we didn't leave with them. She asked me if I knew where to score some booze. She didn't give a damn anymore, either.

Three weeks later, the council found the bodies of these women. They had been attacked. Barely identifiable. The council was unclear if it was Easterners or the Isolationists—men and women who had run into the darkness of the forest before the construction of the compounds—were responsible for the deaths.

Sure, it's terrible. The whole system. But the funny thing about mankind is we have a natural need—a natural will to live. So many of us would rather have a life of nothingness than risk not living at all. And the council knows this.

As the click of the door unlocking stirred me from my recollections, I noticed my supervisor staring at me. Something about the look on her face, the weariness of it, caused me to take a step back.

What was waiting behind that door?

"Now you listen to me, girl. When we go in there you are not to say a word. Nothing. You will not speak of this to anyone. If she says something to you, you will ignore her. Do you understand?"

I nodded. Somehow I couldn't find the courage to speak to this woman as we entered the room.

Lying on the bed was a young girl with her back toward me—the two glaring red slash marks standing out against the pale skin of her neck. She was curled into a ball, her hands pressed against her heart. Spots of blood covered the sheets. As I stepped farther into the room, I began to see how wild this girl looked. Her nightgown barely clothed her body, and she made no attempt to cover herself as we approached.

"Help me get her up," Gwen commanded.

As my hands made contact with her arm, the girl shrieked. She began to blindly lash out, hitting me in the arms.

"Calm down, child," I heard Gwen say from somewhere in the darkness. "Damn it, girl! Make yourself useful and help me hold her down!"

I applied as much pressure to the girl's body as I could muster. I was barely able to hold her in place as she continued to squirm with a force that seemed unnatural coming from someone so small. How old was this girl? She couldn't be sixteen. And yet one was not allowed to take on someone's punishment until she was of age.

My supervisor pulled a syringe from her pocket and without hesitation stuck it into the girl's arm. I felt her body begin to convulse. Tears ran down her face and she attempted to yell out, but all she could do was grunt.

Slowly, the girl became still. I could hear her breathing return to normal. She was mumbling something as the contents of the syringe lulled her to sleep, but it was difficult to make much sense of it.

"Stay with her. Don't let her move. I will be right back," my supervisor said coldly. She was beginning to be a mystery I knew I would never want to understand.

The girl continued to mumble, and I felt the need to hear what she was saying. Maybe it was my endless fascination with other people's pain, my constant need to know I was not alone in feeling the world offered me little else. I sank to my knees and leaned closer to the girl. Without warning, she clamped her hand onto my arm. In her grip existed a strength that didn't seem possible.

"I thought I said no," she gasped. "I thought I said no."

She began to cry again. I tried to pull my arm from her grip. I knew my supervisor would be back any minute, but she held on tightly. She kept muttering the same words over and over.

"What the hell do you think you're doing?"

My supervisor stared down at me with contempt. I couldn't find my voice. I yanked with all my strength, stumbling and landing on my backside.

"Get up and help me wash her," she snapped, throwing me a rag.

I felt uncomfortable as I helped my supervisor undress the girl. The sight of her nakedness caused my skin to erupt in patches of heat. I couldn't imagine ever being so vulnerable. The girl had slipped into unconsciousness; I wondered, had she been awake, if she would have protested our actions.

Her words still rang in my ears: *I thought I said no.*

Her body was so marked up, the attempt to destroy it, own it, rewrite it so painfully obvious. I wanted to ask what had happened. But I couldn't speak.

I helped to clean the blood that was smeared on the insides of her thighs. I wiped down her arms that appeared to be covered in newly formed bruises. I washed her neck, which was strangely covered with bite marks.

I cleaned it all away.

It wasn't so different from the blood I'd helped clean down below. It was just another Templeton secret that I was helping to keep hidden. And for some reason, I felt terrible doing it.

When we were done I followed my supervisor out of the room. My head was throbbing in a way that had suddenly become unwelcome. I didn't want the pain anymore. I had felt enough pain for one day.

Enough for a lifetime.

"Wait," I whispered as my supervisor moved to go down the stairs.

She stopped, keeping her back toward me. "I didn't think you would ever speak."

"Why?"

"Excuse me?"

"Why did you bring me in there?" I knew I shouldn't care, but the question sat burning in my throat. My pulse sped up as I waited for her answer.

I watched as her hand reached for the banister. Her fingers curled around it. "I needed help."

"But you could have asked any of the girls. Why did you choose me?"

Finally she turned to face me. She offered a thin smile. "I asked you because out of all the girls, you are the only one who would see something like that and not care. I knew it the moment I met you. The way you just sat there. Sullen. Self-centered. That's why you'll do so well here. You don't care about anything or anyone."

No. Self-centered? How could I be self-centered when I didn't even know who the hell I was anymore? Everyone was trying to fix me into some place. My father's letter begged me to rage against the life created for me by others. Gwen wanted me to be some silent drone that did her bidding. And while I was so busy working on becoming nothing, everything fell apart. I couldn't be nothing here. The mangled body downstairs. The broken girl upstairs. What would happen to me if I continued to stay silent?

I didn't know who I needed to be to survive this place. All I knew was the rules had changed.

Chapter 10

Gwen left me as soon as we reached the main floor, after saying I was free to report to James now that I was considered his personal servant. She left me standing alone with no explanation of what I had just seen.

My head continued to throb, but a new pain accompanied it now. Even within the silence of the hall, I could hear the girl crying out for someone to care. She was screaming for me. I could feel it in the grasp of her hand on my arm. She needed someone to help, to *want* to help.

Could I continue on with my day as if I had never seen her bruised and battered body? With my sister it had been different. She'd known the consequences of her choices. Part of me would always feel she deserved what she got. Maybe it was a screwed-up way of thinking, but I didn't believe I would ever be able to come back from that.

I knew in my soul, if I still had one, that the girl was a victim. Something had been done to her. Someone had damaged her.

And I was not the sort of person who could watch it and feel nothing. I wasn't a monster.

I wasn't.

I attempted to find my reflection in one of the windows that faced the gardens of Templeton. Nothing about the image was clear; it only whispered a sense of what I really was. Even in the murky shadows, I didn't like what I saw.

When James opened the door, he wasn't alone. Another chosen one. They were both dressed in clothes much too fine for the boys of the compound—starched white button-up shirts with black trousers and a fitted black jacket. While the second chosen one was handsome, as they all were, I soon realized he didn't fascinate me the way James tended to. Was this because I had caught a glimpse of James beyond his physical being? I'd seen something behind those mismatched eyes that didn't belong to all chosen ones. And it wasn't just the scar. There was life behind those eyes, and it was alluringly dangerous.

"If you will excuse me, Tess, I have to help Frank back to his room," James said as he placed his friend's arm around his shoulder.

I nodded and moved to let the two pass. The other boy, Frank, looked a bit ill. Could the chosen ones get sick?

"You go on in. Sorry about the mess," James said, motioning to his room. He attempted a smile as he gave me one last look before heading down the hallway. I knew it was fake.

I wondered if I would ever figure him out.

James hadn't been lying—the room was a disaster. It had only been two days since I had last been here, yet it looked worse than before. The books I had so carefully put away were thrown about the room. The floor was littered with multiple balled-up pieces of sketching paper. There was a pile of clothes lying in a corner.

With a heavy sigh, I began to straighten up. An hour must have passed before I realized James still hadn't returned. The room was presentable, and I wondered if I was supposed to wait around for him. Did he want me to?

The last time I had been in his room he'd seemed distraught. A little wild in his ramblings. So unsure.

My head continued to hum with pain.

I was about to leave when something caught my eye. Underneath a pile of papers on his desk laid the novel he'd snatched from my hands during my previous visit—Mary Shelley's *Frankenstein*. I pulled it out and held it in my hands. It wasn't clear to me what was so secret about this book.

Cautiously, every so often glancing at the door, I began to flip through the novel. It had been years since I'd read one. But it didn't feel like a moment of freedom; it felt like an invasion. Something about this book was so private to James he hadn't wanted me to see it, even when he was so willing to share the rest of his library and music. Perhaps something in this book would reveal why James seemed so different from the rest of the chosen ones.

The binding was worn, evidence that James had read this on multiple occasions. Inside, on the fading white of the pages, he had underlined numerous quotations, writing notes in the margins. Within this story of a man created from the body parts of the working class by a scientist obsessed with producing life, James had attempted to define himself.

One page of the novel was folded in. On it he had circled lines with an evident passion: "I am alone and miserable; man will not associate with me; but one as deformed and horrible as myself would not deny herself to me. My companion must be of the same species and have the same defects. This being you must create."

Around this quote he had written the same sentences over and over again: *I know what she is supposed to be for me. What part of me wants her to be. But I won't be a monster. I can't.*

My skin erupted in goose bumps as if it recognized something my mind couldn't quite comprehend. I forcefully pushed out the image of the girl upstairs that briefly entered my mind. Why I thought of her, I'm not sure. But beneath the fear was something else. The tiniest part of me was desperately curious to know who this girl he wrote of was. Did I want her to be me? It would be impossible. And besides, what would cause me to desire that at all?

Did James feel some connection to these words? Did he feel alone? Miserable? Was it even possible for one of them to feel any of these things at all?

I didn't hear the door open. As I moved to put the book back under the stack of papers, I saw James standing in the doorway. His expression was emotionless, but his hand had begun to twitch. I saw his face slowly transform into fear, then anger.

"I thought I told you to never touch that."

I dropped the book and scrambled away from his desk. I didn't know how to apologize, not correctly. It wasn't something I regularly practiced. James looked devastated, horrified that I had read something so private.

I wanted to know this boy who could play music so beautifully. The boy who smiled despite knowing I was a natural. The boy who took me away from the laughing chosen ones. The boy who was miserable and alone.

The boy who I sensed wanted to know me, too.

The boy who perhaps felt the things I felt.

The boy who could maybe convince me it wasn't wrong to feel them.

"Leave. Now." How strained his voice sounded.

"Please," I begged, "I can explain."

"Just go."

"I meant no harm, I swear it. I saw it lying there and—"

He slammed the door shut, causing me to jump. James moved to his desk, sat down, and started scribbling furiously on a sheet of paper.

"James," I said, caught off guard by the way his name sounded issuing from my lips.

He stiffened. Did hearing it cause him to feel something as well? He slowly put down the pencil, keeping his back toward me.

"I had no right to read that. None at all. But...I liked it. The book. I mean, I can understand it. At least the parts I read. They made sense to me."

I sounded like a rambling idiot. I didn't know how to do this. The pain in my head intensified.

He finally turned to face me, and I breathed a sigh of relief. If he could look at me, face me, maybe we could talk this out. I needed to make things right.

"I told you not to touch it. When I tell you to do something, you are to do it. Or have you forgotten why you're here?"

His words stilled everything inside of me. They were empty. In that moment, he sounded like every other chosen one. I bit my lip and shifted from foot to foot. It took everything in me to control myself. There were so many things I wanted to say in response.

His hand reached for the book and he pulled it to him, looking down at it. For the briefest of moments, in the seconds where he didn't think I was watching, I saw him caress the cover before he put it into a drawer.

When he looked back to me I could see the man he had trained his whole life to become. If I could ignore the shaking of his hands, I might have believed that this was who he wanted to be in life. But I *did* see his hands shake. And I had read the notes in the margins of the books: *What am I capable of? Is there life outside of this place? Do I have a soul?*

"I need you to leave. Go. Report to your supervisor. I'm done with you for today."

"No."

The word had slipped out of me without warning. I felt my heart beat with approval; I felt strength. Excitement. I felt a little like the me I had forgotten.

"Excuse me? This isn't some game, Tess. You can't just go around sneaking into piano rooms and defying direct orders and expect nothing to happen. There are always consequences. *Always*." James curled his hands into fists, placing them against his knees. His words sounded more like a plea than a reprimand.

"So what? Are you going to report me? I can afford another slash mark," I replied with a laugh. I could handle two slash marks. I would never do anything to earn three.

"Stop."

I couldn't. Not now.

"Tell me you want me to leave."

"I already told you."

"Say it again. Say you want me to leave."

The pain in my head was getting worse. It had been a hell of a day. But I couldn't back down.

I watched as he fought with himself. But he couldn't say the words. Instead he looked up at me and asked the question I had been asking since the morning, since forever: "What do you want?"

I took a deep breath. And then I answered him. "I don't want to be a monster, either."

"Tess," he replied, the tone of his voice altering suddenly.

"Yes." I shut my eyes to keep the room from spinning.

"You have blood on your collar."

And then everything went black.

Chapter 11

"Don't touch me!" I screamed.

When I came to I saw James's hands coming toward me to help me up. I moved out of his reach, pushing myself with my feet against the floor to the edge of his bed. His jaw tensed as he stepped away from me. He took a deep breath before pulling a handkerchief from the pocket of his ridiculously formal jacket.

I was mortified. Not because I'd passed out, but because I had regressed into the natural, the girl who feared to be touched by a chosen one. As if somehow I could catch their soullessness by mere physical contact.

I had no idea if he had a soul. I was too busy fighting for mine.

I pulled my knees to my chest and let my head fall forward. "I'm sorry. I didn't mean to freak out." I swallowed, took the handkerchief he offered me, and pressed it against the back of my head.

"You look exhausted," he remarked, sitting on the floor,

leaning against the wall across from me. It was almost as if he wanted me to think we were equals.

"I'm fine. Really, I am. I hit my head while cleaning the banisters earlier today." I'm sure he could tell I was lying.

Maybe he didn't need a book to see a part of me.

The weight of his gaze suddenly felt suffocating. "Please. Tell me something to do. I need to perform a task," I begged quietly.

"I have some clothes that need ironing."

We didn't speak as I worked. Sometimes I felt him looking at me. How strange that a body can feel what the eyes cannot see.

"I'm sorry about the mess. I've never been good at staying focused on one thing. I'll start a project, and some question I have will get me going in another direction completely," he quietly told me as I worked.

In less than half an hour I was done with the task. He mumbled a thank-you and turned back to his schoolwork on his desk. I made my way to the door. My hand barely grazed the knob before his voice halted me.

"You can't go. It's too soon."

"I thought you wanted me to?"

"I don't want you to leave. You seem so tired. Why don't you just rest a bit?" He spoke softly.

I nodded and took a seat in the chair on the other side of the room. "What are you working on?" I asked, nervous to not be occupied with work of my own.

"A project for science class. We are studying the mating habits of rabbits. Completely dull and useless information. There's no way I'll be selected for any medical job," he replied, pushing his book away from him.

"My sister died. We buried her yesterday." I pressed my lips together. I didn't know why I'd spoken up and certainly could not understand why I'd spoken about this thing.

"How old was she?" James asked after a long silence.

"Nineteen."

He inhaled sharply. "You were sent here because of her?"

"She was a silly girl."

"Silly to hope?"

"Yes." I nodded. "Silly to hope where it is impossible."

"There are rumors that certain cases have worked."

"Rumors from a people desperate to believe that God hasn't forsaken them for science," I spat.

I couldn't help it. I knew the anger had slipped out between my words, and I was terrified that my face betrayed it as well. Most of all I was horrified by the way my voice hissed when I said the word *science*.

He cleared his throat. I began to tap my foot furiously on the wooden floor. The dizziness was returning.

"Tess?"

"Hmm," I quietly responded.

"Don't you have any friends you can talk to? Not that I mind hearing about this. I just don't really know what to say. I'm not...I'm not trained for this kind of thing. I will probably do more harm than good."

I offered him a small smile. "You're doing just fine. Besides, I don't really have any friends, so I wouldn't know the difference."

He turned to face me, his eyes still holding the same intensity as before.

"Don't they let you have friends at the compound?"

I frowned. "I choose not to." It was one of the only choices

I was allowed to make in my life, and I had made the wrong one. Maybe if I had someone to talk to, the pain would at least be bearable. I wouldn't have to slam my head against a cement wall to keep from going mad. Maybe I would have been able to help the girl upstairs. At least I would have known what words of comfort sounded like.

His brow wrinkled. "Why would you choose that?"

Because I was scared. If let anyone in, they would see what I had become.

"I'm not exactly a people person," I began.

My father once told me I saw the world differently than others. He said he meant it as a compliment, but I never forgot the tears in his eyes as he'd spoken the words. It was one of the last things we talked about before the council took him.

"I had one friend though. Henry. I mean, I wasn't always a social pariah," I managed. I didn't want James to think I was incapable of human connection. For some reason, I needed him to know I hadn't always been like this.

"What happened? You don't have to tell me, of course." But I could see the anticipation on his face. He wanted the knowledge I could give him. James's fascination with music and books, and maybe even with me, suddenly made sense. He couldn't judge because like me, though for very different reasons, he was also somewhere outside the meaning of humanity.

I swallowed and continued. "When we came to the compound there was a lot of disorder. Back then people still questioned. They still cared. Henry's father, well, he died when Henry was young. In the war. So when Henry came to the compound it was just him and his sisters and his mom. I remember seeing him around, but we didn't really speak. I had my sister…"

I pressed the handkerchief harder, more forcefully against my scalp.

Old habits died hard.

"My sister told me that his mother and sisters couldn't take it anymore. They didn't see the point of the compound. They disagreed with some of the new practices put into place by the council, mainly the ones about our system of punishment."

"The slash marks," James offered. His fingers tapped nervously against the wood floor. I wondered where his tension stemmed from. Was it a burning desire to hear the rest of the story, or fear of what it would reveal?

I nodded. "Yes. So they left. They took Henry with them."

"But it's not safe to leave. There are Easterners and Isolationists out there. Some of those Isolationists are desperate. Men who have been away from civilization too long. The stories they have told us…"

"You don't need to convince me. I know. I learned from Henry." I felt the pain stirring inside of me, but it was not mine, not directly. It was the pain of my one-time friend. The pain I had willingly taken on. "The council found them, his mother and sisters, dead only three weeks later. The things that were done to them." I shivered and my mind momentarily wandered again to the girl upstairs. Was there any place in this world that was safe?

"Henry survived? How?"

"I don't know. He's never talked about it. When he was brought back to the compound, so many people hounded him with questions, like he hadn't been through enough. They wanted to take whatever he had left of himself, too." Something I now understood all too well.

"But you didn't ask him."

"No. It wasn't my place."

"And that's how you became friends?"

I nodded. "One day I just sat next to him at breakfast. I'm not sure why. We didn't talk. It went on like that for days—I would sit next to him, we wouldn't talk. One day he asked me if he could have my leftover pancakes. And that was that."

I couldn't help but smile at the memory and was surprised that James was smiling, too.

"What changed?" he asked.

"Things always get more difficult for our kind as we get older, especially between males and females."

His smile faded.

"When you're young you don't know. And nobody talks about it. The adults just sit there and leave you to figure everything out on your own. I never understood the danger that surrounded our friendship, never suspected it carried with it a threat. How could I? How could I ever fathom that one day he would stop seeing me as Tess, his best friend first, and a girl second—to a woman first, and then as his friend? I never realized the way time worked. It was always against us."

I had never said these things out loud.

"He knew it long before I did," I whispered, more to myself than to James.

A powerful sigh shook my body and I dug my nails into my knees. "Henry started to distance himself. At first, I felt betrayed. I didn't know what was happening. Only recently did I understand. When he left me—"

"He was saving you," James spoke up. My eyes pounced on his.

"In his own way, yes. It never would have come to that. That's not how I thought of him. He wasn't that type of soul mate."

"Soul mate? I'm afraid I have never heard the term," James admitted.

I laughed harshly. "It's silly. Something my sister used to talk about all the time."

"Tell me. Please." I could hear how his voice wavered between issuing an order and asking for a favor. How it must feel to constantly be stuck between having complete authority over someone and wanting them to willingly give in of their own accord. None of this was easy for him, either.

"It means someone you are destined to be with, to love forever. I never really agreed with that definition of it though."

"What is your definition?" James asked.

"I believe a soul has many different aspects, different levels to it. And there are people who can fill a part of you, make it stronger. The part of my soul that longed to be carefree, the part that didn't know fear or disappointment, that was the part of my soul Henry belonged to. He took it with him. But at least I know it was for the right reason."

I was stunned by the honesty of my words and hopeful that I could still believe in them.

"I can't figure you out."

I glanced up at James. He had a way of utterly confusing me, dragging me out of my own world, and I craved to know how he viewed it. Did he find me as interesting as I found him? As different from the others around us?

He cleared his throat. "I know how I am supposed to feel. About your kind. God knows they've given me enough reasons to think that way. But everything I hear, everything they tell us about the naturals, it…it just doesn't…it doesn't explain *you*."

I wasn't sure if I felt insulted or a sense of pride from his words. But I felt *something*.

"Well, if it makes you feel any better, you don't exactly fit my definition of a chosen one, either," I offered with a slight smile. How strange to smile after such a morning.

James's face clouded over. He pushed his hand through his dark brown, almost black hair. "I don't think I fit anyone's definition of a chosen one."

"I'm sorry. I didn't mean…"

Did he want to fulfill the council's expectations? Or was he merely feeling the pain of being an outcast? A pain I was beginning to realize existed not when one failed to fit the mold created for him, but when one didn't even know how to define that mold.

"Don't worry about it," he replied. I watched as his eyes traveled back to his desk, glancing at, seeking comfort from, the book.

"What about you? You must have loads of friends."

"If you're referring to Frank, we're not exactly friends. He just turned to me because I am the only one foolish enough to care."

"Is he all right? Is he sick?"

"Tess, there are things I can't talk about. Things I don't want to talk about. This is one of them."

I nodded.

James stood up and stretched. I wondered if it was unnatural for him to sit still so long with no other purpose than to simply have a conversation. I took him in, allowing my eyes to travel across the boy who stood before me. I could see the hint of muscles under the tight tweed coat that covered his arms. My mouth went dry.

I did enjoy looking at him.

Especially that scar.

He moved with a slowness that seemed foreign to him, hesitating as he stood in front of me, reading something on my face, wordlessly asking me for permission to be this close. I knew if I looked down, he would move away.

I didn't want him to.

He took a seat in front of me, and my knees almost touched his. He glanced at his hands for a long while. Then, with a sigh that spoke of uncertainty, he turned back to me.

"I think maybe we can be friends."

His words caught me off guard. It sounded more like a question than a firm declaration. I picked at the fabric of my skirt, unable to look up at him. Did he really, truly, want to know who I was?

"Why?" I asked quietly.

Was it just to satisfy some bizarre fascination, some need to know the girl who didn't have a place with her own people? Or did he actually like the small, almost undetectable glimpse of me I had allowed him to see?

"I... Would it work if I said I didn't know? Would you settle for me saying that it's just something I want? Even if I know it is wrong to ask for it."

"Yes," I breathed.

He hesitated before continuing. "I won't... If you're worried about... I swear it wouldn't be like that."

I looked away, no doubt blushing. I hadn't exactly thought something of that nature was a possibility. In fact, if I were honest, it was part of what attracted me to him. I knew I could never do anything of that sort with someone like him. And he wouldn't want to with me. Or would he?

I did find him attractive.

No. I sought friendship, nothing more. It wasn't safe to become close to someone back at the compound—friendship there would be too oppressive. I couldn't hide from it. I would only be spending nine months at Templeton. If this fell apart, I never had to see this boy again. But I would be stuck at the compound for the rest of my life.

Besides, there was nothing natural about a relationship between one of my kind and one of his. The thought of it was wrong, and yet...

"You are right. Perhaps we can be...friends."

A note of mischief flitted in his eyes. In a quick series of movements he had opened a trunk and returned holding out two dark, tattered, worn books. I instinctively sat up straight and held out my hand. In it he placed one, *Jane Eyre*.

"Have you read it before?"

"No," I said hoarsely. I wanted to cry at the sheer beauty of it.

His face became even brighter. "How splendid."

Our bodies were nowhere near touching, but the sense of him so close both attracted and amused me. He cleared his throat. "What about this one?" he asked, holding up a novel called *Tess of the D'Urbervilles*. I shook my head. "Your namesake," he replied, setting the book on his desk. "We'll save this one for another time. Don't think we're quite ready for it yet." A slight redness colored his cheeks.

I gently opened *Jane Eyre* and started reading the first page out loud.

Chapter 12

I was fourteen when I lost my best friend. This was when Henry left me. Growing up in the compound would have been beyond boring had it not been for him. Our friendship probably seemed strange to those around us—we hardly talked. We didn't need to.

A lot of the time, especially when we first became friends, we spent just with each other. I didn't have the words to talk about losing my parents or the music and books that I loved. Neither of us knew how to talk of the things we had seen. Neither of us would ever force the other to talk about it, either.

As we got older, we became little smart asses, experts at mocking everyone and everything around us. We had secret nicknames for people. And nothing could touch us.

But change is inevitable.

Fourteen was an awkward age for me. I had grown in places Emma never had, and her hand-me-downs never fit right. I once even stole some tape from the supply closet and tried to flatten my growing chest. If Henry noticed, he never said anything. I was becoming the monster the council constantly warned us of.

Eventually, Emma secured me clothes that fit. She traded laundry duty with Sallie Jo for three months for them. I was beyond thankful. I still felt weird in my new body, but at least I could cover it up.

I wasn't ready to become a woman.

One morning, as I sat with Henry at breakfast, I caught Joseph Nickerson staring at me. It was the first time I'd seen anyone look at me in such a way, but I recognized the suggestive gaze from the videos. I tugged self-consciously at my blouse, making sure I was covered. Henry's brow wrinkled as he sought out the cause of my discomfort. When he saw Joseph continuing to stare at me, the fork dropped from his hands. Then *Henry* was staring at me.

His look was unfamiliar. Without a word, he got up from the table. When I tried to visit him later that afternoon, I was told he was ill. Three days passed without me seeing him. It left me antsy.

Finally, I found him pacing out behind the compound—one of our favorite activities.

"You're okay?" I asked.

He shrugged.

"Were you even sick?"

He shoved his hands into his pockets.

"What? Why are you acting so weird?"

He was staring at me again. I took a step away from him. I didn't know why I had the need to distance myself, but I felt it in my core.

"It was harder than I thought it would be," he replied quietly.

"What was?"

"Staying away from you."

"Why would you purposely do that?" Was it because of what I was becoming? I had no control over that. He had to know I would still be different than the other girls. I wouldn't be controlled by my emotions.

Henry took a step away from me. That one step, that one moment, and everything we had was gone.

"I can't…"

"Henry."

"I can't, Tess."

I knew what he was waiting for. He was waiting for me to tell him to stay.

But I didn't know how to ask that of anyone.

The words of *Jane Eyre* skipped through my mind. How deceiving they were. No wonder the council had outlawed books. Stories enabled you to forget your life and your limits. They urged you to reach for a world that was never meant to be yours. There was nothing more dangerous than an imagination.

As I walked to the mess hall, I knew I looked like hell. I didn't bother to tame my hair, which was no doubt matted with blood. I didn't give a damn. Life couldn't be one extreme or the other—feeling nothing *or* being a slave to my emotions. There had to be some sort of middle ground. I wasn't able to live on one side of the spectrum.

There were ways to relieve some of the pressure of everything that weighed down on me. I would give in to what my heart demanded, but only a little. I would control it still. I had learned sitting in the room with James, listening to the words of Jane, that everything was about moderation. Reading the book, however wrong it was, allowed me to escape. But I would have to watch myself. I could not become seduced by the ideas belonging to the story. Perhaps it wasn't so bad to feel a little, but I would have to be careful. I had to remember how weak my species was.

I wanted to see Henry.

The mess hall was loud, much too loud. It was so bright that it was as if my senses were on overload. I needed sleep. After searching for a while, I spotted him and stopped dead in my tracks. There he was, as if he had always been there. And I realized he had seen me, too. He stopped and stared straight back at me. We must have only been ten feet apart, but neither of us took one step in the other's direction. I felt the fingers of my hands reach for him on their own. He seemed to sense this and took a step back.

Our gazes still never broke. I held my ground, refusing to free him from my stare, and he didn't try to escape. He looked so different from the boy I remembered. Our meetings were moments trapped in short glances—this was something different. While he was still rather lanky, his arms were toned. His sandy blond hair was longer than most of the boys. It was painfully obvious that any trimming he did by himself. His bright green eyes still entrapped me as they always had. He was nowhere near as beautiful as James, but genetics certainly hadn't been unkind to him. I actually smiled.

After a long pause, Henry smiled back. I noticed the pain in it, the pain I wished I could take away. A smile full of the sacrifice he had made for me. I nodded and he returned it. Then he walked away.

I can't say how long the interaction had lasted, but it had

been enough. I needed to know he still existed; I needed him to know *I* still existed. He represented a part of me I was beginning to wish back.

The pain that threatened to crush me ever since Emma died didn't seem all-powerful. I knew the feeling wouldn't last, but I would hold onto it for as long as I could. I noticed a bounce in my step. I felt light.

I knew the smile still lingered on my face as I walked back in toward the serving line, and I made no attempt to wish it away. But when I turned and quite suddenly found myself with Robert, it grounded me. He stole the smile from my face.

He looked worse than I could have ever imagined. Wild and unkempt. I could feel the hate sliding off my skin: it was liquid, electric, flowing from inside me, down my legs onto the floor. His face twitched as if it were struggling to hold something back. I stepped to move around him but the sound of his voice made me stop.

"Tess? Be on your guard. Templeton isn't safe for you."

I flashed him the dirtiest look I could muster.

"What concern of yours is my work detail? I'm only there because you couldn't resist having a go with my sister."

I didn't hear the next words he said. My eyes had somehow found Henry again in the crowd. He sat at a table with a girl who seemed faintly familiar. When he moved his hand to brush a piece of hair from her forehead, I felt my breath catch in my throat. He scooted closer and began to whisper something in her ear.

"Who is that?" I asked Robert, motioning to where Henry and the girl sat.

"Were you even listening?"

"Who is it?" I snapped.

"Julia Norris."

I watched as Henry's hand moved to Julia's stomach. With a gasp, I noticed she was with child.

"Did you know she was a Templeton girl?" Robert asked. I could tell by the tone of his voice he was on the brink of falling apart. He was so weak.

"Yes."

I didn't wait to hear what he said next. The sight of Henry and Julia Norris made me sick. Was the child Henry's? How could he be so stupid? How could he choose her?

I walked away without hearing the rest of Robert's warning.

I felt cheated, like I'd lost something that was never mine in the first place. Henry had gone on living without me.

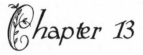

Chapter 13

James hadn't asked for me to visit for a few days, so I was left to clean the many classrooms of Templeton. Even Gwen didn't bother to check up on me. I felt alone. After the scene with Henry, it was the last thing I wanted to feel.

There was only one place that could make me feel better. I crept into the piano room, making sure there was no one around before entering. I even pressed my ear to the door to check that it was quiet. It was.

As soon as I was inside, I felt calm, my mind only concerned with one thing: the feeling of the keys beneath my fingers. Yet I couldn't help but reflect on the ways in which my life had changed since first entering this room.

The piano was humming for me, calling out, and I was its gracious victim. My fingers rested gently on the keys. They felt cool to the touch as I began to play, the same song from the day I'd met James. The song my father taught me. It was mesmerizing and I couldn't stop. I kept playing the same notes over and over again, rocking in accordance with the tune; it was the closest I had ever come to dancing. I wasn't sure how I looked while doing it, but it made me feel graceful for once in my life. Perhaps it was because I was fully in control, something always desired but never fully obtained. It was my revolution, and I would emerge myself utterly in it for as long as I could.

As I continued, the hairs on the back of my neck stood on end. I stopped playing when I caught something out of the corner of my eye. Someone was standing next to the piano.

It was George—the boy James had taken me from.

He smiled. His eyes were feverish with excitement as his fingers ran across the keys without producing any sound. It made me jealous to think he was touching them, as I almost felt like they belonged to me. Anger was quickly and most certainly replaced with fear when I realized I wasn't supposed to be in there. I had a feeling George wouldn't let the transgression pass as easily as James had.

"Looks like someone has a naughty side," George said with a lazy grin.

I stiffened.

"Don't worry; I won't tell. I like a girl who can keep her mouth shut about breaking the rules."

I knew he could destroy me with only a few words. I also knew George could sense my dismay, and he was enjoying it.

"Do you know I could smash every last key of this piano with very little effort? Really, I could do it without even breaking a sweat," George said.

I glanced toward the door, trying to estimate how long it would take me to reach it. I wondered just how desperate his need for validation was.

He glanced there as well. "Oh, leaving so soon, Tess? That is your name, right? I had to ask around. Shame James snatched you up so quickly."

"Yes. I'd like to leave, please," I whispered.

"Well, since you said please," he replied in a much-too-sweet tone as he motioned toward the door.

I wasn't going to overanalyze it. I began to walk as quickly as possible to my escape. His arm was blocking the doorway in a matter of seconds.

"Not so fast. I think there are some things we should settle first." He ran the back of his hand down my face as if it were nothing to touch me. I cringed.

"There she is. I can see her now. The part of dear little Tessie that thinks she actually has a say concerning anything in her sad, pathetic life. I figured you must be different, since James took an interest in you. You're more foolish than the rest of the girls if you think you have any control over what happens to you here."

I smacked his hand away. I knew it was a bad move as soon as I did it, but adrenaline was coursing through me, and it was the only thing keeping me from going to pieces. George forced his hand roughly onto my throat, knocking me back against the wall. My hands scratched at his, trying to loosen them. He was choking me.

"Now, now, Tessie, stop fighting and I will let you go," he growled. It was the only time I had heard him lose his sickly, sugary tone.

I didn't want to stop; I wanted to hurt him. But somewhere inside I knew I could never win. I grabbed tightly onto the fabric of my jacket in an attempt to control myself, and he loosened his hands from my throat. My body was racked with painful coughs.

"This is certainly not how I planned our conversation to

go today," George said, his usual tone back. He grabbed me by the elbow and led me to the piano bench. I could still feel my body demanding a fight, and I clutched the seat to keep me in my place.

My place.

"Such a rude little thing, and here I have come to offer you my assistance. If you ever need anything, all you have to do is ask. There are so many wants I could fulfill." His fingers rubbed against my slash mark as he said this.

I tried to crawl inside myself, someplace where I could hide from this. I wasn't sure how much longer I could control the thirst for violence that surged through me, or fight the deplorable repugnance for his touch that threatened to destroy me.

George cocked his head to the side. "What's going on in that insipid brain of yours? You don't actually think you can refuse me, do you? This is all a ruse, you know. I'm a chosen one; I can have whatever of yours that I want."

I clamped my mouth shut.

George rolled his eyes. "This is boring. You're no fun, all quiet like that. I thought you had a bit of fight in you." He sighed. "Guess I'll be going. But do remember, Tess, this is our little secret."

If George hurt me, I suspected that James would want to hurt him, and I couldn't imagine what the consequences would be for James if he betrayed one of his own for one of my kind. I wouldn't tell James about this encounter.

George crouched down so his eyes were level with mine and his hands were firmly on my face, holding it in place so my eyes were forced to stare into his. "You two really think you can fool me? I half expected him to walk through that door by now," he said with a small, knowing laugh.

I was so thankful he had not.

"I'll find you out, Tessie. Not that it really matters anyway. Soon James will realize what you really are and what he is made to be. We were given the power for a reason. We were chosen."

The nightmares were back.

I was at Templeton but I was alone. Well, almost alone. She was there, Emma. My dead sister. God, she was still beautiful. No one, except for perhaps Robert, had ever found her to be as beautiful as I did. To others, her nose was a bit off center, her teeth slightly too big, her upper lip too thin, but to me she was heavenly. I had always thought so.

Even in my dream I knew she was dead. As I slowly turned around I shuddered, waiting to see the signs of decay mar her lovely face. But as she faced me in the dark hallway of Templeton, she looked radiant.

Emma reached out her hand to me. I rushed to her and clutched her palm to me with all my might. I should have known it was a dream then; in reality, I would never be able to openly express such emotion. She reached up and tucked a piece of hair behind my ear and tapped my chin with her finger.

But as I looked down to take in all of my sister, to convince myself she was really there, I saw it. Her death. There was no running from it. Her white dress was saturated in red from her waist down. Blood sloshed onto the floor, leaving evidence of her secret for me to clean up later.

Even the blood couldn't keep me from her. As I followed

Emma up the stairs to the servants' quarters, I didn't care if I stepped in the blood that flowed from her in a never-ending stream. It was too much a part of me anyway.

There were so many things I wanted to tell her, but even in my dream the emotions sat rotting in my throat. My sister stopped in front of the door that I'd entered to clean up the girl who had been attacked. She wanted me to open it, and she began to pull her hand from mine when I hesitated. I clutched onto her fingers, forcing her to stay by my side. If only I could be by her side forever.

I opened the door and the air was sucked from inside me. There laid the girl on the bed. Just as before, she had curled in upon herself. This time I could see bloody scratches on her back, working their way through the thin white fabric of her nightgown, fighting for recognition. My sister thrust a bowl and washcloth into my hand.

The girl moaned in pain as I sat her up to pull off her nightgown. That was when I saw him: James, standing in the darkness of the corner. He looked past me as if I wasn't there. Then he walked slowly to the girl, crouching in front of her.

"I'm sorry. I didn't mean to," he whispered.

I felt the world tilt. Had he done this to her?

"You have to see what's real and what's not," my sister said from behind me.

Suddenly, I wasn't looking at James anymore, but instead at George.

The girl's head fell to the side—she was too weak to hold it up on her own. I pushed the girl's hair from her face. Then I dropped the bowl to the floor with a crash that rang of finality.

I was looking at myself.

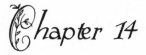

Chapter 14

The next time I saw James was at a party late one night at Templeton. It had been a week since I had last seen him, and I wondered if his offer of friendship was still valid. Every time I met my supervisor to receive my tasks for the day, I both feared and desired another meeting with James. I liked his company. It was the only company I could one day cast off, which made it all the more alluring. It allowed me to see what I could feel without the pressure of anything permanent.

But I also knew there were many things to fear in this world. I had little knowledge. I didn't think I needed to be afraid of James, but maybe I did. Templeton held more secrets than I'd thought was possible. My meeting with George had proven that.

In the end, I merely wanted James to distract me with his music and books. I needed an escape, to close myself behind the door of his room, hoping for a place where I could practice being me. Or at least find out who I was before I finally had to give her up for good.

But a week had passed and he hadn't called for me.

A select group of girls were told they would need to stay late at Templeton—we were to help with a social event that was being held for the boys. We didn't know the purpose of the party, what they were celebrating. All we knew was what to wear and where to be.

Our usual uniforms were replaced. We were forced to wear long satin dresses. I had never worn the material before, and it felt invasive over my skin, settling and emphasizing places on my body that us girls were always told to hide. Each of us wore a different color. Blues, reds, yellows, and pinks filled the rooms, reflecting off the marble floors like someone had figured out how to trap a rainbow in the mansion. The front and back of the dress dipped dangerously low in a V-neck shape. The bottom of the dress flared out. We were told that our hair was to be left down. I'm not sure why, but I'd begun to panic at the thought of it. I couldn't even bring myself to look in the mirror with my hair so free, so unrestrained. It made me feel open, naked.

For most of the night I stayed in the kitchen. When they asked for volunteers to wait on the boys in the study, I let the other more willing girls take their desired places. I couldn't count how many glasses of champagne I filled, how many trays of unfamiliar appetizers I put together. Alcohol and ridiculous finger food seemed so wildly out of place in my hands that often I would lose myself to simply staring at the absurdity. I had no idea these sorts of things still existed. *Decadence* was a word that could have very well been erased from the naturals' dictionary.

But these boys weren't naturals. James was not a natural.

• • •

It wasn't until late in the night that I was summoned to enter the study. The room was smoke-filled and warm. I recognized the chosen ones—all the same boys from before. They were dressed to the nines in black tuxedoes with little bowties. My leg muscles tightened and my stomach clenched. I felt fear as I searched the room until my eyes found James. He wouldn't look at me. But damn if I didn't enjoy looking at him all dressed up.

"Well, hello there, Tess. I've missed seeing you around."

George. Here. He moved closer to me in an obviously exaggerated way. His eyes were big and his hands were out by his sides. The boys behind him snickered.

"Why so scared? Do I frighten you? We're all friends here."

As if to prove his point, he hit the backside of a girl walking by with a tray of empty glasses. She yelped in response, then tried to cover her fear with a sort of giggle.

I was not giggling.

He clapped his hands. "Come, enough of this silliness. Step into the light so we may see you better."

Still, James wouldn't look at me. He kept his eyes on the floor.

I stepped clumsily into the center of the room, crossing my arms protectively across my chest. George laughed again. I wanted to rip the chosen ones apart. I wanted to trash their pathetic room. I wanted to smash their champagne glasses and throw their food trays against the wall, to rip apart their fancy clothes, clothes that no natural man would ever be allowed to wear. Clothes that screamed of the chosen ones' obsession with the past, a past they were never even a part of.

"Aren't you a sight?" George's words snapped me from

my spell, pulled me out of my slow retreat into anger, the descent into myself where darkness thrived.

"Here," he continued, handing me a glass of champagne.

"No thank you."

"I insist." While a pleasant sort of smile crept across his face, I could hear the implication in his tone—I had no choice.

I glanced at James as I brought the glass to my mouth. It felt too thin, too empty against my lips. Had I ever drank from something other than tin? Slowly, as if the whole world moved with one glance, James looked up. George turned back to him; grabbed him roughly, playfully around the shoulders; and pulled him in front of me.

"About time we let her join in on the fun. Right, James?"

James smiled and patted the boy on the back.

No choice.

I opened my mouth and gulped. The bubbles fizzled in my throat, each one trying to inch its way out of an unfamiliar home. I gagged as champagne dribbled down my chin. The boys began to laugh hysterically.

"Aren't you just darling? James did say you were quite pretty. I tend to disagree with almost everything he says, but for once he seems to be right." George winked, taking the glass from me. "I think we're going to have a lot of fun tonight."

I wanted to remind him that he had called me ugly only days before, but I sensed he was trying to get a rise out of me. He was baiting me—reinforcing the knowledge that James wasn't the only chosen one I kept secrets with.

Before I could make sense of anything, James grabbed me by the wrist and led me out of the room, closing the door behind us. I leaned against the wall, my arms crossed, my eyes down on the floor. The faint echo of a song traveled from inside. How I wished James and I could be listening to the haunting waltz in his room and not at some ridiculous council-sponsored event I didn't even understand.

The murmur of the boys and a few girlish giggles from inside almost ruined the song.

"Tess—"

"What are they doing in there?" I interrupted.

James cleared his throat. "I believe they are dancing."

"Dancing?" I asked, raising an eyebrow. "Chosen ones dance?"

James shrugged. "Why not? Might as well enjoy ourselves now, right?" he answered, a note of bitterness creeping in.

"Right, because playing maid is my idea of a hell of a time," I replied. I pressed my lips together as my cheeks burned red. We may have been friends, but this wasn't the way a natural talked to a chosen one. I was surprised to hear James chuckle.

"Would you like to dance with me? I've never actually done it before," he said, taking a step toward me.

"I-I don't. I mean…maybe," I stammered.

"For purely scientific reasons, of course. I mean, it's my job to understand the naturals' culture, right? You'd be helping me out. Besides, it's less time you'd have to be 'playing maid.'"

I took a deep breath and nodded. It would be harmless. I felt myself swaying along with the current of the music, and I suddenly found James close to me. Usually, this would have been frightening, but in that moment the music was calling us both.

I could see hesitation in his eyes. He cleared his throat and slowly placed his hands on my waist.

I should have moved away. I could feel the electricity in

the air, but I didn't want to be even one more inch from James. I placed my hand lightly on his shoulder, hoping to urge him on. His free hand grabbed mine. It was how I had seen dancing done in movies long ago, but I never could have imagined the tension associated with it. It pained me to be this close when I knew I could be even closer. There was still a part of me that refused to allow this to happen, and I was almost thankful for that.

Almost.

I wanted to let someone carry me for just one moment.

We were moving together. I wondered if my breathing had become louder than the song. I could barely hear the music at all, but still we swayed. It was as if some stronger force were directing us.

Dancing was heavenly.

This was being a teenager.

It was easily the most dangerous thing I had yet done in my life, and at the same time the happiest I had been in years. I inched my body slightly closer to his and he welcomed it, wrapping his arm tighter around my waist. I knew this was my limit, but how wonderful it all still was. The song ended far too soon and we were left frozen in our position, staring into each other's eyes. I could feel my chin lead me forward to his face but struggled fiercely to control it. James took a step back. At least one of us was being reasonable.

I followed suit and casually moved myself away, crossing my arms. "That was nice," I mumbled, feeling my cheeks blush.

Before he could utter a reply, the door behind us swung open. George stumbled out, laughing, pulling one of the Templeton girls with him. When he saw us, he stopped dead in his tracks. "I knew Tessie had a bit of life in her. Come here and dance with me."

I didn't have time or the right to utter a refusal as he yanked me from James and crushed me against him. I couldn't stop myself from struggling. The more he forced my body to move with his, the more I fought back. And the harder I fought back, the tighter he held onto me.

And James did nothing to stop it.

The other boys filed into the hallway to watch, laughing. Always laughing. I couldn't help the angry tears that filled my eyes as George pushed me into the arms of another waiting boy. This sort of connection was so different than the moments spent with James. I cringed at their touch. It felt wrong, like they were taking something from me they shouldn't be allowed to have. As I was thrown into the arms of a third boy, my body covered with their fingers, I tripped over my skirt and fell to the floor.

James rushed in and helped me up. He didn't let go of my hand as he led me down the hallway, the boys' snickers echoing off the walls.

He gently brought me into a closet and shut the door behind him. We were shrouded in darkness, the only sound our breathing. His was much heavier than mine. I didn't speak. I didn't want to.

"Tess," he whispered.

"Don't."

I wasn't sure if the word was meant for him or me. I didn't want to hear his excuses or lame promises of friendship. He was just like them. No, he was different than them: he was scared. He was the weakest among the chosen ones.

And I wished desperately that I didn't want to hear his excuse.

He had abandoned me. Why was I not used to that by now?

I tried to shift myself around him to get to the door.

"No. You can't leave." It was a command. I heard his power slither out between the short letters of the word.

"Why not? Is there something you need? What would you like from me, *sir*?" I could hear it, the voice I had become so used to hearing come from my mouth. The voice that made others shy away from me. It sounded empty.

"You don't understand."

"Of course I do. Now what do you need me to do, *sir*?"

"Tess. Enough."

"Would you like me to stop talking, *sir*?"

"I swear, if you call me sir one more time…" I had never heard him sound so hard, so cold.

I shook my head as I once again moved to leave. James grabbed my arm and pushed me deeper into the dark room, my back against the wall. He leaned his forehead close to mine. "You can't leave yet."

I gritted my teeth.

"What are you thinking?" he asked suddenly.

I bit my lip. He didn't want to know, not really.

"Tell me," he replied as if he could hear my thoughts.

"You're just like them." There was no anger to my words, only truth. I wouldn't let this bother me. It was fact.

Fact.

I always knew this. Always. It was the grief that had fooled me.

How could I have ever thought he would allow me to be myself?

"Please, don't say that," he whispered.

"You let them. You let them…"

Suddenly, the door flew opened. A Templeton boy was laughing and dragging a worker with him. She was laughing, too. She was drunk. The boy mumbled an apology.

James turned to me. I could see his face now as the light from the hallway revealed it.

"Just go, Tess. Go."

I started to leave but something inside of me wouldn't let me move. I had a voice; I just needed to use it. I reached my hand forward and grabbed the doorknob, pulling it shut.

"What is this place?" I asked.

I could feel James stiffen. We weren't touching, but we were so close I could sense when he moved. The air between our bodies shifted with us, connecting us. "It's a training center."

His voice was emotionless.

"Don't," I warned, knowing I was getting closer to the point where I couldn't turn back. I took a deep breath. "Last week, my supervisor made me do something. Something I didn't quite understand. There was a girl and she was hurt, really hurt. Do you know anything about it, James? I mean, this is a training center, right? Shouldn't this be the safest place for us naturals?"

I thought about my run-in with George, and how I'd promised myself never to tell James. It felt like I should tell *someone.*

"Safe?" James scoffed. He turned to leave but I grabbed onto his arm and he froze. I could feel him begin to shake as I moved my hand from his. Did something about me frighten this boy?

"Tess," he replied. "This place isn't safe for anyone."

The heavy silence that followed filled in the empty spaces between our words. Without a noise, he grabbed onto my hand.

The feeling of his fingers wrapped so tightly around mine stole the breath from my throat. It wasn't a completely unwelcome sensation, just new. He pulled me gently from the closet and began to lead me to the third floor. We didn't speak as we moved through the halls of Templeton. All I could think about was the feeling of his skin against mine. It was warm. Nice.

We stopped at the entrance of his room. James still didn't look at me as he opened the door. I knew I could speak if I wanted to, but I didn't. My mind was still reeling from the events of the night. When he returned to me, he held the book in his hand. His book.

"I want you to take this," he said shakily.

"But—"

"I'm sorry about tonight. I should have stopped them. I'm not...I don't know how to do this. They don't teach us about this..."

"About what?"

We were whispering even though no one was around to hear us.

"About what it means to want something outside of this place. I wanted to speak up. I just didn't know if I could. I'll regret it for a long time."

He gently lifted my hands and placed the book into them. "Please, take this. I need you to see who I am and what I want to be."

"You don't have to," I offered, knowing I would never be so brave.

He shook his head. "Yes, I do. Because when you find out what this place really is, what it means to be sentenced here, you knowing that I mean you no harm is the only hope I have of protecting you."

• • •

As I made my way through the quiet compound, my fellow naturals sleeping, I held Shelley's *Frankenstein*. While I felt some jealously over the fact the chosen ones were allowed books, I wasn't surprised their library was only filled with ones belonging to the time period so beloved by their creators. It seemed that even the chosen ones were forbidden to experience things outside of what their council deemed appropriate. Maybe they were no freer than us naturals.

I found a place that I knew would keep me hidden and safe.

The Void.

I couldn't recall the origin of the nickname. It was a room kept for the purpose of holding naturals selected during a wrangling, a time when a natural was to be accused of a crime. They would stay here before facing their public trial and, in most cases, execution. When I was little I always thought it would be the perfect hiding place during a game of hide-and-seek. But even then, even before I knew what the world really was, I never stepped foot near The Void. Stories of men going crazy in the enclosed space were tossed around the compound. It was said that once a man clawed out his own eyes.

It was merely a room devoid of light. People would whisper that the space must be haunted, or some unnatural presence must have driven these men to the brink of insanity. But I had another theory. Our world was one where we were told what to think. When you were in The Void, you had no one. Just yourself.

And that was scary as hell.

I opened the door and stepped inside. Here, no one would

bother me, not that anyone besides Robert even checked on me at all. I knew some part of him once cared about Louisa and me, but I think the part that felt anything true must have died with Emma. How could it not? He only looked to us now out of obligation.

I sat against the wall of the black room, lit the lamp I had stolen earlier in the night, and pulled the door shut. Slowly, I brought the tattered book out from inside my shirt. I held it in my hands for the longest time before opening it. I was slightly afraid of what lay in these pages. Not of the story but of James's interpretation of it.

I began to read.

Hours later, halfway through the book, I found myself exhausted from the text and James's notations. It wasn't a very pleasant story. It was a narrative of violence and struggle, love and loss, creation/birth and death. The story of a man who attempted to reach for seemingly unattainable knowledge—the ability to create life outside of God's will. The man, Dr. Frankenstein, succeeded only to later be horrified by his own creation. The creature, left to devise his own understanding of the world, turned to violence.

But the real story held within the pages of the book belonged to James. He questioned everything, almost obsessively. Sometimes he wrote so furiously it was difficult to construct meaning from the sentences. He wanted to know if, like the creature, he was doomed to destroy.

Near the end of the book, my name appeared. How strange to see writing in a book and know I was part of the story. I mattered. Even if it was just a little bit.

The book became almost like a journal. Some of what James wrote was painful. He had guessed my outcast status. He wondered why I had chosen to distance myself from my people. He pondered what I thought of him. Was I repulsed? Or could I see beyond the reasons he was created?

He wrote about how pretty I was. But this wasn't a good thing. It made him nervous, even frightened. He spent so much time writing about how it was wrong to think such things, convincing himself he would never reach for me. But constantly wondering if I would allow him to if he were human and we lived in some different place and time.

He wrote about how strange it was to look at me and feel the things other boys, other chosen ones, had described to him so vividly. Things he thought he would never feel. He wrote about the way a loose strand of hair always seemed to fall and graze my shoulder. How hard it was for him not to reach for it. The way I bit my bottom lip when I was deep in thought. Attraction. His teachers never explained what it meant to want to touch. All he had was what the other boys said.

He wondered if what his teachers told him about my people was true? Or if I was merely an exception.

I didn't finish the book. I only read till the place where James's notes stopped. I was left breathless by the end of my reading. Never in my life had anyone shared so much of themselves with me. Not Emma or even Henry. Those I was once close with remained guarded. But this boy let me see everything.

Maybe he didn't have a soul. But maybe something else made one a human. Maybe us naturals had forgotten what it meant to be one. But this boy, with his questions and insecurities, seemed more human than was possible.

And it was beautiful.

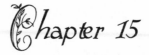

Chapter 15

"So tell me," James urged.

"Tell you what? You need to be a bit more specific than that." I laughed.

"About the book, of course," he said, lightly tapping me on the head with the treasured novel, the forbidden fruit.

We had just finished reading *Jane Eyre*.

When I had returned James's book, we didn't speak of it. He simply took it from my hands and placed it back inside the drawer. I knew when I was ready to talk he would be there to listen. I'd still made sure to smile when he opened the door, though I wanted to somehow communicate to him that I understood the things he wrote, the parts of himself he had revealed, even though I didn't have the words to tell him.

I insisted as I entered the room that he give me some task to complete. I needed boundaries to remain in this new friendship. After I dusted his room, James suggested we read more of *Jane Eyre*, and I didn't refuse. I wanted to read more. I wanted some sense of normalcy before it all got so complicated.

And I knew it would.

The things he wrote and the things I saw would force us into a place where we both would have to re-examine everything. I knew that now.

But not yet.

I didn't pull away from him when he carefully grabbed my hand as we sat on his bed reading the novel and his fingers interlaced with mine. It was a simple gesture. A safe gesture. Yet it caused me a moment of hesitation. Is this where it all started?

But as we delved deeper into the story, I couldn't move away from him.

"I thoroughly enjoyed it," I replied.

"But…you're holding back something."

Was I that easy to read? Or did he just know me?

I hesitated. "Well, I don't think she got it exactly right."

He wasn't letting me off that easily; he simply sat there, expecting an explanation. I had to remind myself not to stare too long at his wondrous face. He cleared his throat.

He thought I was pretty, too.

I licked my lips. "Well, she makes it seem like Jane and Mr. Rochester are two halves of one soul."

James nodded at my assessment. "But you believe the soul has many parts. I remember you saying so."

"You remember that?"

"I remember everything you say."

"Um, well, yes, that's what I believe. I think there were others who had a claim to Jane's soul."

He raised an eyebrow.

"Her aunt who made her feel so insignificant certainly

claimed a part. Jane spent her whole life wanting to fight this sense that she was worthless, unlovable. That fear and her aunt's malice most certainly possessed part of her. It's not only love, affection, that can touch one's soul."

The words had all come out in a rush. I was afraid to look up at James, afraid that his face would show me how stupid my thoughts were. I picked at a single thread on the blanket of his bed. But I knew I wasn't done.

"I think in the end, Rochester won her soul, just as she won his. But there was always a battle for it. From the very start, before she even knew him—a battle between the light and the dark. And even in the end, he didn't have her whole soul; he had what was left, what survived. And that was enough."

I brushed a loose strand of hair off my face. The room had become stifling.

I saw his free hand gently caress the book's cover. He was silent, his eyes somewhere else. But then, quickly, they found mine.

"Is that how you feel about your soul?"

I was caught off guard; I could feel the blush creep into my cheek.

He seemed to sense this. "Am I making you uncomfortable?"

I shook my head, mostly in an attempt to clear it. "No, it's just, I didn't realize. I didn't remember how overwhelming a good book can be."

"Yes, overwhelming." He chuckled. "What about his secrets? Mr. Rochester's? Jane was such a good sort of girl, a bit stubborn, but good to the core. He, on the other hand, left something to be desired when it comes to fictional heroes. How do you feel about him and all his dark secrets?"

What secrets does James have left?

I shrugged. "Not sure I really thought about it. You're supposed to believe they were made just for each other. They exist for each other, despite his secrets. They exist for each other despite everything."

James shifted. It seemed like he was uneasy. Was it my imagination or had he moved away from me? Still his hand clutched onto mine.

"And do you think it is possible," he continued, "that two people can exist for each other despite secrets, despite everything?"

It was as if all the air had been sucked from the room. I could feel my heart begin to dance, to bounce against my chest. My mind was racing, always coming to the same image—the way Robert had appeared at her funeral.

I looked away from James. "No. Not in the real world. I don't think that is possible."

I was unsure why, but I felt angry. I pulled my hand away from his, and I stood up quickly. "I think it must be time for me to go."

James glanced at the clock. "Yes, I think so." His voice sounded so formal, so controlled.

For many days after that, we avoided talking about this new, strange thing between us. I would spend my mornings cleaning around the estate house and my afternoons with James. There was always something to tidy up in his room. I wondered if the boy ever slept. He would always insist I didn't have to do anything, but it helped me control the nervousness that consumed me around him.

I wasn't afraid of him. But that was the problem.

We would spend our afternoons reading or listening to music. James would hold my hand, or his knee would graze mine as we sat on his bed. His hand would touch the small of my back as he walked me to the door. And every time he touched me, I wanted more.

I wondered what it would feel like if he touched my face or brushed my hair from my forehead. I would find myself glancing at his lips, imagining what being kissed felt like. I wasn't thinking of consequences in those moments; I was only thinking of want.

Desire.

Need.

I would think about the consequences of such feelings later, on the transport home. I would convince myself I was only experimenting, that I would never fall in love or get married. But did that mean I had to give up everything? Did that mean I couldn't allow myself anything at all? Couldn't some sort of balance be found?

Besides, soon, once some member of the council claimed him, he would be gone. He would leave me before it could progress anywhere. What harm could a little handholding really do?

Later in the week, my supervisor once again informed me that I was to help her for the morning instead of the usual work around Templeton. I felt my whole body slump with the news. Of course I knew why she'd selected me; she had made it very clear. But she was wrong.

We continued our usual routine of not speaking as I followed Gwen down into the lower levels of Templeton. I knew where we were going—the place where the young chosen ones slept. It was where I'd scrubbed the blood from the floor and walls, hiding the evidence that one of them had been found deficient.

As we passed through the room with the incubators, I couldn't help but look more closely at them than I had before. Had James woken up here? Was this the very room where he had slept so peacefully till it was time to enter into the life that was chosen for him?

They seemed so helpless amid the tubes and machines that kept them alive.

We continued to the back of the room, stopping in front of the door where I had found the mangled body. I took a deep breath to try and stop the panic that began to work its way through me. It had been weeks since my last attack, but I didn't know if my damaged senses could take what was waiting beyond the door.

It was Frank.

When we entered the room, he was sitting on the metal table. His hands held tightly onto the edges and his head hung low. He had lost so much weight since I'd last seen him. As he looked up to find out who had entered, I noted the dark circles under his eyes. Had there ever been a chosen one who looked like this?

"Helloooooo, ladies!" chirped the man who had no doubt killed the defective chosen one. He wore the same silly grin that I'd seen when I cleaned up the blood—he really enjoyed his work. I watched as my supervisor's mouth formed into a tight smile in response.

"Tess, we are to help the doctor make Frank feel better."

"Yeppers! Going to make Frank here as good as new. He's

got himself a little transformation fever," replied the creator as he slapped Frank on the back. The movement caused Frank to erupt into a fit of coughs. "Now, Frank, we're gonna need you to lie back."

Frank, visibly trembling, lay down on the table.

"I'm ready for you, ladies," said the creator.

"Right. If you will help me strap him down, please," my supervisor instructed me, moving toward the cabinet stationed in the corner of the room.

"Why? Why do you need to strap me down?" Frank asked nervously.

"Because you chosen ones are big babies when it comes to this medical stuff. I guess never being sick makes one mighty scared of doctors when you *do* have to see one," the creator replied with a laugh.

His demeanor, the artifice of it all, made me angry. It was hard to believe someone could really be so heartless.

Gwen handed me a set of restraints before she went back to Frank. She secured the top part of his body, and when she motioned for me to do the same with the lower half, I closed my eyes and tried to will my hands from shaking. With a deep breath, I worked on strapping Frank's body to the metal table.

"Wait. Don't I know you? You're James's girl, right?"

I didn't want to look up and acknowledge him.

Would I run from this as I had run from the girl upstairs?

"Yes. I know you," I replied quietly.

I watched as my supervisor's face transformed into a mask of shock. I also saw the warning in her eyes: I wasn't to speak again.

The doctor returned from the cabinet holding a syringe. "Now, Frank, this here is going to make you feel all better."

Frank began to thrash against his restraints, painful, guttural coughs breaking through the noise. "No. You're... going to...kill me."

"What reason would I have to kill you? You have been chosen," replied the creator as he stuck the needle into Frank's arm.

Frank closed his eyes. I watched as tears fell down his face.

"Tess, you will stay with him till the end. The doctor will be busy in the other room. When it is done, you will inform us."

"When what is finished?" I asked, rounding on my supervisor. But neither she nor the doctor bothered to answer my question. They simply left. What had I ever done to this woman to make her hate me so much?

Frank, much like the girl from before, began to settle down. I knew, without a doubt, the creator had just killed this boy, and I'd stood by and watched it happen. I felt the walls of the room crawling toward me. My breath came out in uneven, desperate puffs. I closed my eyes in an attempt to keep it under control.

The truth was the council wanted us all dead—anyone who they saw as weak or useless meant nothing to them. They didn't want to protect us. They wanted us gone. Now that I saw the truth, what could I do with it? It wouldn't save the girl who'd died or the boy who was dying in the room in which I stood.

"They'll come for him, too," Frank whispered.

A feeling of dread settled over me.

"Come here. Please. I don't want to be alone."

I moved so I was kneeling next to Frank. I watched as he attempted to keep his eyes open, fighting to stay alive.

"Why did they do this to you?" I asked. Somehow I felt

it—a sense of camaraderie between the two of us. I knew nothing about him and he knew nothing about me. But we were connected.

In this moment, we were human.

"Because I got sick. I wasn't what they wanted us to be. The kicker is, I bet they could fix me. If they really tried, they could fix me. But they don't bother because I am nothing. I can be replaced."

"That's not true," I replied. I said it for his sake, even though we both knew it *was* true. Maybe I said it for my sake, too. I didn't want to be replaceable, either.

A sob broke through as he clutched to the side of the medical table, his face turning red and sweat appearing on his brow. I wiped his forehead with my sleeve. "Shhhh. It will be over soon, I promise." I wondered if my words sounded like comfort or damnation.

"Do you think I will go to hell?" he spat out from clenched teeth.

I didn't know how to answer his question. Did the chosen ones, children of science, have souls?

"Probably not, huh? No heaven. No hell. Just nothingness. God doesn't care enough to send us to hell."

"Shh. Just rest."

I didn't want to think of James in such a way. It was too painful. Too final.

"No one will even care when I am gone."

I brushed the hair from Frank's forehead. "James will care," I said with certainty.

These words seemed to bring a sense of calm to the dying boy. "You're right. He might just be the best of us. But they'll hate him for it. They'll see it, and they'll punish him."

I shook my head. He had to be wrong.

I couldn't lose James.

"Will you hold my hand until this is over?"

He sounded like a child. But I held Frank's hand until he died. I did for him what I had been unable to do for my sister.

On the transport home, I said nothing to anyone. This wasn't different from the usual routine, but unlike the other days, today I *wanted* to talk. I wanted to tell someone how much I missed my sister. I wanted to inquire about my father, to find out what had happened to him. I wanted to confess how I was the one who found my mother hanging in the shower. I wanted to understand the feelings I had around James, to ask if it was wrong for me to want him to touch me so much. I wanted to shout to the world what the council was doing to both the naturals *and* the chosen ones.

But I didn't know who to talk to. As I made my way through the compound, I stumbled into the only place I knew I could be alone, a place where I could let it all out.

I didn't hesitate before shutting myself inside The Void. There was something alive inside of me that was worse than my childhood fear of this dark room. I stumbled against the wall, sliding into an almost sitting position. My shaking hands moved to my hair, and I began to pull it tight from my scalp. The tension of the panic attack was getting stronger.

My hands made their way over my mouth.

I did feel. I felt too much. All the time. I could barely hold on.

My hands weren't enough to keep the scream, the pain, inside of me. I felt pain all the damn time. Every second of my life. I just needed to control it.

But not now.

Asking for control was asking too much.

I pressed my mouth against the cold cement walls of The Void. I hoped the pain felt by so many others who had shared this space lived inside its walls. I wanted their pain to consume mine.

With my lips against the wall I began to scream.

And scream.

And scream.

The council wanted to take all they could from me.

They wouldn't stop.

Unless I made them.

Chapter 16

TESS,

IT'S BEEN MONTHS SINCE I HAVE SAT DOWN TO
WRITE TO YOU. SOMETIMES I WISH YOU WERE OLDER SO I
COULD SAY THESE THINGS ALOUD. MAYBE THEY WOULD BE
EASIER TO BELIEVE THEN. I CAN HARDLY BELIEVE ANY OF
IT MYSELF.

THE THINGS I HAVE SEEN.

THE COUNCIL TRUSTS ME; I DON'T KNOW WHY.
IT'S BEEN EASY TO WORK MY WAY UP AT THE TRAINING
CENTER. TWO WEEKS AGO, THE WESTERN SECTOR VOTED
TO ALLOW THE CONTINUED CREATION AND TRAINING OF
THE CHOSEN ONES. DEMOCRACY? RIGHT. LIKE THE VOTE
REALLY MATTERED. THEY HAVE BEEN WORKING ON THIS
FOR YEARS, DECADES. IT'S ESTIMATED THEY ALREADY
HAVE AN ARMY OF FIFTY CHOSEN ONES READY TO FIGHT,
AND SEVERAL MORE BATCHES NEARING COMPLETION.

APPARENTLY, THIS HAD BEEN IN THE WORKS EVEN BEFORE THE GREAT WAR. THEY'LL WRITE THE HISTORY SOON, AND THESE FACTS WILL BE HIDDEN AWAY.

TECHNOLOGY WAS ADVANCING AT SUCH A FAST RATE IN THOSE DAYS THAT THE UNITED STATES FELT GENETIC ENGINEERING, CREATING AN ARMY BECAUSE ITS OWN PEOPLE WERE SO UNWILLING TO FIGHT, WAS THE ONLY VIABLE OPTION.

DID YOU KNOW WHEN THE BOMBS FELL THE FIRST PEOPLE RUSHED TO SAFETY WERE SCIENTISTS?

A CREATOR HAS TAKEN ME INTO HIS CONFIDENCE, TESS. I DON'T FLATTER MYSELF TO THINK HE ACTUALLY LIKES ME—HE WANTS TO BRAG. TO SHOW SOMEONE HE CAN PLAY GOD. AND I'M JUST SMART ENOUGH TO PRETEND HIS TALENTS FASCINATE ME, TO PRETEND HIS WHOLE LIFESTYLE DOESN'T MAKE ME FEEL SICK. SO MANY OF OUR PEOPLE ARE STARVING, TESS. YET LIFE IN THE TRAINING CENTERS IS ONE OF POMP AND CIRCUMSTANCE. IT'S A PLACE FILLED WITH ART. EVERY DAY FOR LUNCH THIS CREATOR EATS TWO PIECES OF BUTTERED BREAD WITH HIS MEAL. BUTTER? BUT OF COURSE I SHOULD SAY NOTHING. HE'S CREATING AN ARMY OF MEN WHO WILL CHANGE OUR WORLD.

HE IS GOD.

ALL THOSE PROBLEMS THE COUNCIL PROMISED WOULD GO AWAY HAVEN'T. IT'S LIKE A VIRUS—THEY JUST FOUND A WAY TO MUTATE AND ATTACK AGAIN, BUT THIS TIME THE COUNCIL IS SMARTER. THEY REMIND US OF THE PAST AND ALL ITS DEATH. THEY PASS OUT PAMPHLETS ALONG WITH SOUP IN THE SHANTYTOWNS. THEY PROGRAM TELEVISION DOCUMENTARIES FOR THOSE OF US LUCKY ENOUGH TO STILL

HAVE SOME SEMBLANCE OF NORMAL LIFE. AND AS THE PEOPLE WATCH, THEY BECOME MORE AND MORE WILLING TO GIVE UP THEIR RIGHTS. THE COUNCIL IS SO DAMN CONVINCING. FLASH THE CARNAGE AND DESTRUCTION OF OUR RECENT PAST AND WE ARE WILLING TO GIVE UP ANYTHING TO AVOID GOING BACK THERE.

TWO MORE LAWS WERE PASSED IN THE NAME OF PROTECTING THE WESTERN SECTOR. NOW THE MILITARY CAN ENTER ANY TOWN AND DEMAND ROOM AND BOARD. THEY SAY IT'S TO PROTECT US. MORE AND MORE SKIRMISHES ARE MAKING THEIR WAY TO OUR BORDERS. THE BATTLES WITH THE EASTERNERS THAT USED TO EXIST IN THE MIDDLELANDS, THE BATTLES OUR GOVERNMENT COULD DENY BECAUSE NO RIGHT-MINDED CITIZEN WOULD TRAVEL THERE, CAN'T BE COVERED UP ANY LONGER.

I THINK THEY HAVE DIFFERENT REASONS FOR THIS LAW. I THINK BIG CHANGES ARE COMING TO THE WAY THEY WILL ALLOW US TO LIVE.

THERE IS ALSO A NEW PROGRAM AIMED AT OFFERING EMPLOYMENT TO THE FATHERS AND SONS LIVING IN THE SHANTYTOWNS. THEY ARE TO CONVERT OLD FACTORIES AND BUILDINGS DAMAGED BY THE GREAT WAR INTO LIVING QUARTERS. THIS WAY SO MANY OF OUR PEOPLE WON'T HAVE TO LIVE IN TENTS ANYMORE. JUST LIKE THE APPEARANCE OF OUR ARMY, I THINK THESE LAWS ARE TO WEED OUT THE RATS. ANYONE THEY BELIEVE COULD CAUSE PROBLEMS WILL BE MARKED. THEY CAN WATCH US NOW, AND WE CAN'T SAY ANYTHING.

When did my own home become so dangerous?

Even the appearance of our hodgepodge army of men, who were forced to volunteer in an effort to feed their families, sends a message. As they replay over and over again the scenes of the chosen one killing those terrorists, we can look to the men who walk our streets and see the difference. We can witness our own human weakness. Physically, of course, the weaknesses are obvious, but we can detect another weakness, too—weakness of purpose. We don't want to fight. We want to live. Something in us questions the need to destroy. The chosen one who fought those men held nothing but determination in his eyes. We can see the difference between them and us, and we want the chosen ones to fight our battles.

This creator told me that for many, many years they were unsuccessful in their attempts at artificial life. They didn't just want to create humans; they wanted to perfect them. He said they lost hundreds of these things before finding the right way to bring them up. They could, for lack of a better term, grow them, but struggled with how they would be programmed. They had to be different from us naturals. They had to believe in the cause so much they wouldn't hesitate to die for it. You could make them strong and agile, but if you couldn't make them believe, none of it would matter.

You can put weapons into the hands of men, but if

THEY CAN'T BE CONVINCED TO USE THEM, IT'S POINTLESS.

IN THE EARLY DAYS, THERE WAS NO INCUBATION PERIOD. A WOMAN WOULD BE INSEMINATED WITH THE PERFECT EMBRYO, PAINSTAKINGLY DESIGNED TO REPRESENT OUR COUNTRY'S GREATEST NEEDS: STRENGTH, AGILITY, PERSISTENCE, ENDURANCE. ONCE THE CHILD WAS BORN, THE MOTHER WOULD BE PAID AND SENT ON HER WAY. THEY TRAINED A GROUP OF NURSES AND PSYCHOLOGISTS TO RAISE THE CREATIONS, BUT MANY WERE FOUND WANTING. TOO MUCH HUMAN CONTACT, THE SCIENTISTS PROCLAIMED. IT DIDN'T MATTER WHAT TRAINING THESE NURSES AND PSYCHOLOGISTS WENT THROUGH, THEY COULDN'T KEEP OUR WEAKENING EMOTION FROM THEIR VOICES OR THEIR TOUCHES, AND IT MADE THE CHOSEN ONES WEAK AS A RESULT.

THEY KILLED MORE THAN THEY KEPT DURING THOSE EARLY DAYS BEFORE THE WAR, BACK WHEN IT WAS ALL SECRET. AND AFTER THE GREAT WAR, IT WAS A RACE BETWEEN THE EASTERN SECTOR AND WESTERN SECTOR TO SEE WHO COULD CREATE THEIR ARMY FIRST. THE CREATOR SAID THEY DIDN'T CARE HOW MANY CHOSEN ONES WERE KILLED IN THE PROCESS. THEY WEREN'T CHILDREN TO HIM ANYWAY. THE CREATOR TOLD ME THESE THINGS WITHOUT EMOTION. I THOUGHT OF YOU, AND I WANTED TO VOMIT.

BUT SOON THEY CAME UP WITH A WAY TO LIMIT HUMAN CONTACT. THEY BUILT MACHINES THAT COULD SIMULATE A MOTHER'S WOMB. IT WAS DECIDED TO KEEP THE YOUNG CHOSEN ONES IN A COMALIKE STATE FOR THE MAJORITY

OF THEIR CHILDHOODS, AS THIS WOULD ELIMINATE HUMAN CONTACT AND INFLUENCE OUTSIDE OF THE SCIENTISTS' CONTROL.

IT'S SO BIZARRE. THERE ARE ROOMS AND ROOMS OF THEM, TESS, EACH HOLDING A DIFFERENT BATCH. A DIFFERENT AGE. THREE-YEAR-OLDS, FIVE-YEAR-OLDS, TEN-YEAR-OLDS. THEY JUST LAY THERE. THEY HAVE NO MOTHERS OR FATHERS. THEY WON'T EVER KNOW WHAT IT'S LIKE TO BE SCARED OF THE MONSTER IN THE CLOSET, OR WANT TO HOLD A DAMN TEDDY BEAR. INSTEAD, FOR TWO HOURS EVERY DAY US WORKERS ARE ASKED TO WHEEL IN GIANT PROJECTORS. ON LOOPS, THEY PLAY THE SAME EDUCATIONAL VIDEOS. WE HOOK CORDS FROM THE PROJECTORS INTO THEIR BRAINS. THEIR BRAINS, TESS. EVERY TIME I DO IT AND LOOK DOWN AT THOSE CHILDREN'S FACES, I WANT TO SCREAM.

BUT THEN I WATCH THE VIDEO. IT'S ABOUT US— OUR PEOPLE, OUR FAULTS, OUR NEED TO SELF-DESTRUCT. COUNTLESS IMAGES OF WAR, GREED, LUST, AND DESTRUCTION PLAY ACROSS THE SCREEN. AND I CAN'T ARGUE AGAINST IT BECAUSE IT'S ALL TRUE. EVERYTHING THEY SHOW IS A PART OF OUR HISTORY, OUR HUMANITY. BUT THEY DON'T SHOW THEM THE WHOLE STORY. THEY DON'T SEE LOVE OR AFFECTION. AND I KNOW THAT WHEN THESE THINGS GROW UP, THEY'LL HATE US.

THEY'LL HATE YOU, AND I CAN'T STOP THEM.

THE NATURALS THINK THE COUNCIL HAS CREATED AN ARMY TO PROTECT US. THEY DON'T UNDERSTAND THAT TO THE CHOSEN ONES, WE'RE THE VERMIN THAT NEEDS TO BE

EXTERMINATED.

I COME HOME EVERY NIGHT AND I WANT TO HUG YOU AND YOUR SISTERS. I PRAY YOU CAN FEEL THINGS LIKE LOVE AND SHOW IT. I CAN'T. NEVER HAVE BEEN REAL GOOD AT IT. BUT IN THE END, I THINK OUR CAPACITY TO FEEL THESE EMOTIONS FOR ONE ANOTHER MIGHT BE THE ONLY THING THAT MAKES US DIFFERENT FROM THE CHOSEN ONES. IT MIGHT BE THE ONLY GOOD THING ABOUT BEING HUMAN.

I HOPE YOU'RE DIFFERENT THAN ME.

Chapter 17

No matter how much I scrubbed, I still felt evidence of the crime on my hands. I had helped the council kill Frank. I had strapped him down. I'd ended a human's life. I should have said no. I couldn't just separate people into chosen ones and naturals—the council was to blame for all of this. I understood whom to hate now. There would always be bad people, chosen and natural alike, but the council had played us all.

How long would I let the council control me?

I didn't hear her come into the bathroom. Julia. She was blocking the entrance as I made my way to leave. "Can we talk?" she asked. Her eyes were blotchy and swollen. She made no attempt to look presentable. Her hair was disheveled and her clothes wrinkled.

I didn't know if I wanted to talk to Julia, after I had forced myself to forget her. I didn't want to be reminded of what could happen, what would happen, if I for one second lost control with James. Everything in life seemed to be so tightly wound, so controlled that it left one damn near exhaustion. No wonder so many around me simply gave up.

But then I remembered lack of communication was what had gotten her into this mess.

"Sure." I nodded.

It was late and most people had turned in for the night. She glanced at herself in the mirror and frowned. A ticking time bomb. How strange it must be to know the very thing that lived inside of you would be your death, and yet you had to carry it around for nine months. Did knowing how it was all going to end make it easier?

I wished I had asked Emma.

Just thinking her name caused me such an intense, overwhelming amount of pain that I was unable to look at Julia again. Instead, I stared down at my feet.

"I wanted to warn you, Tess."

I shook my head and swallowed the lump in my throat. "You don't need to warn me. I know how this all works," I said, my eyes darting to her stomach.

"Look, this isn't easy for me. I don't really know you, but Henry cares about you, and I care about him," she confessed, wringing her hands. She took a deep breath. "I'm not really doing this for you. When I'm gone, you will be all he'll have. The least I can do is help you out."

She tilted her head to the side. "You have to know why they make us girls work there, right? We're the entertainment. We're expendable. And it doesn't matter if you say no; they will just take it from you."

I thought of the girl I'd helped clean up.

Julia cleared her throat. "There are ways to protect yourself, things I didn't know about. He didn't use them, of course. He also didn't force me, but that doesn't mean one of them won't. I can get you some—"

"I don't understand how what you and Henry did has anything to do with me," I said. I didn't even want to think of *that.*

"It's not Henry's."

I felt the blood drain from my cheeks. "You mean, a chosen one and you…"

"Yes. I thought he liked me. He offered me anything I wanted. Books. Cigarettes. Alcohol. All sorts of contraband items. His name was George. Do you know him?"

I shuddered. I knew him all too well.

"Watch yourself, Tess. Let me know if you need anything." And without another word she walked over, kissed me on the cheek, and headed out of the room.

I had a mission. And it made me feel alive.

I sat down at one of the mess hall's tables, waiting. He noticed me instantly. Caught my eye, blushed slightly, and turned to walk out of the room.

I jumped up. The sound of the chair falling to the floor didn't stop me. "Henry!" I knew it came out as a yelp—I hoped he could hear how desperate I was. How much I needed my friend. After my conversation with Julia, it was clear he needed me, too.

He stopped, frozen in his tracks. He didn't turn to face me, but he didn't walk away, either. I slowly approached him until we were inches apart. Then I reached out and touched his shoulder. How good it felt. He tensed but still didn't turn around.

"Please. I need to speak to you. I wouldn't ask, I wouldn't dream of bothering you, if it wasn't terribly important."

He turned to face me; the passion in his eyes was frightening. A look I never saw in our childhood. I realized he was a man now, not the boy I'd known. I withdrew my hand quickly.

"You could never bother me."

His voice sounded so different. It caught me off guard. Such sadness as he said it; he was breaking my already sick heart.

"Will you take a walk with me?" I asked.

"No."

I inhaled sharply.

"Please, Henry. Please, just a small little walk."

"It's not good if we're seen together," he said roughly, glancing over his shoulder.

This confused me. Who here would care if we talked?

"Then let's go somewhere we won't be seen," I countered. I grabbed his hand and it felt so warm. "Please."

He didn't say anything, but at least it wasn't no.

"Please," I said again.

"All right." I could see he felt defeated.

We didn't talk until we were outside the compound's walls. As we stood in silence, both of us daring the other to speak first, I saw him glance toward the forest line—the forest where once he and his family had attempted to run off.

This was going to be more difficult than I expected.

"I need you to tell me what happened when you tried to escape."

He went pale and took a step back from me. "Don't."

"I need to know."

"Please, don't ask me to do this."

"I don't have a choice. Not anymore."

"We've known each other over a decade and you've never asked me before. Why now?" he replied angrily, throwing his hands into the air.

"Templeton," was all I offered.

He took two steps toward me, bridging the distance between us, almost close enough to touch me. Whatever anger he had was now replaced with fear. "That place isn't safe, Tess."

"I know."

Utterly unsure of myself, I slowly placed a hand against his chest. He swallowed and looked away from me. It felt different from touching James, but I didn't mind it as much as I should. "It's important, Henry. Please. Tell me."

He grabbed onto the hand on his chest. "I've been so lonely without you. Did you know that?"

I felt my throat go dry. "You have Julia," I charged.

"She isn't you. I mean, I care about her, but damn, she isn't you. Hell, she's half crazy, I think. She spends more time ranting about the council than trying to have any sort of relationship with me. But I guess that's part of the appeal."

I frowned. She cared about more than that. She cared enough about him to warn me. But maybe she hadn't mentioned our talk to him. "What happened when you tried to escape?" I asked again. I had to change the subject. We were getting too close to discussing things we could never come back from.

"They did it."

"Who?"

"The chosen ones. They attacked us."

I shook my head, but Henry continued. "They caught my

family. I thought they were going to take us back. I wanted them to; I didn't like being out there. I watched what they did." I tried to pull my hand from his, but he only held on tighter. "What? You said you wanted to know."

"You're lying." I stepped away from him.

"Am I?" He grabbed me by the arms and pulled me to him. I tried to get away, but he held onto me, pressing his chin against my forehead. His breath tickled me as he spoke.

I had awoken something in him that would never be able to sleep again.

"The council couldn't let us get away. If we did, then anyone could leave. We would have destroyed the sense of fear they'd worked so hard to create."

"Why didn't you tell anyone? And why would they let you live?" I asked.

"Because I was a child. I didn't understand what I saw. Hell, maybe some part of me was convinced they'd deserved it. I buried it inside me. And they let me live because they needed a symbol. I was the boy who was saved. They wanted the naturals to trust them."

Henry touched my cheek. I was surprised by the goose bumps that appeared down my arms as I struggled to catch my breath.

He watched me in silence for a long time before stepping away. "But I'm going to show them they can't keep me quiet."

He sounded so dangerous, so crazed.

"What are you talking about?"

He stopped and stared at me. He looked like a man destroyed. "They took her, too."

"Julia?"

"Yes. I liked her. I was beginning to forget you, and she

was good. I knew there were limits, but I finally felt normal. Then it happened, and she got so messed up. Talking crazy. And I started to believe her. I started to agree. I don't think I could go back to what I was before."

I nodded.

"Our women are theirs to screw with. And if the chosen ones can kill them in the process, so much the better."

"They're not all like that," I whispered.

"Oh, Tess. Don't tell me they got you, too."

"No!" I exclaimed, almost offended. "I haven't…I wouldn't. It's just, I've seen things since I've been there. And it's not all black and white."

His jaw clenched.

"Yesterday I watched a creator kill a chosen one because he was sick. Something was wrong with him, and they ended his life. Like he was nothing."

"They *are* nothing, Tess. They aren't even human," Henry replied through his teeth.

"That's not true! I know one of them. He plays the piano and reads. He doesn't want to be a killer. He would never."

"You sure about that?"

"Yes. I am."

And despite not being sure of anything, I was sure of James. Call it instinct.

Henry shoved his hands into his pockets and stared at me. "You said you watched them kill one?"

I nodded.

"How?" he asked, his voice taking on a different tone. He almost sounded calm.

"They injected him with something."

"That simple?"

"There was nothing simple about it."

He was silent.

"Maybe it's not the chosen ones' fault. At least not completely," I said. "My first day there they brought me to this room down in the lower level of Templeton. They were just lying there, young chosen ones. Alone, waiting to be awakened. They had no sense of the world around them. And even when they open their eyes, they have no choice over what they are shown in the videos. If most of them are monsters, it's because the council made them that way."

Before I knew it, Henry's hands were holding my face. He was making me nervous. This wasn't right. It wasn't safe.

"What do you want from me, Tess?"

He was scaring me. Not just the desperation I heard but also how close he was. He abruptly let me go and began backing away.

"Wait. I want you to help. We have to find a way to fight back, to stand up to the council. This can't be the only life I get to live. I refuse to accept it," I proclaimed.

"Did you ever wonder what makes someone a terrorist?"

"What?"

"Those men who strapped the bombs onto their children's chests? You ever wonder what would drive someone to do that? I have. I think I can understand it now. Some of us can't just sit silent waiting for it all to end. We want to end it ourselves."

His words caused a chill to settle over me.

"Besides," he continued, "if I was on the winning side, the side with the power, they wouldn't call me a terrorist. That's the jacked up thing. Even more so than the violence and death."

"Shut up. Stop talking like that. There has to be another

way. Maybe if we could get the people of the compound to listen, we could do something."

"What, and wake them from their naps? No one would listen."

"Then maybe we can try and leave. Take our chances in the wild."

"You really think they would just let us?"

I sighed with frustration. I wasn't going to give up. Henry's story had only fueled my fire.

"Please don't ask me to see you again."

"I won't," I said, biting my cheek to stop the pain that threatened my heart.

"I would give anything for things to be different. Anything. If I could be your friend, Tess, if I could…but it wouldn't be good for either of us, especially now." He stopped and muttered what I thought was a curse. Then he threw one more glance to my face and ran.

I felt it again: loss. Except this time it seemed permanent. I was alone.

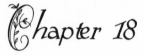

Chapter 18

You want what you can't have.

You want it because it will destroy you.

You want to be destroyed.

You want to destroy him along with you.

I could hear Henry's voice inside my head saying these things to me. Was he right? Was the only reason I sought out any kind of relationship with James because I knew where it would lead me?

Henry seemed bent on destruction. Was I the same? I knew the rules. And there were rules about everything. But I seemed recklessly willing to break them all. Was I doing so out of some need to rebel against a system that had taken so much from me? Or had I merely found another way to end my pain—the destruction of myself?

The need to touch and be touched was like a drug.

As I walked to James's room after spending the morning scrubbing the countless windows of Templeton, I feared our meeting. I had not seen him since Frank died, and I had been unable to shake the guilt that overwhelmed me when I thought of the incident. I still wasn't sure I could have done anything to stop his death, but the fact that I did nothing at all left me feeling bereft.

When I reached James's room, the door was already open. James lay on his bed, his arm thrown carelessly over his eyes.

I sat down on the bed next to him and gently shook him.

"James?"

With a heavy sigh, he slowly sat up. I grabbed his hand and held it in my own. "I'm so sorry."

"How did you know?" he mumbled.

Could I admit my part in Frank's death?

"You know what? It doesn't matter," he said. "I don't know why I'm so surprised. I knew they wouldn't choose me."

"Wait. What?"

"No one chose me, Tess. They didn't want me."

The Introduction Ceremony. James had not been selected by any of the subcommittees. He didn't know about Frank's death. Instead, he was feeling the pain of rejection. James would be left to a life of glorified babysitting. He had been labeled forever as insignificant. As nothing.

"I knew after the interviews…"

"What happened during the interviews?" I asked.

"I couldn't answer the question."

"Which one?"

"The one about our purpose, our reason for existing. I don't understand why the hell the naturals need us. And then when they started asking me what I thought about your people, I froze. Because I didn't know how I felt. I haven't known how I felt in such a long time."

James began to pull away from me, but I grabbed onto his

arm to stop him. The movement caused me to be closer to him than I had ever been before.

James noticed, too. "You are so beautiful," he whispered.

I let out a shaky laugh. "You're talking crazy. I'm not."

He shook his head. "No. You are," he replied, scooting away from me, sitting up against the wall. "I...when the other boys would talk about the female naturals, the Templeton girls, I never got it. Sure, some were attractive, but I never felt that thing, you know. I mean I would read about it in books. But I never understood it. Then I saw you in the damn piano room. And I felt it—want. I wanted you."

I could have stopped him, but I didn't.

He reached for my hand. "But I won't ever, Tess. I promise. I understand the rules."

"Do you want to kiss me?"

I said the words without really thinking about what they would mean to each of us. I was tired of life always being difficult. I knew what it meant to want, but I was sick of how tainted my wants had become. Everything I wanted came at a price. I couldn't let the council, or Henry, or Julia define my relationship with James. *I* had to define it.

I needed to trust myself.

There were a million reasons I shouldn't have asked him this question.

But the want was there all the same.

"You can if you like," I continued, wondering where my bravery was coming from.

James grabbed me by the arms and pulled me toward him. An unfamiliar panic began to run through me—I had never let anyone kiss me before. James slowly, painfully slowly, leaned toward me. I felt a shiver run down my spine at the mere thought of what was about to happen. When his lips pressed against mine, it was so light I wondered how a kiss could ever be considered a sin. When his hand moved through my hair, I pressed against him harder. My heart sped up. This was the line it was so dangerous to cross.

This was the line I wanted to cross and never return from.

I pulled away from James and practically jumped off the bed. I couldn't look at him, was afraid I would read disappointment on his face. I knew how the kiss felt to me, but what if he didn't agree? I mumbled something about meeting my supervisor and stumbled out into the hallway.

As I walked away, I became aware of how noisy the mansion had become. People were shouting and running. Farther away from me I could see a fellow natural sitting against the wall, crying into her hands. A group of chosen ones were huddled together, talking quickly, as if devising a plan.

I turned to see James following after me. "Tess, wait. We need to talk," he called out. As a chosen one passed us, he reached out and grabbed James's arm. The two of them bent their heads in conversation. I watched as the flush in James's cheeks disappeared. And I saw fear.

He walked toward me in a daze, his hands shakily holding the wall.

"What is it?" I asked. I had to fight the growing need to place my hand upon his in comfort. It was okay in the privacy of his room, but I couldn't in front of any of these people. Doing so would make them a part of our relationship, and I wanted them to have nothing to do with it.

"They're all dead."

"What do you mean? Who?"

He kept shaking his head.

"Who?" I asked again.

"The young ones. The chosen ones."

He must have meant those still in the incubation period. Had the council found something wrong with them? Had they wiped them out? I couldn't imagine how much blood there would be down there.

"A natural did it."

Clearly I had misheard him.

He pushed past me and began to walk down the hall.

"W-wait," I stammered. "What do you mean a natural did it?"

"Exactly that," he replied, refusing to look back at me. "A natural committed murder."

Chapter 19

The alarm was never good. Used to warn of impending attacks during the early days after our move into the compound, it had now come to stand for something else — a wrangling.

The alarm was used to assemble the compound. Someone was being taken. This was beyond merely being reported; an alarm, a wrangling viewed by the whole camp, meant you had already been found guilty. You were to be the lesson.

It meant death.

As I walked through the overcrowded hallways toward the dining hall, I could feel the panic. One question lingered in the air, caressed the backs of our necks, making the hair stand on end: *Who?*

As I stood in my row, I could sense my body reacting. I could feel it betraying my fear without a second thought of loyalty to my defiance. My palms were sweaty. I tapped my foot furiously. I avoided looking around me; I didn't want to see this happen. I began to memorize the floor, every dull and empty inch. I felt the presence of someone beside me, someone familiar. I glanced up and was caught off guard to see Robert standing there. Of all the places, why would he stand next to me? His eyes met mine and they were empty.

I thought back to James's words. A natural had killed the young chosen ones? How was that even possible? The council had created such a general feeling of indifference among my people that I didn't think anyone was capable of even thinking of such an act.

Henry.

No. He couldn't do anything like this. He wouldn't murder someone. I had learned from the other Templeton girls on the transport home that all thirty of the young chosen ones had been killed. The cords that kept them alive, aiding in their breathing, had been pulled from their bodies. The lone creator who worked downstairs, the man who I'd watched murder Frank, had been knocked unconscious.

It wasn't possible that Henry sat and watched thirty children suffocate to death.

It wasn't.

Maybe it was a lie created by the council to keep the chosen ones' hate of us alive, to protect the council's secret that each chosen one was expendable. All they had to do was return to the lab to create more. Maybe something was wrong with the young batch of chosen ones.

The doors slammed open and I froze.

They filed in. Much to my horror, I realized I recognized them—they were the Templeton boys, those chosen ones still training to take their rightful place so far above us. I had only seen a public wrangling twice, but that was before my work at Templeton, before my interactions with the chosen ones. I recognized their faces now, the pawns of the council.

I felt my stomach tighten. It was easy when I didn't know them. I saw George. He stood emotionless like the rest, a perfect representation of the grace of his sect. I saw him, too. James.

No. No, not him, not here, not for this.

My breathing became ragged. The room was stifling. I could feel Robert's questioning eyes on me, but I didn't care. I wanted to get out of there. I needed to leave. But a voice in the back of my head reminded me that it was my duty to watch this.

Duty.

Roll call.

One by one they checked off our numbers. I didn't dare look up when mine was called, but merely grumbled a reply. I couldn't see James there. It would shatter the illusion I'd so mutinously created. I couldn't entirely blame him; logically, I knew that. He had about as much control over his life as I did. Frank was evidence of that.

I vaguely heard Henry's number, Robert's, my younger sister's. God, how I had pretended like she didn't exist. I hadn't even heard her come near me. When her number was called, she sniffled. I hoped it was from fear and not another bout of the mysterious illness that had plagued her throughout her childhood. I reached for Louisa, pulling her hand into mine. We weren't close, but we were sisters.

The room became silent. Insanity forced my eyes up and I wondered why it was taking so long. I saw George again and was unable to stop myself from staring. I watched as the corners of his mouth fought a smile. He nodded to James.

James stepped forward.

No, he couldn't be the one to read the declaration. Please

God, no.

"Will Julia Norris please step forward? Serial number 778234."

The room was spinning. My heart had stopped. It had to be some nightmare, or maybe I was going crazy—seeing monsters everywhere. She stepped forward, the very epitome of calm. Julia? Henry's Julia? Did he know what she'd planned to do? Had she known when we talked in the bathroom that she would end her life in some wild statement of rebellion?

Did he help her?

I searched for Henry among the crowd. I could only catch his profile but my heart ached to see his eyes, if I could only see his eyes.

"Julia Norris, you have been found guilty of the murder of thirty chosen ones. You will be taken from this compound and your life shall be forfeit. It has been decided by the council that you shall be put through the cleansing."

The cleansing—a throwback to the purification rituals of some old-time religion. She would be tortured for days before they finally killed her. They wouldn't care if she were pregnant. Is that why she did it? Because she knew she was dead either way?

I kept waiting for Henry to do something, to show he felt something for this girl. He sat there stoic, unmoving. He looked like me before I knew that not all feelings were wrong.

There was no fancy speech. There were no verses of poetry. There were just simple sentences—a string of words that had the power to end a life.

Some woman began to cry. I could hear a man curse under his breath. I felt in the core of my being the silent screams of my people, Julia's people. I tried to force James to look at me, but he wouldn't even acknowledge my presence. His voice was beautiful, sickly sweet and bitterly cold.

Did Henry help do this?

I remembered his cryptic words in the woods.

If he had a part in this, would he let Julia suffer alone?

I remembered how it was I who had told him about where the young chosen ones were kept.

Did I help him commit murder?

I couldn't breathe. Then came the pain. Unbearable, wretched pain. My chest was burning and it was excruciating. It was a raw, familiar feeling. I was freezing, shivering, panting. I was dying.

Just let it end. Please let it end.

James placed his hands on Julia's shoulders, forcing her down onto her knees. George handed him a black bag and whispered something into his ear. I still couldn't see Henry's face because he kept it down. He didn't make a sound. He didn't fight for Julia.

Her death would be gruesome because she had no female family members to take on part of her punishment. Maybe she deserved to die, but I couldn't watch her suffer. I was so tired of watching people suffer.

It was there, in that moment, that James's eyes briefly met mine.

I saw regret. It was only there for a second, but I saw it.

With a quick and violent motion, James placed the bag over Julia's head. George slowly walked next to her and quietly said something to him. I watched as James nodded to me. In response, George found my face. He kicked Julia forcefully in the gut, his eyes never leaving mine.

Powerless.

I could no longer control my actions. I lunged forward; I wanted to claw George's eyes out. I wanted to silence forever his damn laugh. She was carrying his child. He was the one who had broken her. I barely knew this girl, but I wouldn't let her suffer alone. I couldn't. Not again. I wouldn't keep her pain a secret like the girl I'd helped clean up at Templeton. Did George attack her, too?

A pair of strong hands held me in place. Robert.

"It's what they want," he whispered urgently, protectively. He sounded like the Robert I had admired before Emma died.

I didn't care as I struggled to get away. People were starting to notice. Robert forcefully pinned me to his side, cementing me in place. "Stop this, Tess. It won't help. They'll only get you, too." Louisa gripped onto my hand at Robert's words.

I looked at my sister, her pale blue eyes wide in terror. Gone was the constant smirk she wore on her thin face. I knew the right thing to do was to keep quiet, be there for her. But how could I ever look her in the eyes if I became yet another natural who didn't speak up?

"I'll take on some of her punishment," I screamed.

The room went silent. I would, for once, welcome the notion of suffering for someone else. If Julia really did what they accused her of, she was a monster. But *they* created the monster. The council. They were to blame for this.

George pushed through the crowd with a speed that seemed unreal. He grabbed onto my arm and shoved me to the front of the room. Without warning, he bent me over and slammed my face into one of the mess hall tables. I gasped in pain.

He roughly yanked my ponytail away from my neck, leaning down and hissing into my ear: "Do you know what this means, girl? Your sentence will be extended by years. You'll get another slash mark."

"Good," I gritted.

"Stupid bitch," George whispered so only I could hear.

While George still held my head against the table, I managed to turn so I could see James. I had made a choice. I had used my voice. And I knew how it must have seemed—that I had chosen my people over him.

"I'll need the iron for the branding," George yelled.

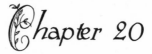

Chapter 20

TESS,

IT IS WRONG TO HATE YOUR OWN COUNTRY?

WHAT DOES ALLEGIANCE MEAN? SHOULD ALLEGIANCE BE TO YOUR FAMILY FIRST? TO GOD? TO YOUR HOMELAND? WHAT ABOUT TO YOUR SELF? I AM CHOOSING MYSELF, TESS. PLEASE FORGIVE ME.

RIGHT AROUND THE TIME LOUISA WAS BORN THE COUNCIL NOTICED A SHARP INCREASE IN THE NUMBER OF DEATHS DURING CHILDBIRTH. BUT THEY NEVER REALLY STOPPED TO THINK WHAT IT MEANT. OUR COUNTRY WAS STILL STRUGGLING. PEOPLE WERE STILL STARVING, AND THREATS FROM THE EASTERN SECTOR SEEMED MORE PROMINENT THAN EVER. WE HAD OTHER THINGS ON OUR MINDS.

DID YOU KNOW WE HAVEN'T HAD A SINGLE SUCCESSFUL CHILDBIRTH IN OUR SECTOR IN YEARS? LOUISA IS A

MIRACLE, ONE OF THE LAST NATURALS BORN. I KNOW SHE'S NOT LIKE YOU, TESS, BUT SHE'S SO PRECIOUS.

IS IT POSSIBLE THE COUNCIL HAS SOMETHING TO DO WITH THIS? I FEEL CRAZY EVEN WRITING IT, BUT IT MAKES SENSE. ONCE WE ARE GONE, THEY CAN RECREATE THE WORLD AS WHATEVER THEY WANT IT TO BE. THERE ARE NEW CRIES TO BAN MORE AND MORE BOOKS. WHAT IF THEY GET RID OF IT ALL? THE END OF THE NATURALS, NO BOOKS, NO WRITTEN HISTORY OF US.

WE NEVER EXISTED.

IT'S NOT POSSIBLE.

GOD, I'M LOSING IT.

TODAY I WATCHED A CREATOR BEAT A CHOSEN ONE SENSELESS. EVEN THOUGH THE TEENAGER COULD HAVE EASILY KILLED HIS OPPRESSOR, HE JUST STOOD THERE AND TOOK IT. PERFECT OBEDIENCE. I CLEANED UP THE BLOOD AFTERWARD.

THE YOUNG CHOSEN ONE WAS BEING PUNISHED FOR ASKING A QUESTION. THE GROUP OF TEENAGERS TO WHOM I AM ASSIGNED WATCHED A VIDEO ABOUT THE TOWERS TODAY. YEARS AND YEARS BACK A GROUP OF MEN FLEW AIRPLANES INTO TWO MASSIVE BUILDINGS IN A PLACE CALLED NEW YORK. THEY SHOWED VIDEO OF PEOPLE FALLING FROM THE SKY.

IT WAS HORRENDOUS.

THE YOUNG CHOSEN ONE ASKED HOW THE GOVERNMENT HAD FAILED THE PEOPLE. THE CREATOR TOLD HIM IT WAS HUMANITY THAT HAD FAILED.

THEY KILLED TWO MORE CHOSEN ONES TODAY. SICK.

Something called the transformation sickness. That's seven we've lost since I have been there. I'm not supposed to talk to them. I'm not allowed to talk to them.

But there is one who speaks.

And it breaks my heart.

He whispers. He asks me about life on the outside. I have shown him pictures of you and your sisters. He thinks Emma looks kind. He wishes he could meet her.

The council will one day make this boy hate your sister.

One day she'll hate him in return.

The propaganda monster is in full swing. Every day there is some new report or pamphlet published discussing our need to hold tight to our morals. Beneath the words, I fear there is a pretty nasty tone toward women. The breakdown of the family. The failure of motherhood.

How can I protect my daughters from this? I think I may have given up on you, my girls. I can only fight for myself now.

Jacobson introduced me to a group of men.

I think we're going to do something.

If I were a good father, selfless, I would stay with you till the end.

I just can't.

Chapter 21

"I hope you don't take this the wrong way, but you aren't looking so good," said a girlish voice that shattered my trance. It pulled me from my numbness, the only thing keeping me from screaming.

The crowd was tense. It had taken hours to transport everyone to the square, an abandoned airfield used in the early days of the war. Most of what lay outside of the compound was rubble. The heat was wretched. There was little water. It smelled of death.

I was saving my strength for when I would need it. Standing up for Julia had reduced the torture to a simple death by decapitation.

And my new slash mark burned. It had taken everything in me not to cry when the searing metal was placed against the back of my neck as the entire compound watched. They had to take Henry out of the room because his protests over the action became too loud and violent. He fought for me, but not for

Julia.

Unlike when I'd received the mark for my sister, this new mark, the mark for Julia, was excruciating.

That's what I got for allowing myself to care.

Robert had found his place next to me after the wrangling. "Are you all right?" he asked quietly.

I shook my head, and he placed a reassuring hand on my shoulder. It was getting harder and harder to ignore him. He was all I had left of Emma.

I felt the sun burn my cheeks. I would welcome the rawness of my skin later. The sun could char me straight through if it so desired, and I wouldn't move to shade myself.

"I thought they would be here at least," the same girlish voice repeated.

"Who?" I mumbled.

"The boys from Templeton."

Louisa. Always looking for something or someone to love. I was so wrong—Robert wasn't all I had left of Emma. Louisa looked more and more like her every day. Louisa had always been a little sickly, but there was now a fresh blush to her cheeks. Her blue eyes seemed to become brighter and brighter. She was with me. Alive. My sister. How could I have been so blind?

I cleared my throat. "The chosen ones aren't what you think they are."

She rolled her eyes in response. "Says the girl who gets to spend all day with them. They're perfect, Tess. They protect us. And they seem loads more interesting than the boys around here."

"Perhaps we can save this conversation for another time?" Robert said in a gentle tone.

Yes. I would need to have this conversation with Louisa. I would tell her the things that had never been discussed with me. I would protect her. She would never go to Templeton. Ever.

My head had started to hurt from all the noise. I sat there listening to the conversations of those around me, refusing to take part.

"Tess, what's the matter?" Henry asked suddenly, a note of true concern in his voice. Where had he come from? It was as if he appeared from thin air. And in that moment, I didn't know if I wanted to hit him, yell at him for his actions, or fall into his arms, glad he was safe.

Henry didn't wait for my response. He never waited for me. He grabbed my arm and started to pull me along with him through the crowd. I vaguely heard Robert and Louisa protest.

It was then I realized he was walking me away, carrying me from the square. A guard asked where we were going, and I heard Henry explain that I was sick. My vision blurred and I could feel my heart pounding in my ears. Henry rushed me through the crowd.

Amid my pain, I began to hear the pain of others. I heard the crowd gasp and some begin to cry. It was happening.

Please! Please! Please! My voice made no sound. A wave of nausea hit me.

They were asking Julia for her last words. As the sound of her voice settled over the crowd, everything inside of me stopped.

She began to speak: "I am alone and miserable; man will not associate with me; but one as deformed and horrible as myself would not deny herself to me. My companion must be of the same species and have the same defects. This being you must create."

The crowd fell silent. The words from James's book? What nonsense was she speaking? I didn't understand the meaning of her words, but it sounded like blame. It felt like blame.

No, I was stronger than this. I wasn't completely useless. I tried to focus on Julia. My hands gripped Henry's shoulder, and I blindly hit him as hard as I could. The shock of it caused him to drop me to the ground. This brought on another round of nausea. I fought to hold it back as I scrambled to get up, trying to make my way through the crowd. I didn't get far.

Henry grabbed me from behind, one arm around my waist, holding me in place. I knew I didn't have much time. Two naturals were lowering Julia to her knees. She slowly, gracefully held out her arms. They, her own people, people forced into this position by the chosen ones, serving out their punishment because they had no female to speak up for them, tied her arms behind her back. She kept her eyes forward. They brought out the blade. She seemed ignorant of this, almost peaceful. Her gaze wandered over the crowd.

Then everything went black. Henry had forcefully placed his hands over my eyes.

"No," I managed to say weakly.

The crowd was screaming, a mixture of sadness and anger. It chilled me to the core.

I tried to struggle, but Henry was too strong. He forced me to the ground. He stayed there next to me, hands never leaving my eyes.

The crowd was suddenly silent and I heard the *swoosh*. It was followed by a *thud*.

Then screaming, unstoppable screaming.

It filled my ears. It electrified my pores. I then realized it was my screaming. And I couldn't stop.

"Why?" I whispered when he finally let me go, the crowd bumping against us as they headed back to the compound.

"I knew you would feel guilty. You'd blame yourself. And this has nothing to do with you," he replied stoically.

"Doesn't it? I told you how. Dear God, Henry, what part in this did you have?"

"You wouldn't understand," he replied, a note of frustration creeping into his voice.

I felt my stomach drop. "You *did* have a part in it. How could you let her die for you?" I charged.

Henry ran a hand over his face. "She didn't die for me. She died for something greater."

I took a step away from him. "I don't even know you."

"Maybe you never did."

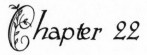

Chapter 22

I was to serve thirty years at Templeton, one for every young chosen one killed. I didn't have anyone's sympathy. They all wondered why I'd stood up for Julia—they couldn't understand that I didn't approve of what she'd done. My people were still happy to go along with the whole ruse the council had created. They weren't ready to rebel.

The more I thought over my punishment, the more I wondered about the Isolationists. What was it like in the wild, living in the destruction of the Middlelands, caught in the middle of a war between Easterners and Westerners? Had they found a way to be free?

It didn't matter. Maybe before I could have managed at least an attempt to run off, but the council would be watching me now. I couldn't earn another slash mark; I didn't even know what happened when you did. I also had to protect Louisa. And somehow, I knew if I earned a third mark, I'd be leaving her alone.

I was to live at Templeton now. I would only be allowed to

return to the compound on Sundays.

It didn't really matter.

On my fist day back at work my supervisor met me. They were going to make an example out of me. "You've really done it now, child," Gwen said, shaking her head.

"Be quiet," I muttered, unable to take another minute of her damn superiority. She was nothing. Just some sad, pathetic natural who was stuck here, same as me.

"What did you say?"

"Let's get this over with."

Today's assignment?

We were to get rid of the bodies.

They had been transported to deep in the woods behind Templeton, where a huge hole had been dug. My supervisor and I, along with the newly bruised and battered creator, were to pull the bodies from the transport and place them into the mass grave. There would be no words spoken over the dead. No pretense of religious ceremony.

It took hours to move all thirty bodies into their new home, their eternal resting place. While my supervisor had given me a mask to cover my nose and mouth, the stench of decay was overwhelming. The bodies were heavy. I tried to convince myself the children were simply sleeping, but they weren't. They were death personified. I felt the softness of their skin, the vulnerability of it. They never had a shot at life, never felt a thing. They never knew what it was like to be touched. They had no mothers or fathers to weep over them.

And I had helped kill them.

I had told Henry where they were kept.

I destroyed these unlived lives.

When we finally finished, I was covered in sweat and dirt.

There was a noticeable chill in the air and the sky had become cloudy and dark.

"Am I done?" I asked dully.

"Yes."

"May I stay here for a while?" I didn't see why it would matter if I did. My shift was over but I couldn't really leave. Templeton was my new home.

My supervisor nodded. I could almost detect a look of understanding on her face, but it was too brief to be sure.

I waited. Staring at the bodies, waiting for the sky to open up and cry.

Then, it was pouring. Every inch of me was covered with it. I sat on the ground, my knees clutched to my chest, shivering. I wasn't sure if it was because of the rain and cold or the guilt over what I had done. I'd stood up for a murderer. I'd helped a murderer.

I had allowed myself to feel and hope.

And this was my punishment.

For a few crazed moments, I contemplated laying myself down within the hole. Needing them to bury me with the rest of the rejects.

I heard a twig snap. I wasn't the only one here. Who dared to enter this space?

It was James.

His face showed apprehension. Did he really think he could fool me into thinking what we once had still remained? He must hate me. I had chosen Henry over him. I had chosen to align myself with the naturals. Before, I had begun to think neither the terms *natural* nor *chosen* could describe James and me; we were outside the council's definition. Not anymore. We couldn't run from who the council needed us to be.

It was ridiculous of me to think I could be anyone else.

Don't feel.

Don't feel.

Feel.

Feel.

It would always be chosen versus natural. The council set it up that way.

He would destroy me.

"What are you doing here?" I snarled.

"Tess."

"Don't you dare," I warned. "Don't you dare say my name. You have no right. You have no right to any of me." Some small part of me knew he wasn't the enemy, but I couldn't yell at the council. And God, I needed to yell. My hands were shaking. I was losing it. I was on the verge of an attack and didn't care if I could fight it off.

James stepped forward.

I would not back down, regardless of the consequences. I held my ground. This seemed to scare him, and he paused. I took two quick steps closer to him. We were inches apart.

"We need to talk about this. I did what I had to. She was a killer."

I slapped him as hard as I could. I did it without thinking— it was pure instinct. It stung my hand. It thrilled me.

I saw him flinch. Shock crossed his face, but he said nothing, did nothing.

This made me even angrier. "Don't you feel *anything*?" I screamed. I knew in the back of my mind I was no longer talking to him. It was as if the panic, the fear had finally found its voice.

"I wish it had been you. I wish it had been you they took!

You deserve it! You're the villain, the monster. You made Julia and Henry do those horrible things. He was such a sweet child. You took everything from him; you left him with nothing to want. And when you are left feeling like that, you fear no consequences."

"What are you saying, Tess? Let's talk about this."

"Don't stand there staring at me as if you can understand my pain. You're not even *human*. You feel nothing. You are nothing. You think it means something, you reading that book?"

His hand twitched.

It was too much; I was suffocating. I felt my eyes begin to water. I couldn't hold it back any longer. I would explode.

I was sobbing hysterically. I was being ripped open, and I wasn't sure when or if the flood could stop. Everything flashed before my eyes—my father being taken, my mother holding the bottle of discount liquor to her chest, the way Robert looked at the funeral, how Emma held out her hand for me to take, the loneliness I felt when Henry had abandoned me, the day with the piano and James, *Jane Eyre*, the evil way George had grinned, the laughter of the Templeton boys, the excruciating pain of receiving my second slash mark.

I sank ungraciously onto the dirt. I wanted to crawl inside of it. In the quickest of moments, James was on his knees, reaching for me.

"No!" I shrilly screamed, blindly lashing my arms against him. "Don't you touch me!"

I could faintly see a devastating look of pain on James's face, but I didn't care. I curled myself into a ball, letting the emotions take me where they willed. I could sense that James was still there and I had no idea why.

Suddenly, I felt extremely tired.

"Just do what you want with me. Have your fun and get it over with. I can't take any more. I won't scream. There isn't anyone now who would care. It's what you want, isn't it? I know what it means to be a Templeton girl," I managed to gasp through the tears.

I heard him inhale sharply, and I could feel him move away from me. But I knew he was still there, somewhere.

I closed my eyes. They were burning, dry, unprepared for the exercise they had performed. But something was different; my heart, it purred. Fluttered. I slowly sat up, my body sore from my crumpled position. I felt the sheen of tears dried to my face. My hair was wild, untamed. I searched for my ribbon. I saw James holding it in his hand.

I wanted desperately to hate him, but I knew that I never really could. He had a part of my soul. And as much as I wanted to claim it back, I believed I wouldn't. How long could I survive through this, the slow destruction of my being?

James walked over to me, stopping a short distance away. He crouched down so his face was on my level and gingerly held out the ribbon. His face was emotionless. The rain continued to whip me in the face as I took the ribbon, turning my back to him, trying to tie my hair into some sort of order.

My knees seemed wobbly as I stood up, but I somehow managed it without falling. I walked past James without a second glance. Part of me wished he would just leave, but the other part didn't, and that's the part that hurt the most.

"I know I betrayed you. Why are you out here pretending you care?" I said, my back still toward him.

He laughed, slightly losing it himself. "It's *all* I care about. You were wrong—I believe someone *can* have all of your soul.

Don't you see? You have all of mine."

I wanted to tell him that was impossible, that he had no soul. But I couldn't. I turned to face him quickly. Too quickly. I felt dizzy and closed my eyes to try and stop the world from spinning out of control. I couldn't put the words together.

His eyes found solace on the ground. "I had to do what I did. Maybe they would have grown up to be these things you detest, but they were just children. They knew nothing of what it means to be human. And if I refused to help bring in a natural, they would have guessed my secret."

"Secret?"

"George. He suspects you. He suspects me. He can tell."

Did James somehow know of my run-in with George?

"Tell what?"

James hesitated. "He can tell it is…that we aren't normal. This, us, it scares the other boys."

He was near me in an instant, his hand reaching for my face. I froze; he did, too. James dropped his hand slowly to his side. "They know that you have power over me."

"Power? I don't even have that over myself."

The tears were coming back. I took a deep breath, trying to calm myself.

"I've already caused the other chosen ones to suspect me. If I made a big deal about the wrangling, they would realize you don't mean to me what the other girls are to them. I don't know what would happen to me then. Which I don't care about, not really. This isn't much of a life anyways. But I had you to think about…"

"But—"

"You have to believe me. I can't go on knowing you think that I could willingly hurt you. This is who I'm supposed to be.

What choice did I have?"

I took a step closer to him. "How can I trust you? How can I trust *anyone* who belongs with them?"

I knew the us-versus-them argument was illogical. I had seen too much to pretend it could be boiled down to these simple components. I just needed to hear that I was right about him.

James shifted uncomfortably. "I don't belong with the chosen ones. Sometimes I don't feel like I belong anywhere. Except maybe with you."

I felt the honesty of the words as if they were my own.

"You say you see me differently than the other boys? The other Templeton girls? I saw one of them, James. I think she may have been forced…"

His jaw clenched. "Yes, I heard of it. George. It's why he wasn't chosen either. The council, Templeton, they don't care if we…if one of us has…with a Templeton girl. It doesn't matter because—"

"We're dying anyway. Because they think we're worthless."

He nodded. "But George made a scene. He wasn't even secretive about it. He stalked this girl and then took her. Secrecy is essential. It's the only thing that keeps this horrid world together."

I was feeling dizzy again. I was falling. James's hands were there to steady me, one on each of my arms, my support. My body heated up instantly despite the chill in the air. I could smell him, could feel his breath on me. He was so close, and for once I didn't care. I wanted him to be closer. I don't know how long we stood there—a minute, an eternity. It didn't matter. Everything was so disjointed, I couldn't see sense, could only barely control the surge of emotions running through me.

"I am sorry," he whispered.

I didn't know what I was doing. It was as if some force was alive in me, controlling me. Maybe I was finally losing my sanity. I slowly raised my hand to his face, hesitating before placing my palm against his cheek. He sighed and closed his eyes. I closed mine, too. The rain had slowed, but I could hear the wind picking up, hear it howling, moaning. Strangely, I didn't feel it. All I knew was my palm against his skin. How strange that such a small gesture could cause such emotions.

Such feelings.

This wasn't just about the need to touch anymore. It was so much more than that. The council called it weakness, but I didn't *feel* weak.

James leaned forward and gently kissed my forehead. "Tess," he breathed against my skin.

God, I loved how he said my name.

I couldn't answer. I was overwrought with the sensation of human contact.

"Tess," he repeated.

"I'm sorry, too. There is no right side. But you're not the enemy. The council is."

He tugged me toward Templeton. "Let's go home."

I offered a short laugh in response.

"James?"

"Hmmm."

"What do we do now?"

He wiped the remaining tears off my face with his thumb, his hand resting on my cheek. "I have no idea."

Chapter 23

James held my hand all the way back to Templeton, but the minute we neared the entrance, he let go. The council would barely notice we were together, as long as it was physical, not some mutual exchange of true feelings. They had plenty of disdain for relationships between naturals; a real relationship between a natural and a chosen one was unheard of.

Maybe if the Templeton girls would talk to one another, talk about something of substance, they could prevent it. But when our parents never taught us about sex, irrationally hoping by not talking about it we wouldn't think about it, they set us up for failure. We didn't know how to handle any of it. Maybe some of us didn't even know we could say no.

But if the council saw the way James and I looked at each other or the way we clutched so desperately onto each other's hands, they would know we'd changed the rules. They already suspected us. They knew James questioned the whole thing. And I had aligned myself with a rebel, a terrorist.

We had to be careful.

"Meet me in the piano room?"

"Are you sure?" I asked.

"Yes," he said, walking slightly ahead of me in the hallway. "Most everyone is asleep."

As I closed myself within the darkness of the room, I forced away the memory of George threatening me the last time I'd been there. He would not own this space.

I sat down on the piano bench and pressed my forehead against the keys with as little pressure as possible. As much as I wanted to play, tonight might not be the best time. And it felt good to just touch the keys anyway.

When the door opened, I couldn't fight the wave of nervousness that hit me. I would never be able to forget what this place was. James offered me a small smile as he shut the door and set a lantern on the piano.

This is where we met.

How my life had changed since then.

I suddenly felt shy, self-conscious. I was shivering, soaked, and embarrassed by my appearance. I knew the pale tint of my skin was showing through my wet top. I made an attempt to cover myself by crossing my arms over my chest.

He seemed to sense my discomfort, pulling off his jacket and handing it to me. It was oversized, but it was a part of him, and I welcomed it.

"You have questions? I know I would. I figure we've got a lot to discuss," he said, sitting next to me on the bench.

"Yes." I nodded.

He waited for me to continue, not an ounce of frustration on his face. Just patience.

"I...well, maybe you could..." I had so many questions. I

wanted to know more about how Templeton worked, as well as how James fit into the whole scheme of things. I knew he wasn't like the others, but it was time I found out as much as I could about the life I was given. I just didn't know where to start.

He laughed gently, took my hands, and placed them on the keys. He didn't press down, either. Maybe the illusion that we could was all we needed.

"Maybe you can just tell me something I don't know about you."

He took a deep breath. "Three nights ago, I discovered my gift," he replied with a forced smile.

"Gift?"

"Yes. When I was born…made…when we are created, they enhance us."

So the rumors about the superpowers were true. What gifts did the others have? We really had no idea of the power the chosen ones held. I couldn't help but cringe at the thought of George with even more power than he already had. The council had a plethora of weapons.

How many lies had the council told us? If they were making the chosen ones with these abilities, how powerful would the council become? Did the naturals even have a chance of surviving?

"You don't have to tell me any more," I whispered. I wasn't sure I wanted to know.

"You'd let me off that easy?" James asked, running his fingers up and down my hands as they rested against the keys where we had made music. Together.

All I wanted was to touch him. Now that I had allowed the weakness to come through, I didn't care what it meant. I was already damaged too much for it to matter.

"It's not who you are. It doesn't really matter," I replied. It *did* matter, but I didn't want to think about it tonight.

"No," he said, grabbing my hands in his, staring at the way our fingers fit together. "I want to tell you. I want to tell you everything. Is that crazy?"

"Completely."

He laughed, and it sounded genuine. I was amazed by the gamut of emotions we had both exhibited that night.

"When we are made they give us a gift, an ability. To let us know we are—"

"Special," I interrupted.

"Yes, special," he said, rolling his eyes, "or freaks."

"You're not a freak." I gave his hand a squeeze.

Because if he was, then I was, too.

James took a deep breath before speaking again. "My creator has a weird sense of humor. A real humanitarian, if you can imagine that. He's not very popular with the council. I only recently figured out what it was he'd given me. *You* made me realize what it was."

"Me?"

"Yes. I had a dream about you weeks ago. I saw you here with George, and he threatened you. I thought it was just a nightmare, but then I overheard him bragging about it the other day. Why didn't you tell me?"

I looked down at the keys. "I didn't want to cause any trouble. I didn't know I had the right to tell," I admitted.

He lifted my chin, forcing me to look at him. "You will tell me if it happens again. My gift isn't perfect, and I can't guarantee that I'll see every threat to you before it happens."

I nodded.

He cleared his throat. "I talked to my creator because I was curious. They say that around this age your ability starts to show itself. Not at full power of course, but in spurts. Puberty, I guess you could call it."

I let free a shaky laugh. "Lovely."

He laughed, too. "Yes, even we go through some of that awkwardness. The pure power of science is no match for the grueling years of being a teenager."

He was back to looking at our hands.

"You still see your creator?" Was it possible that he had some sense of what a family was?

James shrugged. "Sometimes. He was there when I was awakened. Every year the creators come here to visit us, to see their work. Usually they are busy with the council. But my creator, well, he must have done something to really piss them off, because he works at the sector's inspection center now. That's a real downgrade for him. Most creators were selected because they were the best of the naturals. The scientists, doctors…the greatest natural minds. Most of them wanted nothing more to do with their own people. So to be stuck inspecting naturals isn't their dream job. No offense."

I shrugged.

"But it means I get to see my creator more than most," he said.

The inspection center. The place that would forever mark me as proof of my people's extinction. A rite of passage.

"From what my creator told me, it's like a sixth sense. I can feel things about those I am close to, care about…"

I turned away, hoping to hide my blush.

"He says I will get better at controlling it," James continued. "Right now, since I don't understand it, I can't just use it whenever I want. That's why he thinks it happened in my dream, through my subconscious." James fell silent.

"Sounds like a useful gift," I offered.

He sighed. "I was beginning to wonder if I even had a gift. Some of the others have been developing theirs for a while now. Probably one of the many reasons I wasn't chosen—late bloomer. Hell, I think they were worried I was getting the transformation sickness or something."

Frank. Is that why the council had killed him? How long till they found a reason to kill James, too?

"Why would your creator give you that gift? I mean, don't get me wrong, I—"

"Yes, I know, not a gift you can see being particularly useful in combat," he said with a dry laugh.

"Unless they wanted you to guard someone," I offered.

He looked at me, puzzled.

"I mean, it would be pretty useful then. They pair you with someone, someone you can feel close to, and you would know if he were in trouble."

"A bodyguard," James said with a slight shrug. "I guess it could be worse. Too bad that's not going to happen—they'll ship me off to a compound soon. The council doesn't even think I'm good enough to guard one connected to a training center."

I didn't want to think of him being anywhere but with me. I couldn't acknowledge that one day he would leave Templeton. His place wasn't here, and mine always would be.

He wouldn't be able to protect me during my now-thirty-year sentence at Templeton.

"And George? You really think he will just let me be?"

"He won't hurt you. I swear it." The fierceness in James's eyes frightened me. I wouldn't want the two of them to fight, especially since I didn't know what George's gift was.

I cringed. "What is it exactly that you do all those hours you spend away from me?" I asked, hoping to change the subject. Besides, we both seemed bent on asking all of our questions tonight. "Other than the physical training," I added. I didn't need any reminders of how strong they were.

James shrugged. "Mostly classes. Not unlike when you still had school, I assume. Math. Science. Literature."

"Sounds amazing," I replied, trying to keep the jealously out of my voice.

James nodded slowly. "There are other classes as well."

"And your least favorite would be…?"

"Human Ideologies."

I raised an eyebrow.

"It's where we study the mistakes your people made." James sighed. "How the naturals just let it all slip away. How the original creators were gifted men, men far above others in intelligence, and their creation of the chosen ones would ensure the world went on. We would have no family ties. We would be trained to control our emotions. Everything that made the naturals so weak would be weeded out of us. We would fight in the wars the naturals no longer had the numbers to win. We would continue humanity in a world where women were no longer needed…"

I inhaled sharply. I could hear my father's words mingle with his, almost as if they were cut from the same cloth. But their lives couldn't have been more different. Perhaps there were some ideas that transcended time and circumstance, a desire to define ourselves instead of letting others define us that burned unceasingly. Perhaps it was this need that connected the naturals and the chosen ones; it was what made us human.

tiffany truitt

"These aren't my thoughts, Tess. But the council believes they can create a perfect future, one where they will have full control over subsequent generations. They will choose how to educate them. They will train them to fight. And if they need more? They'll just create them. We're the perfect citizens because we are expendable."

"It's not fair," I whispered. We both sat silent for a long time.

"We should probably go. It's late. You have work and I have class in the morning. And let's not forget all that pretending we have to do. Like pretending I don't want to spend every second with you." Coming from anyone else it would have sounded cheesy, but when I heard the pain behind his words, I heard them as truth.

I swallowed. "Before we go back, I want something just for us. Before we need to start pretending again."

"Anything."

I reached out and placed my hand against his neck. He stilled at my very touch. "I want to kiss you again," I whispered. I stood up and grabbed James's hand, pulling him toward me.

He slowly leaned his face down. He hesitated as his lips were only inches from mine. I was tired of waiting for something that I wanted. I didn't have time to wait anymore. Life was too damn short.

I stood up on the tips of my toes and pressed my lips against his. They felt soft and warm. A strange sensation that seemed to stir from my center spread across my body. My skin was tingling. The hair on the back of my neck stood up.

I pulled away.

Before I could tell him how nice the kiss was, James pressed his lips against mine again. A sound escaped my lips. Was that a moan? I reached my hands up and pushed them through James's curly black hair and he grunted in response. His hands were on my face. His lips opened and I felt his tongue. We only stopped to take a wild gasp of breath and then we were back to kissing. I was moving backward, away from the door that kept the whole world at bay. I stumbled awkwardly against the piano bench, James leaning over me, still kissing. My elbow accidentally pushed down on the keys and we froze with the noise.

We remained silent, the sound of our heaving breaths the only evidence of our transgression. James closed his eyes and kissed my forehead. "Thank you."

"For what?" I asked, still struggling to breathe normally.

"For seeing me."

I smiled.

"Can you meet again tomorrow night?"

I knew, without being told, my afternoons spent with James would have to stop. The council couldn't know what we felt. The day was too bright, too many eyes watching. They already suspected us.

It had to be secret.

He nodded. "And what shall I bring? What book should we venture into?"

"Surprise me," I said, handing him back his jacket.

I saw his eyes for the briefest of moments glance onto my bare arms. He cleared his throat. "Surprise it is. I will see you soon." He turned to leave, but I grabbed his arm.

"Wait, I have something to give you." I undid the ribbon in my hair and placed it in his hand. "I know how you adore contraband things. And what could be more outlawed than this?"

• • •

As I walked back to my room, realization dawned as I finally understood the way my sister had felt for Robert. It was like I was standing over an abyss, and any second I would throw myself right in, just to see if it were possible for the darkness to end. It didn't make Emma's actions any less selfish—but at least now I understood why.

Chapter 24

Someone had been pounding on the door. The noise echoed in my ears much too loudly as my feeble hands instinctively tried to block out the intrusion. My mother said nothing, just sat with her bottle congealed to her hand, rocking ever so gently back and forth. I could hear Louisa crying somewhere off in the distance. I wanted to go comfort her but fear had frozen me in place. I heard the gruff, raw punches of male voices outside the door. Who were they? Why were they here? And what could have possibly happened to make them so angry?

My father was pacing. I had never seen him like this before. He was always so easygoing, so calm and collected. Occasionally, he would run his hands through his hair, but mostly they stood limply by his sides, the only part of him that appeared in control. I could see that he was sweating. Sweating! My father didn't sweat; he was above that. He was a God.

"Emma, your sister," he barked suddenly.

Emma's face was white but she didn't say a word. Just

quickly disappeared from the room. I had forgotten she was even there.

The knocking was becoming louder, demanding, taking all sense of sanity from the room.

Without warning, my father stood still. He was staring at me. I could see his mouth twitch; he was trying to smile. The smile I adored. But something inside of him would not allow it. Then I saw pain—pure, unquenchable pain. He kneeled in front of me so his eyes were level with mine, placed his hands on either side of my face, and proceeded to kiss me on the cheek. It was the smallest of moments, one most would think insignificant, but my father was not an emotional man. He had never been a hugger and I couldn't recall him telling us stories before bed. He was always laughing and joking and pleasant to be around, but never one to wear his feelings for the world to see. A wild, ferocious fear stemmed through my body. Something was horribly wrong. Why did I feel like he was saying good-bye?

I heard the crack of wood against the wall. I looked away from my father's face and realized the door was off its hinges. Two of the largest men I had ever seen stood watching my father and me. I could see the veins protruding from their much too lean and muscular bodies. Yet they were beautiful. I couldn't help but stare at them—I didn't want to look away. There was something hypnotizing about the mismatched color of their eyes. Were there chosen ones in my house? They seemed different than how they appeared on TV—somehow improved, better.

My father moved away from me, held up his hands. His jaw was clearly clenched. I shook my head, trying to clear it. Did he actually have tears in his eyes? No! It was impossible.

He was the bravest person I knew, the comforter when the sirens went off, always ready with a joke. In the quickest of seconds, I saw one of the men throw my father against the wall. I started to scream but couldn't move my feet. How gut wrenching to feel the need to help, to save him, but unable to move an inch. Fear had complete control over me.

I saw his blood smudged on the wall where his head had hit, and I couldn't look anymore. I shut my eyes tight, waiting for it all to end. Somewhere in the distance Louisa was still crying. I was retreating inside myself when a voice caught my attention, halted my surrender. It was my father's. "Emma," he yelled hoarsely, "Louisa will need her medicine. You have to ask one of our friends for a loan to help pay for it."

My eyes shot open in time to see the taller of the two men backhand my father. I shuddered. My father twisted and kicked the man holding him. The man stumbled into his partner's arms as confusion swept over their faces.

My father was back in front, clutching me to him, wrapping his arms around me as if I were a butterfly stuck tightly in a protective cocoon. His lips were close to my ear and he was whispering frantically.

"You must be brave. Promise me you won't ever believe their lies. Promise me you won't believe what they will tell you about me. Don't believe what they will tell you about yourself!"

This was all he was allowed. Out of the corner of my eye I saw a fist fly into the side of his head. My father crumpled to the floor, lifeless, weak, destroyed. I could see he was still breathing but it didn't change anything. For the first time in my life, I knew that my father was human, and I was angry—not at them, but at him.

. . .

When I awoke my entire body was trembling. It had been years since I'd last dreamt of the night the chosen ones came for my father. It was during the early years, right before we were mandated to move into the compounds. Somehow my father had found a way to hold onto our house while many of our neighbors were forced to abandon their homes for tent city. In the early days we were allowed to leave, take our chances in the Middlelands, and I imagine he wanted to move out into the wilderness, but my mother had a need for her material things. She couldn't be guaranteed her bottle in the place where civilization ceased to exist. Louisa couldn't be promised medical aid out there either.

So we stayed. I never knew what my father did to cause the chosen ones to take him. I never asked my mother. I was certain he must have deserved it. I always blamed him for leaving, for choosing some stupid idea over his family.

But now I understood.

If he had stayed, it would have been worse than death to him. He would have become nothing. He would have hated his life and himself. He would have hated us, too.

You can't care for someone else if you don't care for yourself.

Call it selfish, but he chose himself. He was the brave one, not me.

I didn't belong with the chosen ones *or* the naturals. I needed a place for me, but I was afraid, too scared the chosen ones would come after me. I feared losing James. I was petrified what it would mean to have no excuses for not being true to myself.

I pushed my pillow against my face and began to sob.

I cried for realizing I had a dream I would never be brave enough to chase.

I cried for my father—the man who gave up everything to be free.

He even gave up me.

"What are you thinking this very moment?" I asked James as we sat on the floor in the piano room late one night. I was sitting in front of him, my legs tucked underneath me. He rested his hand on my knee.

"How very glad I am to see you."

"You don't look very glad."

"Because I shouldn't be this glad."

I frowned. "Oh."

His hand found mine in that instant. "No, I mean—I don't know what I mean. Can we talk about something else?"

I felt his hand leave mine, and I instantly wanted it back. He retrieved a giant book from his bag. While it would have been just as safe, or reckless, to meet in his room, we often didn't go there. We did this for many reasons really—the bed being the foremost.

He placed the book in my open, empty hands. It was heavy.

"Shakespeare," he said, his face lighting up.

I raised an eyebrow. "And where would we even start?"

"Your choice, of course," he replied.

I flipped through the giant compilation of works, recognizing titles as they flashed before me. I smiled as I thought of my father trying to pass as many stories to me as he could before he was taken. I saw *Romeo and Juliet*. No. Definitely not that one. *Macbeth*.

I remembered something about witches and decapitation. No, that wouldn't be good. *The Merchant of Venice*. I hadn't heard of it. Considering books had been outlawed for years, I was pretty impressed I knew any of these at all. In the early years of the compound, some of the adults would gather the children around and tell them stories, passing down their favorite narratives orally. But eventually that ended, too.

I chose *The Merchant of Venice* because it seemed safe.

James glanced down and nodded.

Safe.

The first act was more unsettling than I could have imagined. Shylock, a Jew, was presented as evil, licentious, someone not to be trusted. In my mind, Shylock was the chosen ones, though I wondered if a part of James saw my people and me as Shylock—someone outside of normal society. He was portrayed as something to be disgusted by and feared. The racism, the prejudice in it appalled and upset me. Yet I was unable to deny how true to life it was. How easy it was to rewrite people in our own misconstrued ways, in an attempt to make ourselves feel safe. I didn't want to do that to James; I wanted to see who he really was, not who I imagined him or needed him to be.

I looked up from the book and found James staring at me. I turned away. "I think I need a break from the Bard."

He nodded. "Agreed." He took the heavy weight from my hands and placed it away, hidden in his bag.

"Did the story upset you?" James asked suddenly.

I knew I wouldn't be able to lie to him; I didn't want to.

"Yes. A little."

"It upset me, too." James took my hand back in his. "It's better knowing what the other is thinking, right?"

I squeezed his hand. "Yes. I always want to know what you're thinking."

After a prolonged silence, James said, "Your name is on a list."

I froze, fear flooding every inch of me. Having your name on any kind of list usually wasn't good. It was better to go unnoticed. But I hadn't exactly done a good job with that as of late.

James shifted and lifted my chin so I was looking up at him. "From what I've gathered it's merely precautionary. You have a meeting at the inspection station in a few days. I just thought it would be wise to give you some warning. I know we aren't always the best at that."

Oh, yes, the inspection station—I was considered an adult now. I hadn't even realized my birthday had passed. How could I have forgotten my own birthday?

"Do you know why? Is this normal?" he asked. I could hear the mistrust of the council in his voice.

It made sense that he didn't know. He was very young and all of his life had been spent in Templeton. He didn't have the knowledge base that I did. But it also alerted me to something else: he questioned more than he trusted the things his comrades told him. I wondered if I was slowly destroying his world by finding a way to survive in mine.

I nodded. "Yes, it's normal. We have to be checked." I shivered. I could feel the bile creeping up my throat.

"Checked?"

"To make sure. To confirm that we're infertile."

He dropped his hand from my face.

I rolled my eyes, trying to ease the panic in my mind. "It's all sort of silly, really. So unnecessary. Many of the girls get their hopes up that they will be different; they don't want to accept one day our kind will be gone, extinct. I think the council only conducts it to give us some small amount of hope. It's stupid I even have to go. I don't need or want the hope." I knew my attempt at easing the tension sounded more like bitterness. I also knew James wouldn't miss it.

"Did your sister know then, when she…"

I could tell he was uncomfortable asking the question.

"No. She knew it was a risk. They told her during the inspection. Some of my people think your kind lie to us. Some believe the council tells us we can't bring forth new life in order to discourage us from trying to save our species. My sister believed that. She was wrong, as you can see."

"And you, what do you believe?"

"I believe history has proven there are other, faster ways of getting rid of a group of people. If the council wanted us gone they could easily do so. You know that."

He didn't reply, just nodded.

"We are the weak. Nature has decided the strong will stay and the weak will go."

His hand was on my cheek in the briefest of moments. My eyes met his. "Please don't speak like that. I don't like to think of a world without you in it."

"I don't think you will have to worry about it so much," I said with a small laugh. "I think we will both be long gone before the end of my people. Well, maybe. I'm not even sure what the average life span is for your kind."

He shrugged. "Depends. Though I guess we average ninety to one hundred years."

My eyes grew wide in amazement. "Wow."

The average life span for our kind was fifty. He could live twice the time I would on this earth.

Another difference.

"Can't we talk about something lovely? Something besides the naturals and chosen ones?" I begged. "Or can we at least talk about how we're the same? I am so tired of knowing how odd I am."

"Yes, you are odd," he said, tapping my nose with his finger. There was an amusing air to his words and I could feel the stress begin to leave. "Hmm. And how do you think we are alike?" he asked, stretching. It was getting late and I knew it would be time to leave soon.

I bit my bottom lip. "Well, we both love to read and listen to music."

"Yes." He laughed. "We both love reading and listening to what others have demanded that we should not be allowed to."

I nudged him with my elbow. "Very true. And what do you have to add to our list?"

"We both don't get enough sleep."

I scrunched my nose. "What a compelling addition. I can see I'm going to have to do all the work."

"Fine, fine, I can do better," he said, holding up his hand.

I crossed my arms in front of my chest, feigning mistrust.

He cleared his throat. "We both have a serious lack of logical thought when it comes to the other."

I could feel something inside of me want to crawl away; this was not a conversation I could have. I just wanted it to be easy. I wanted to spend time with him without thinking of anything but us. And it was then I knew he was right. I nodded.

Without warning, he pulled me into an embrace. I could feel a desperate longing connected to it. He moved his face so his lips met mine and I craved them. We were kissing with a passion I had not yet experienced, and we were touching. He pulled me from off my knees practically into his lap. His hands ran up my back and into my hair. I leaned against his chest. Every time one of us pulled away to breathe, I wanted to tell him to stop. No. I didn't want that, but I *should* have wanted it.

His hands began to slide down from my hair to my neck.

I didn't want him to stop. I felt all warm and lightheaded. Tingling.

I couldn't do this.

I roughly pushed him off of me and scooted away, drawing my legs against my chest. My eyes were glued to my feet, refusing to look at him. He was silent; I half wondered if he even existed at all. I could only hear my own ragged breath.

"I am so sorry," he whispered.

I couldn't speak, only nodded once.

"I think you should go," he replied.

I stood up and headed toward the door.

I turned to face him. "We have to remember the rules, James. If we can't then I won't be able to come here. And I don't think I could keep myself from wanting to see you."

His back was toward me, his hands curled into fists. His voice sounded so far away. "Yes, I can keep my promise."

"I'll see you tomorrow night," I said, once more heading for the door.

"Tess?"

I couldn't turn to face him. I kept my hand on the doorknob as I answered. "Yes."

"Can you do me a favor? Ask around, maybe your supervisor, and see if anyone has heard anything about Frank."

I could have told him right then what I had seen and done. But I simply nodded and left. I lied to the one person I had asked to be honest with me.

And there are always consequences.

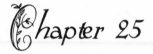

Chapter 25

"You have to stop moving around so much." Louisa sighed, clearly frustrated by my inability to remain a statue while she measured.

"This is stupid," I muttered. Spending so much time altering my uniform for Templeton seemed like a waste of a Sunday.

"Ugh, cheer up! I can't believe you actually get to attend an event with the creators tomorrow," she chirped as she pulled my skirt tighter.

"I don't really consider anything about my time at Templeton fun, Louisa."

My sister shook her head, motioning for me to take off the skirt. When I handed it to her, she sat on the cot and went to work. "I would gladly take your place. It must be so cool to be surrounded by all that glamour and wealth. This stupid, dingy compound is all I can remember. And the boys! I wouldn't mind looking at them all day."

I took a deep breath. This sisterly love thing was new for

Louisa and me, and I didn't know exactly how to do it. I gingerly took a seat next to her on the cot, thankful our bunkmate Grace was off somewhere. "Templeton isn't what you think it is. That place isn't an escape from here."

"Of course *you* would say that. No offense, but you're not exactly the type of girl to enjoy a place like Templeton. I don't know why they won't just let any girl from a family volunteer to work there. Why does it have to be the oldest? Besides, as one of the last born, I'm about as special as the chosen ones."

Louisa brought this up at least once a day. I should have stopped her then, told her about all the horrors I had seen at Templeton. But I couldn't. I saw the excitement in her eyes. Why not let her have it? She would never go there—I'd make sure of that. Why destroy the dreams of a thirteen-year-old girl? Dreams were all she had left.

"Here. Good as new," Louisa said, handing me back my skirt. "You've really got to stop losing so much weight."

"Thanks."

I only had Sundays left at the compound now. I would dedicate them all to her.

"Here, I got you something for your birthday. I didn't forget, you know," she said.

That made one of us.

Louisa placed a bright yellow ribbon in my hands. "For your hair. I traded Grace laundry duty for two weeks to get it. Wear it tomorrow to the picnic."

It wasn't my style at all. It would match Louisa much better, but I loved it. I smiled and was happy to see Louisa return the smile as well.

It was a start.

. . .

Only the "real" Templeton girls, those of us lucky to have the back of our necks forever graced with two slash marks, were allowed to wait on the attendees during the event that celebrated the matching of chosen one and committee. I guess the council figured we wouldn't dare reveal any secrets. The third slash mark was always in the back of our minds.

Even those like James and George who had gone unselected would attend. The chosen ones were dressed sharply in tweed trousers and dress shirts, some of them even donning vests. Like they'd stepped out of one of the books James and I loved to read.

The girls carried around trays, stopping and smiling at council members and chosen ones alike. The members of the council stood out like sore thumbs, their faces a sometimes disastrous display of uncontrolled genetics. Their skin sagged with age. And while they were dressed in the finest clothes around, their faces were covered in wrinkles and liver spots—the science they'd used to create the world couldn't save them from time.

It was rumored that naturals used to cut up their own faces to appear younger, but such surgeries were now seen as superficial. Only the chosen ones could remain sublimely beautiful. It was odd to see them in person. Like they were some Gods who descended down from Mt. Olympus to mingle with us humans. These were the men who reigned over everything.

You never would have guessed it by looking at them.

I moved around the massive lawn as quickly as possible. Each table was decorated with crisp white tablecloths and a bouquet of wildflowers. In the center of the lawn a space was cleared for some sort of event. A group of council members played on violins while everyone mingled. Apparently, scientists and doctors weren't the only ones selected for the council. They kept the artists for themselves, too.

I didn't try and chat with any of the boys like most of the other Templeton girls, though I knew it would be easier for me if I did. The more I looked closely at Templeton, the more I saw how the system worked. Julia had been right. You did your job, flirted with the boys, allowed them a little touch or kiss, and you got what you wanted. Extra food. A cigarette here and there.

In some ways, it wasn't so different than James and me. But in the important ways, it couldn't be more different.

The clinking of silverware against glass pulled me from my thoughts. I followed the other more experienced girls who hustled to stand in a line opposite the speaker, who now rose up. Council member after council member stood with their selected chosen one like it was a giant game of show and tell. They would list their committee, and the chosen one would demonstrate his ability.

Something I'd never seen before. The only reason we were allowed to watch this was because we were permanent Templeton girls. Templeton's secrets were now our own. None of us girls knew what a third mark would mean for us, but the threat of one was enough for us to fall in line. Or at least pretend to.

The things the chosen ones could do were mind-boggling. These weren't the ones flashed before my eyes as a child. Who had changed the design without informing the naturals? A boy could move from one side of the lawn to the other in the blink of an eye. One second he was there, and the other he was gone. Another launched himself in the air like it was nothing. Part of me wondered if he could actually *fly*. Was he holding back? Were they all holding back? One merely twitched his fingers, and almost every glass shattered into a million pieces.

At each demonstration, the council and girls cheered in amazement. I didn't. I *couldn't*. What had we created? If the chosen ones were the weapons of the council, how could we ever hope to rebel?

Did I even *want* to rebel?

When the crowd broke up to mingle after the show, I felt a gentle tug on my hand. Looking up, I saw James. Relief flooded me. He wasn't scary like the rest of them. He placed a finger over his lips and glanced toward an archway created by a row of trees—it could keep us hidden.

When I was sure no one was watching, I made my way to meet James. As soon as I reached him, I wanted to throw myself into his arms. To remind myself that he was human like me. I needed to hear his heartbeat.

We didn't speak at first. I self-consciously tugged at my yellow ribbon.

James sighed. Apparently, he didn't find today's proceeding particularly celebratory either. "If my people were never created, yours would not suffer. You would have a much different life."

"And who is to say that life would be better? Maybe it would be. Maybe not. The war changed us all, and honestly if it wasn't for your people I don't know that any of my kind would have survived. You can't control what life you're born into."

"I wasn't born," he said harshly, bitterly. I wondered if my undying hatred had seeped into him. Hadn't I once thought this very thing about him?

"I'm a freak," he continued. "You are marvelous, innocent. How can I accept a world that dictates the manufactured over the natural?"

The pain in my chest was pulsing. I placed both of my hands alongside his face. "Your body may have been produced, or manufactured as you say, but your soul, your being, that comes from God, and he has given you a miraculous gift. He has given *me* a miraculous gift. We are so lucky to have each other. Don't forget that."

His brow wrinkled with thought. "You speak of my soul with such certainty. I hope you're right. But where did this hope come from, when you've denied it so long?"

I pulled away. Not because his question bothered me, but because it actually took some time to consider. What reason had I to hope?

My heart beat wildly against my chest. It was because of *this*. Because I had finally realized what power it had over me, and I welcomed it. It was because I knew that I was loved without having to hear the words—because for better or worse, I was alive. And I would never again allow myself to shrink away from life. It was meeting my self, my true self, not the self I had taught myself to create. I didn't know her completely yet, but I did know that for once in my life I was welcoming her into existence. I hoped…because it brought me joy to know that my greatest exploration, my greatest adventure would be discovering who she was.

How could I possibly put all of that into words? Words never seemed to be enough to encompass what I was feeling or thinking these days.

"I think, well, maybe I'm…" I stumbled.

I took a deep breath before continuing, feeling the weight of James's eyes on me. "I don't really know how to explain it," I admitted. "I just don't think I would survive very much longer without it, especially when you're gone. Maybe it's my secret weapon, *my* gift," I said, trying to lighten the tone.

I reached up to tuck a loose strand of hair behind my ear and James caught my wrist. He ran his thumb gently over the numbers lasered there.

"Did it hurt?"

"No," I replied. Not physically, at least. It was a deeper pain, the pain of entrapment.

"Maybe our intentions were good, but somewhere down the line we got too damaged," James offered.

"Perhaps. Sometimes I can't really blame the chosen ones, not completely. I blame us. I blame my people for allowing it to happen. We let ourselves get taken in; we let ourselves be fooled by the propaganda. I blame our own ignorance."

"You were just a child, Tess."

His words were simple but they stung. Who could I blame then? My parents? *Their* parents? Had the series of events long before been set in motion? Could all of it have been stopped?

I opened my mouth to speak when we both heard someone call James's name. He leaned down, gave me a quick kiss on the cheek, and hurried off. Our time still wasn't our own.

Chapter 26

It was supposed to be a milestone in my life. I would officially be told I had no future. It certainly wasn't a day to be taken lightly, but that was exactly what I tried to do. To think of anything besides the fact I was going to the medical center.

I could feel the sympathetic eyes of Louisa follow me all Sunday morning. It was strange. I'm not sure how she knew I was getting inspected, but she seemed to feel sorry for me. Maybe the sympathy was also for herself—soon she would be the one to go to the medical center. Soon it would be her time to realize that a part of her had long ago died.

Even Robert seemed aware of the fact. He placed himself opposite me at the breakfast table, quiet for a long while before speaking. I'm not sure why, but I felt a small sense of comfort having him there.

I held my neck to the side in an effort to alleviate the stiffness from my perpetual lack of sleep. Robert noticed, and it was then that he first spoke.

"You look horrible."

I cringed. "Thanks. Good morning to you, too."

He sighed. "Sorry, that was rude."

I gulped down some water to keep myself from falling back to the days when I'd considered him a friend, a brother.

"I just meant you look like you haven't slept in days. I'm sure today has you worried, but it's all very normal. You'll only be there a few hours and then, God willing, you won't have to go again."

That was a small comfort. Most illnesses were dealt with inside the compound. It was only for severe injuries or inspections that one had to travel to the center. That's all a sector needed to survive—compound, training center, and inspection center. That was our civilization, everything we could ever dream of.

"I guess it's my rite of passage or something," I mumbled, stuffing a piece of pancake into my mouth.

He merely nodded.

I looked around and lowered my voice before asking my next question. The cafeteria was filled with people, and I didn't want anyone to hear the questions I needed to ask him. "Robert, was she nervous when she went?"

They had already been sweethearts when Emma went for her inspection. I remembered seeing him around during our early days at the compound. At first, it was obvious that he was trying to ignore my sister, but as time went on we saw more and more of him. This didn't upset me at first. I thought he was merely her friend, just as Henry used to be for me. In fact, I enjoyed his company, even when he was being irritable and aloof. These moods became less and less frequent as he continued to hang out with us. I even thought that maybe he was my friend, too.

One day that illusion was shattered when I caught them

in the laundry room. Robert's arms were wrapped about her, her hair out of place. They broke apart at the sound of my entrance, both of their faces flushed from the heat of the room and the closeness of each other. Emma tried to explain, but I didn't wait around to listen; I just ran. I caught the look on his face before I did, and it only held one emotion—guilt.

Robert gripped the edge of the table as he spoke. "No, she wasn't nervous. She was glad. Excited."

"What about you? You had to know she was being ridiculous, just lying to herself." I was whispering now, afraid of how he would react to my much too personal question.

He placed his face into his hands. "How can I explain what you'll never understand?"

"Try me," I countered. When he didn't reply I asked again. "Don't you think I deserve to know? Today of all days?"

"Telling you I loved Emma wouldn't be enough. It was more than that. I was obsessed with her. There wasn't anything I wouldn't do. Every second of every minute that we spent together, I knew it was wrong, insane, but I couldn't help it. I didn't care. I thought I deserved her, that she was my reward for…"

I was aching to know what he meant, but he quickly skipped over that part.

"I knew there were ways, things you could obtain from the underground that would prevent pregnancy. I knew she didn't have to fall into that trap. It was dangerous to get them, of course, but I didn't care."

I wondered if these were the things Julia had spoken of.

For some reason, I found myself blushing at the mention of this. I looked around me to make sure no one could hear our conversation.

"Then how? I mean if you were being safe."

The words hung in the air. My face was blazing with heat.

"These sorts of things aren't foolproof, Tess. I can't be sure if it was just some sort of freak accident, some vengeful joke of fate, or if it was her."

"What do you mean?" I asked. I was sweating.

"She wanted to try, saying it was her duty to her people. I told her she was being irrational, but I can never be sure that she didn't stop taking the pills."

I could feel my hands begin to shake. She had done this to *herself*? With no care for me, or Louisa, or even Robert?

"She was a damn fool," I spat, standing. I wanted to be anywhere but there.

Robert was up instantly. I was prepared to receive his wrath, but it never came. Instead, he took one of my hands and covered it with both of his. "I'm sorry if I upset you. But please don't be angry with her. She was the most selfless person I ever knew. Place your anger back on me; I can take it."

I ripped my hand from his. "You say selfless like it's a good thing."

And I walked away.

The waiting room was an icebox, and I was shaking from head to toe. I occasionally snuck a look at the receptionist, who didn't seem to be even remotely chilled. I hid my hands under my legs in an attempt to keep them warm. I noticed the slash mark on her neck as she turned to file something away.

The room was devoid of any other color besides metallic grays and blues. I was quite sure the lack of color was not helping.

I tried to think of James, but it didn't help. Thinking of him in this place, of all places, felt wrong. I didn't want to associate him with this experience.

The seats couldn't be any more uncomfortable either. Hard metal benches with no backs were packed into rows in the tiny waiting room. Of course, I was the only one waiting. Like I needed anything else to make me feel alone. I thought somewhere I smelled coffee, but naturally, none was offered to me.

The door swung open. I tensed up. "258915?"

I stood up at the sound of my number. Did they even care that I had a name? "Yes, sir."

"If you will come this way, please." I noticed how he drew out the word *please*. I wanted to laugh. Like I really had a choice.

The doctor led me into a much smaller room. On one side there wasn't a wall, simply glass. I peered through it but couldn't see a thing. I was sure that someone on the other side could see in, though.

The doctor threw what appeared to be a paper sheet into my hand. "You'll undress now."

I expected this, but suddenly the thought seemed horrifying. Was he going to stay in the room? What about the glass? Was someone watching? I couldn't *possibly*. My heart was racing, screaming. I wanted to run, bolt through the door. The doctor, a disgraced creator, rolled his eyes as he moved to leave. "Just knock when you are changed," he said, obviously bored. This was routine.

There was still the problem of the glass wall. How could I be expected to just undress knowing I was exposed? Didn't they care at all for my modesty, my dignity? There had to be a better way than this.

I turned my back to the window and with shaking hands began to take off my clothes. It was like removing a second skin. With each button I undid, I felt a part of my shell leave as well—the shell that took sixteen years to surround myself with. I felt tears spill down my face and didn't even try to stop them. I was mortified.

This wasn't right. Never before had I been more aware of the lack of choices in my life, how little the council trusted us. What if I didn't want to know? Just because my parents and their parents before them decided to give our government complete control didn't mean I had to. Shouldn't my government be what I wanted it to be?

As I stood there naked, I'd never felt more vulnerable. I'd never wanted to fight back more. I was no different than the girl upstairs at Templeton. The paper gown I put on wouldn't protect me.

I knocked on the door as quickly as humanly possible, jumping ungraciously back onto the bed. I curled my legs under me and wrapped my arms across my chest as tightly as I could manage. I needed to try to protect myself somehow.

The men who came to inspect me were not chosen ones, but instead creators who had fallen from favor. I wasn't even important enough to be examined by a chosen physician. I was an afterthought.

Dr. Kendall, as his nametag read, and two other men entered the room. I felt my throat closing up. How many of them would it take? How many really needed to be there? The paper dress crackled loudly.

While the other men were bent over clipboards, Dr. Kendall took a step toward me and smiled. It didn't seem threatening, but I knew how easy it was to lie. He reached over and gave me a small pat on the knee. "James was right. You are awfully pretty," he whispered to me. I cringed. I didn't ask for this compliment.

I didn't ask to be here.

And how could he know James?

I didn't have time to ask before the men started their examination.

First, they scanned the number lasered on my arm. I was officially in the system as an adult, as a woman, but I never felt more like a scared little child. They told me to lie back. Of course they explained to me what they would be doing, but all I heard was sound. I couldn't make sense of the words they were saying. I was letting myself shut down, crawling somewhere deep inside where no one could get me.

I wanted my mother. I wanted Emma. I even wanted my supervisor. I could faintly feel the doctors' hands everywhere, prodding with their cold instruments. They didn't talk anymore, just moved me when needed.

I wanted to scream. I wanted to hit. Every second their hands moved across my body, methodically, as if *I* were the experiment gone wrong, I felt something inside of me harden. I didn't shut down the feelings anymore. I held onto them. I heard my father's voice inside my head. And Henry's. I understood them now.

I had been inspected and it was worse than I could have ever imagined. Worst of all was the fact that these were *my people*. They were my flesh, my blood, my bone, my people. These were the ones responsible for it all, and I couldn't deny my connection to them. They were the creators, but *we* had created them.

They left me in the waiting room by myself until the transport came to take me back. Even the receptionist had mysteriously vanished. I was alone except for three cages filled with bunnies. Who knew where they came from? It was just me and them, me and the animals. They thought of us in the same way.

I didn't even question why the bunnies were there. I assumed it was for some experiment, some inspection. Some horrific moment of invasion.

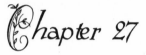

Chapter 27

I didn't want to see James. Today he was one of them, one of the chosen ones. I didn't think I would be able to separate his inner grace and truth from its outer shell.

All we are is the flesh we wear.

While I didn't particularly find joy at our meeting, I knew I would go.

I made no attempt to smooth out the wrinkles of my clothes before heading toward his room. The only part of my physical appearance I paid attention to was my hair. It was pulled tight against my head in a refined and constraining ponytail. The yellow ribbon tightly imprisoned it. Somehow this seemed appropriate.

James opened the door the minute I knocked. His face was pale, his hands curled into fists. I quickly walked past him and sat myself on his bed. I pulled my knees up to my chest and wrapped my arms around my legs, resting my chin and staring at the floor. I hadn't spoken since my inspection. I wondered if I could even speak at all.

James took a seat at his desk and picked up a book. He began to read silently, though every once in a while I could feel his eyes on me. I knew he was giving me my space, and I welcomed it. I reached out for the copy of Shakespeare, opening it to where we'd left off in *The Merchant of Venice*. I didn't think he would mind if I finished it without him. I didn't think he enjoyed it much. Neither had I, but now the story held a certain level of interest for me. I wanted to see how it all ended.

It was painful.

The way they treated Shylock disgusted me. He was painted to be the villain, when clearly he was a victim of the bitterness that results from intolerance. I felt my heart struggle for stability as I read his impassioned speech. The complexity of it seemed to sum up my whole world. He used language to demand that the others recognize he was human. He had a heart that feared and loved, and in the end, his words were used to damn him. Shylock's speech confirmed their fears—if he could look, talk, and move just like them, then how could they mark his difference, his inferiority? For my people, it was us, the women. Women were no longer able to create life. We were the chosen ones' strongest propaganda.

Maybe we should have allowed the world to end. It might have been God's will that we were destroyed by the bombs, weapons put into the hands of men who most likely had no idea why they were fighting anymore. Maybe we were *supposed* to die out. Living inside compounds, too afraid of the world around us, that wasn't a life. This thing I found myself slugging through day in and day out meant nothing.

I was just biding my time till it all ended.

"James," I whispered.

His eyes pounced on mine. I wondered if he had ever really

been reading at all, or if he was merely waiting for some sign from me that I wanted his company.

I gripped the edge of the wall in an attempt to stand up. James followed suit and we were soon inches apart from each other. I briefly saw his hand reach for me, but he just as quickly placed it back by his side. I stared intently at his daring hand. It would be easier to look there, look to my ally.

Feeling a sudden fiery burst of self-revelation, I pulled James to me and pressed my lips hungrily against his. I felt him pull away and vaguely heard him mumble something about this not being the right time and asking if I was all right. But I didn't care. I forced myself against him. I knew what he wanted. He couldn't fight me forever.

I licked his bottom lip and he groaned, falling against me. We stumbled back into the center of the room. I desperately clung to James, pushing myself against him as hard as I could. His hand traveled down my back and he gripped onto my hip. We stumbled some more, falling against the wall. He hiked my legs over his waist and began to kiss my neck.

I moaned.

All this life was about was death. We were meant to die.

So what if it happened now?

I felt him moving against my body, and I could barely contain the need that stemmed through me. I moved my hands to his shirt and began to unbutton it. His hand reached up and gently pushed my fingers away, but he continued to kiss me. His hand moved from my waist up to my chest. I had never been touched in such a way. I moved my hand from his chest down to his waist, and he pulled away abruptly. His sudden removal caused me to fall ungraciously against the wall.

We were both left panting.

"Why?" His question was simple, but I could hear the torrent of emotions under it.

"Because I'm dead already."

"That's not true."

"I won't be able to just sit by and deal with it all. It's not the life I want. So we can do this, you know, now," I replied.

He stiffened. "Don't say things like that."

"Like what? The truth? This place, this world, is nothing but death. My father, my mother, my sister, Julia—all of them dead. My people? Dead. Or they might as well be for all the living they do. I can't even want you without being reminded of death. I'm not supposed to survive this. Can't you understand that?"

"You're being ridiculous!"

"No, you just can't see it yet. But you will. You will when I tell you what I helped the council do."

"Tell me what? This whole reckless routine you have going on is starting to drive me a little mad, Tess. This"—he pointed between the two of us—"is hard enough without you throwing caution to the wind."

"Is that what I'm doing?"

"First, you don't tell me about your run-in with George… and now you act like this. I'm trying to keep you safe, and you're bent on destroying yourself!" he retorted. I could see the anger work its way through James. Perhaps he was angry with me for telling the truth—a truth he had to know deep down.

I needed to make him understand. Even if it meant the destruction of my last hope at some sort of meaningful relationship. "What could you do about George? Threaten him? Then what? You've already been marked as insufficient. What would they do to a traitor? Because according to George, according to the *council*, that's what you would be. They would find a way to do to you what they did to Frank."

He stilled. "What are you talking about?"

I took a shaky breath. "He was sick. He had the transformation illness, whatever the hell that is, and they killed him."

"How do you know that?"

"Because I helped them do it. They didn't bother trying to fix him. He wasn't worth their time. What's one when you can just create a whole lab full of replacements? Of course, in retrospect, they didn't see Julia's little plan of action, now did they?" I asked, near hysterics—a strange place between laughter and tears.

I watched as the anger slipped away from James. He sat down on the bed, staring at the floor. He wouldn't look at me again—I could see it in the way his shoulders hunched over and his head fell into his hands. This boy was heartbroken. "What do you mean you helped them?"

I figured I'd break my own heart as well.

I fell to my knees in front of him, but he still refused to look at me. "While I berated you for your part in Julia's death, I was just as guilty. I watched as they killed Frank. I kept it secret. Maybe because I didn't think his death meant as much. Or maybe some part of me wanted him to die. Who knows? It doesn't matter."

"Yes it does," James whispered. "You didn't tell me. I would tell you anything you wanted."

"I know. I don't have any valid excuses. And I'm not stupid enough to think this won't change things. But you should know the council *will* find a way to kill you, too. Someday they'll come for you. You're not going to survive this either. You're not like the other chosen ones. You won't make it."

He was silent.

"Go ahead," I said, standing up, "tell me you want me to leave."

"I want you to leave."

And I did.

Chapter 28

My eyes frantically searched for James as I followed the other girls out onto the lawn. There was to be some sort of mass meeting for all of the Templeton staff and chosen ones. When I found him, he didn't look worried. I sighed in relief. He hadn't talked to me in a few days, and I didn't blame him. I saw George slither his eyes between James and me, a silky smirk on his face the whole time.

He was planning something.

It was then I noticed Jacobson, his lip bloodied and swelling larger by the second.

No one else seemed to be paying Jacobson any attention. Were they blind? I pushed my way around my fellow workers and placed myself beside him. I could feel George's eyes follow me as I did so; I couldn't help but throw him a quick glare before turning my attention directly to Jacobson. I pulled a handkerchief out of my pocket and placed it in his hand. His eyes never left the floor but his cheeks flushed with embarrassment.

"Jacobson, are you all right? What happened?"

He didn't reply, but I couldn't miss that his eyes briefly landed on George. I felt my nails claw into my thighs. "George? George did this?"

"It was an accident. Don't worry your pretty little head about it," he mumbled, his attempt at sincerity failing miserably.

"What sort of accident?"

"Tess, please, just let it be."

"I certainly will not," I said, feeling the heat of rage bearing down upon me. Bitterness, a constant companion in my life, was urging me to join George's game. My eyes sought him out, and I realized something was happening. The Templeton boys were forming a semicircle as George stalked into the middle. He was grinning, holding his arms out for a bow. It was followed by a round of cheers from his fellow mates; their laughter caused me to shiver.

"What is this?" I spat out angrily.

"Training."

"What sort?"

"Well, they're going to fight, miss. One boy goes in the circle and asks if anyone challenges him. Then they both go into the circle, neither one allowed to leave until the other surrenders."

"How humane," I replied, rolling my eyes. "Let's go inside and get you cleaned up. We don't need to watch this," I said, moving to grab his hand.

Jacobson didn't budge. His eyes met mine and they were filled with an ancient sadness that sucked the breath from my chest. "We have to stay. They called us together to watch."

Of course; they wanted us to know that any second they could crush us. They wanted to remind us of our place, that they wouldn't shy away from hurting us, not even an old man. They wanted to make it quite clear that they could kill a sixteen-year-old girl for simply existing. I interlaced my fingers with Jacobson's—at least we wouldn't watch it alone.

My stomach churned. James had stepped into the circle. What was he thinking? Or was he thinking at all? Was I responsible for this? Was my new recklessness somehow contagious? I began to tap my foot nervously. Jacobson sensed this and patted my hand again. If only he knew the real reason for my anxiety. I feared for the one person who bothered to know me at all.

I suddenly found myself angry as I watched both George and James unbutton their cotton shirts and each hand theirs to a friend. How could James expect me to sit there and watch this, especially without betraying my emotions? It took all of my will to keep the muscles on my face contorted into a neutral appearance, though I was quite sure my eyes betrayed me.

George said something, a silly grin plastered onto his face, and James's fist curled in response. I couldn't be sure of what was said, but it was obvious it had something to do with me. I heard the hoots and boos of the crowd as several of them glanced my way, laughing. I wanted to choke that insipid sound right out of their throats.

The two chosen ones were circling each other now, the group of Templeton boys jostling around them and blocking my view. As much as it made me sick to think of seeing James getting hurt, especially by George, I knew I had to watch. I was meant to see. There are some things in life you can't just turn away from.

Maybe violence calls to our less civilized selves, but I like to think it was a nobler cause that led me to creep forward toward the circle, breaking Jacobson's hold on my hand. I like to think it was a need to protect, my need to protect someone I loved. I didn't know what that love meant—but I knew I loved.

What I could possibly do I wasn't sure; I just knew I wouldn't stand by. I think ever since the first time I'd touched his cheek, neither of us would be able to simply stand by anymore.

I heard the hollow thud of a punch make contact before I actually saw it. George scrunched over briefly, then sprung back up, holding his chin. He craned his neck to the left, then the right, and raised his fist. A smile still graced his face. Their feet were moving much too fast for me to follow, each boy ducking up and down, side to side. It was a much too complicated dance, one I would never be able to learn. This was what they were made for.

Never had it been clearer that James was not the same as me. How did I keep forgetting this?

Suddenly, James was on his back on the floor, George's foot towering down onto him in response. It missed shattering James's leg by seconds. I could feel my throat closing; I knew I wasn't breathing. James jumped up into a crouching position before running straight for George's knees, knocking both chosen ones onto the ground. He was on top of George now, his fist raised back, waiting to be released. I closed my eyes. No, this I couldn't watch. I didn't want this image—the image of James ruthlessly pounding into George's face—in my memory. I didn't want any more reason to fear James. I needed him to be the one thing in my life I didn't fear.

The crowd was vibrating with excitement. They were like rabid dogs waiting to sink their teeth into something, waiting to spread their infection. I heard a chosen one yell out George's name, and the voice was filled with thrill, excitement, and confidence. I demanded my eyes open and I saw George and James both on their feet, George's hands wrapped around James's neck. Each boy's face was now blood-red, sweat covering their brows.

Wasn't someone going to stop this? It was too much; it had gone too far. I looked back at Jacobson. His eyes were on the ground, his hand gingerly touching his lip. Some of the girls watched with dread, but none dared speak up. Much to my horror, a few of them looked like they were enjoying it. Why? Because they were fascinated by the way the boys' bodies moved, or because they were happy to watch our oppressors tear each other to shreds? Of course they didn't know James was mine and I was his.

George leaned close to James and whispered something into his ear. I shuddered as I saw James's face contort in rage as he clutched onto George's wrists and pushed him off. It was then I realized that I was walking closer, my body leading me right to the center of the circle.

"Stop!" I screamed.

James's head snapped in my direction at that moment. That was all it took—one simple distraction. George grabbed onto James's arm and twisted it, and my ears were filled with a sickening snap. James fell to the floor in pain; I could hear him moaning. George backed away, his hands held up in surrender. "I give in," he yelled to the crowd.

It was my fault. I had distracted him, had set him up. It was all happening too quickly now. My ears were buzzing. There was too much sound in them to make any sense. I heard the shouts and seditious laughter of George's friends. I heard James cursing and moaning in pain. I heard the girls behind me talking frantically, throwing around accusations.

Before I could move to help James, he pulled himself to his feet with a grunt. Something passed before his eyes that I had only seen once before—on the videos of the first chosen one killing the prisoners of war. Any sense of humanity that existed in him had slipped away. James pulled his good arm back and let it fly. Even the other chosen ones gasped at the strength and determination he exhibited. He kept hitting and hitting and hitting. George crumpled to the floor, and still James didn't stop.

"James! Stop!" I begged. Some of his fellow chosen ones joined in on my pleas, but he didn't hear us. The James I knew had been replaced with the war machine the council had intended him to be.

And the blood was everywhere. It splattered onto me. It covered James's face. All I could see was how much the substance had tainted my life. Would violence always find me? Of course it would.

If the boy I *loved* more than anyone else could become a monster, what hope did I have?

Chapter 29

I knew the reasons he was created. Violence. Destruction.

Maybe in that room, the moment I'd confessed the lie, told him that even in the council's eyes, the people who had given him life, he was worthless, something in him died.

His humanity.

I talked to no one during my chores after the council dismissed us from the fight. I dusted and mopped as if my life depended on it. It was better to be busy than to think of what I'd just witnessed.

I saw James standing at the end of the hallway.

He didn't move. His gaze was intruding, forceful as he took a step toward me. I took a step back in return. I was done fighting. I simply turned around and walked the other way. I didn't wait to be dismissed.

"Tess."

He was following me. I could feel the weight of his authority swallowing me, he was so close. He almost touched my heels with his toes.

"Tess."

I kept walking. His hands grabbed onto my waist and he pulled me from behind into the shadows of an adjoining hallway. I reached out and touched my hands to the wall, pressing my forehead against its cold stone. He didn't let go of my waist. I felt his breath caress my ear.

"Let me explain." His tone conveyed he would whether I wanted him to or not.

"I don't care."

It wasn't true. I cared too damn much. It was exactly what made James and me so dangerous.

"Don't do that. Don't you shut down on me. You can fool everyone else, but not me," he pleaded.

"I can't do this anymore."

He turned me around so I was facing him. His hands were in my hair.

"Can't you see what they make me do? They want me to destroy you. They want to destroy any sense of self I have. Don't let them, Tess. I need you. You need me. I lost control. It won't ever happen again."

I shook my head. "You can't promise that. This is what you were made for. Violence is your true nature. It's better if we stop fooling ourselves that we can be anything but what the council wants us to be."

"You have no idea what it is like. All day they fill my head with such stories, stories about your people. Stories about waste, immorality, hate. They want me to hate you. I fight so hard against my nature. But I'm no monster. I don't want to be soulless."

He leaned his forehead against mine. "I had another dream, Tess. They're going to come for you. They've assigned me to a compound. I'll be leaving soon. And I don't know if this dream is real or just some nightmare. If it's real we have to come up with a plan. There's something you should know—"

"Let me."

"What?"

"I'm supposed to die," I whispered.

He punched the wall beside my head. I tried not to scream. He forced me to look at him. "I am alone and miserable; man will not associate with me; but one as deformed and horrible as myself would not deny herself to me. My companion must be of the same species and have the same defects. This being you must create."

The words Julia had spoken. What did they mean?

His hands fell away from me. He looked dejected.

"We aren't helping each other. Not really," I said. "Maybe it's better to live in a world you don't understand, because if you understand it, it becomes unbearable. And we keep forcing each other to see the truth." I started to move away from him.

And he let me go.

I was on display in the cafeteria that Sunday during my return to the compound. Everyone was talking about how I'd tried to stop the fight between James and George. What was a Templeton girl doing getting between two chosen ones? Wasn't my job to merely follow orders? Rumors were flying about my relationships with both boys. I was the fallen girl. It didn't matter if the story was true.

I could hear the whispers swim around me, never directly touching me, but never completely leaving my presence either.

They were all talking about it. They all knew. I pushed my plate of food away. It was a pretense; my attempt to pretend that life could go on as normal would no longer work. James had lost control, and as much as I searched for an explanation I could only come up with one—he was made to be violent.

I decided to quit trying to pretend my world wasn't falling apart and attempt to get some sleep. The thought of not seeing James made my heart skip a beat in a most painful and final way.

I stared numbly at the floor as I walked across the mess hall. I almost reached the door when I heard my name called. I knew the voice, of course, just as I knew I wouldn't be able to escape the confrontation. Henry never could just leave things well enough alone. With a heavy sigh, I turned to acknowledge him but found myself unable to look into his face, scared of what I would find there. I flinched as his hand suddenly found its way to my chin, so I would be forced to look at him.

His fingers felt rough against my face, though not in a completely unwelcomed way. I knew it wasn't because it was Henry touching me, but more because I was being touched. Not out of anger but out of something less severe.

Concern, perhaps?

I bit my lip to stop it from trembling. I wanted to fall into his arms, let him keep me safe. Now that my protector had abandoned me I realized how nice it was to have one. I had been on my own so long, I never knew what it could be like to have someone out there in the world who thought of you and your well-being before his own.

"Aren't you going to say something?" I managed to mumble, more to control my bizarre desire to wrap my arms around him than to hear what he had to say.

"What would you like me to say, Tess?" His voice was soft as he spoke, but I could sense something smoldering underneath it. Henry sighed. "We need to talk about some of your actions."

I laughed bitterly. "*My* actions? You're the last person I would take advice from concerning decision making."

He clenched his jaw. "Oh, of course. Obviously you're an expert at making decisions regarding your welfare. Let's see: in the few weeks you have been a part of the workforce, you managed to fall for every one of their tricks. Let's not forget what everyone is calling you."

"Don't you dare," I growled.

"Just listen. Please. What happened with Julia—"

"What happened with Julia proves you're a coward! You helped her and then you let her die," I charged.

"She was dead already. We both know that," he snapped. He took a step even closer to me. Some of the other naturals started to pay attention to our heated conversation.

Henry looked around and then leaned close to my ear. "I am alone and miserable; man will not associate with me; but one as deformed and horrible as myself would not deny herself to me. My companion must be of the same species and have the same defects. This being you must create," he whispered.

First Julia. Then James. And now Henry? My eyes widened. "What does that mean?" I asked.

Henry gave the slightest shake of his head. "Just be ready, Tess. Change is coming."

Chapter 30

Deportation.

It had been quite a while since the compound had gone through a selection. Deportation meant certain members of the community would be transported from this compound to another, for various reasons. Most of the time it was the elderly or the very ill who found themselves on the list. They were sent to compounds better suited for their needs.

Our own medical center was shabby at best, so we were assured our deportees were placed in more comfortable situations. In fact, many often expressed joy at being chosen, rejoicing as if they had won the lottery—dreams of pampered living glowing around them. Others did not. These were the people who made deportation difficult at times. If your name was on the list, it was mandatory. And you—only you—were allowed to go; you couldn't take any other family members. As these people were chosen for the best living conditions, spaces were limited as it was. Still, some of the good-byes were horrendous to watch.

Slowly, everyone in the compound made his and her way into the mess area. It wasn't like the wrangling. People weren't so tense, more like curious. It had been at least a year since the last deportation. I assumed that like me everyone was wondering why now and whom they were going to take. It was a relief to think about someone else's problems for a change. I didn't focus too long on the selfishness of that thought.

I grabbed Louisa as soon as I saw her in the crowd, ignoring her protests that she wanted to stand with her friends. I wasn't letting her out of my sight.

The two chosen ones in charge of our compound arrived.

"Deportation Decree 765893 has been put into effect. Deportation is for the safety and health of all natural citizens. Deportation is mandatory for those citizens whose numbers are called. The selected will have twenty-four hours to get their affairs in order. Only those people may leave this compound. Each selectee will be able to bring with them one bag each."

I couldn't help but smirk as I spied an older man across from me mumbling the words along with the chosen one. We all knew what deportation meant, and I suspected that like myself, the old man hated the formality of it all. The chosen one proceeded to pull out a roll of parchment paper. It was crisp, its glaring whiteness cutting across the room of gray.

"The following inhabitants of compound 321 are scheduled for deportation two days from now: 23647, 36897, 336093, 25670…"

Soon the voice of the chosen one flowed into melodic notes, slithering around my ears. The numbers began to merge one into the other. They were just numbers anyway. In moments like these, it was possible for me to ignore the individual. And for once, much to my shame, it brought me comfort to see someone besides myself suffer. Selfish, heartless girl.

One by one, sporadically placed within the confined space, I saw them react. First, a look of recognition crossed their faces at hearing their number being called. Some, as I suspected, looked relieved—finally, they would have the medical treatments that would ease their suffering. Usually these positive responses stemmed from those people who were alone, no loved ones left to leave. For others, watching the families react when they heard a loved one's number called was difficult. I wanted to engross myself in their pain in order to explain mine. Pain touched everyone. I didn't want to be special.

I saw a woman begin to sob quietly into an old man's shoulder. Could she be his daughter? I saw him whisper in her ear. Words of comfort? I couldn't read his facial expression.

Then I noticed something new. A man was yelling. People were jostling about. I saw Robert dart from my side to help hold a man in place. Was he intending on charging the chosen one? Didn't he understand this was how it worked? Next to him, a woman was clutching onto two children, a boy and a girl, not much older than ten. The little girl had her arms wrapped around her mother's waist, her head buried into her side. She was crying as well. The boy was reaching toward his father; his mother struggled to keep him in her grasp.

I tried to force my mind to separate from the noise in my ears—I needed to understand what was going on. A new outcry distracted me. Another man was now yelling from the opposite side of the room. He moved so he was standing in front of his wife. I could vaguely see her hands shakily reach around his hand in what looked like an attempt to calm him.

The whole common room was talking at once. The chosen one stood still, firmly placed, never budging and never flinching. I realized—this wasn't like before. In the past deportation had been for the elderly and ill, and now they were taking women and children. The definition of deportation had somehow changed without anyone telling us.

More numbers were being read off. The chosen one kept his voice calm, never once pausing to allow the outcries of my people their proper space. I could barely hear the numbers. I didn't want to hear them. I had wished to witness other people's pain but this was simply too much. I'd never meant like this. It was different to take people who truly wanted to leave, but these wives and these children didn't want deportation. Was there nothing left of our own in our lives?

My eyes met Louisa's. How odd they looked. She was petrified. I noticed Jacobson's gaze on me as well. Something cold was sliding up my spine. It crawled inside my veins, wrapping around my heart. Fear. It was in this moment that I saw Henry's face. His eyes were squinting, a vein in his forehead protruding, his jaw fixed rigidly. Why were they looking at me in such a way? I tried to move, to turn from their sickening glances, but my body was trembling. It knew something that my soul didn't yet understand.

Slowly it clawed its way into the dark corners of my soul, the places that still survived—they had called my number. The truth weaved its way in and out of the strands of hope that held my tattered soul together; the one damaged by the loss of my father, the loss of Emma, the loss of Julia, the betrayal of James. James. His dream. He had told me I was on a list, that they would come for me. Deportation didn't mean a better life. It meant no life at all.

I had been wrong. The chosen ones had come up with a way to get rid of my people after all. They wouldn't wait for our slow and sure extinction. The chosen ones had learned from the past, and they would use its secrets to destroy us. We had blindly ignored our history, comforting ourselves with the belief that the horrors of the times before ours could never be repeated. We stupidly believed mankind had evolved.

No, *science* had evolved, and our own lack of perspective would be our downfall. Every number they called, every person that number belonged to, would surely and quickly die. Their deaths would not be mourned. There would be no public outcries, no promises of revenge; the chosen ones had learned how to take those away from us as well. To deport women and children now was to flaunt their growing power. They were no longer afraid to show us they were in control. And there was nothing we could do about it.

The noise was monstrous, growing in strength every second. I felt like I would go crazy from it all. Should I warn those whose numbers were called? Would they even believe me? Would telling them they went to their deaths, forever separated from those they loved not by distance but by blinding finality, keep it from happening? We couldn't stop them. We had let it go too far to turn back.

I wasn't sure I could live with the guilt if I *didn't* tell them. Surely, those husbands who stood by their wives, the sons who were to say good-bye to their fathers, would not just sit idly by. Surely, *some* of my people would want to fight back. It would mean their demise—of that I was certain. Would their deaths then be on my head, too? I wasn't brave enough to make this decision. It wasn't fair. I was only sixteen.

It was stifling inside the mess hall, my skin blotchy and red from the heat. I tasted something unfamiliar in my mouth. Blood. I had been biting down hard on my tongue. I could feel every inch of my body slowly tensing up, attempting to protect itself. I had to get out of there. I knew I had time to think. They wouldn't take us for two days. And I wouldn't be able to think clearly in here.

James.

I wondered if he had seen this. If he knew this was the way it was going to end for me. Did he care? The noise in my head was maddening.

I forced my legs to move, stumbling blindly toward the exit, but then I felt someone grab my hand—it was Louisa. She was crying. This unnerved me. I was already so fragile, and this wasn't the Louisa I knew. I shuddered. She would be truly alone now. Like me, Emma had been her only confidante. Like me, she had lost her when Robert had entered our lives. How pathetic I was to not realize that we would have understood each other perfectly. Would Robert continue to look after her? Maybe Henry? I needed to make sure of it.

"What are we going to do?" she asked, her voice shaky. It was in this moment I knew she was still a child. She had been abandoned by the world that was meant to protect her.

I didn't know if I was strong enough to do what needed to be done. But for once, I would not be selfish. I would place her needs above my own. How I craved to wrap her in my arms, to share one moment of sisterly affection to carry me to whatever fate had in store. This would comfort me but destroy her. It would be easier for her to deal with my absence if she hated me. Yes, that was something I had learned in my sixteen years of life—hatred was its own shield. If I could only make her loathe me, I would save her the pain of loss.

"Stop being a baby. They're simply moving me to a nicer compound," I replied in a dismissive tone.

I saw her eyes well with tears. She was biting her bottom lip. She looked down at our hands before finally saying, "But I don't want you to leave. What will I do with no one here? I know I haven't been the best sister but I promise I will try harder. Please, can't you ask them to let you stay? I swear I will be better."

She was begging now. It was unbearable.

"Just because you're jealous doesn't mean you have to put on such a self-satisfying show. You'll be just fine without me, I promise you."

"Please," she begged once more, her voice cracking.

God was surely testing me. "Stop being pathetic, Louisa. What would my absence mean anyway? Do you think my staying would change our relationship? It wouldn't. We would still be the way we are now. Emma was the only thing that kept us together, and she's gone now. Nothing can change that. Just like nothing can change the way I feel about you." As I said this I tried to muster all the venom I possibly could.

I was wounding her, causing her pain. For once, I was aware of her as a child, as a younger sister, as someone I was meant to keep safe but had only harmed. I'd never loved her as I should have. This would be my act of love, and she would never see it as that.

Louisa stiffened and bit the inside of her lip. It was here, in this very moment, that I watched her grief turn into something else, something I had at once dreaded to see and was thankful for—anger. Her hand suddenly flew at my face. I barely had time to protect my already injured cheek. Her hand bounced off of mine, the hand that was meant to hold hers. It had worked. She was running from me now. I could hear a wild sob break free from somewhere deep inside her.

I was alone now.

They were going to take me away from Louisa. She would go to Templeton in my place. They would get to her. I couldn't let that happen. But, God, if it did, I had to make her stronger.

It was unbearable. My chest felt as if a much too heavy weight was chained to it, and there was no hope of finding the key to unlock it. I was damned. Had I damned everyone else around me as well?

Chapter 31

I was going to run. I needed to find help. There had to be someone out there who could help us. I would gamble with the Isolationists in the Middlelands. Or at least I could scout, find some way to get Louisa and me away from this place. Forever.

I had nothing to take with me, and I had no time for good-byes.

Maybe I would die, but at least it would be of my own choosing. On my own terms. I might only have a day or two of freedom, but that would be more than most got.

There were no guards at the doors of the compound. Why would anyone leave? The council had done a fantastic job of creating a prison of fear. As I stepped out into the woods that surrounded our sector, separating it from what was left of the world, I refused to think of the good-byes I didn't make.

The deeper I got into the woods, the more I was aware of the fact that I was alone. Every noise made me shiver, reminding me I had no chosen one to fight my battles for me anymore. It was so damn dark. I sprinted. Every time I tripped, I pulled myself up. Every time a branch slashed across my skin, I kept pushing. I didn't know where I was going. I just knew to run.

I fell to the ground, my weak natural body not used to such physical exertion. I didn't care that I was covered in dirt and leaves. It was then I heard the footsteps. The hair on the back of my neck shot up, tingling all the way down my spine. Something told me this was wrong. It wasn't James. No, of course not—there were two sets of footsteps. It was someone else. Someone must have followed me. I began to tremble.

When I slowly turned around, two men I had never seen in my life stood before me. Chosen ones. I couldn't miss them. Beautiful, just like they all were, their blue and green eyes shining through the darkness of the night. One held a black bag in his hands.

No! It was all happening too soon. I wasn't ready.

The men took a step forward. Why couldn't I move from the ground? Why wasn't my body fighting back? My heart was screaming. I was shaking so much my teeth were slamming against one another.

Maybe something inside of me wanted this to happen. Maybe I wasn't strong enough for this place, this prison.

"We can do this the easy way or the hard way. I'm sort of hoping you want me to do it the hard way," one of the men sneered.

I still couldn't move. The other chosen one squatted in front of me, roughly grabbing onto my arm. His breath was next to my ear. "I do so like when we get to take the girls. The council usually lets us play with them a bit first. Funny how they knew you would run for it."

He proceeded to yank me from the ground, positioning me so my back was against his chest and I faced his partner. He was grinning. These men were not from Templeton; they were beyond training. These were chosen ones, already selected, already working. Had the council sent them for me? Why?

He held the bag open in front of my face.

"I hope you aren't afraid of the dark."

We were in some sort of vehicle. My captors had roughly pushed me into the back, and the vehicle was speeding, thrashing about here and there. I often slammed against the ceiling or bumped against the car door. I would be bruised by morning. If I even saw morning.

I hadn't cried. What good would it do? Instead, I'd tried to lie as still as possible. To disappear. To not exist at all. Existence was painful.

I didn't even listen to what my captors were discussing. I refused to think about Louisa or James, to think about the world I was leaving. I just focused on breathing, for as long as they would allow me to do so. Suddenly the car came to a halt. I flew into the seat in front of me and felt my head begin to throb. We had stopped. I didn't care why.

Only now was I beginning to realize how many mistakes I had made. I didn't know it was possible to make so many in such a short amount of time. Only sixteen years. Sixteen years I had wasted.

Someone yanked me out of my introspective haze, pulling me through the now-open door of the vehicle. My futile attempt to bury my pain had been in vain; it had always been in vain. I failed because I was never brave enough to face the darkness of my life. I always found ways of avoiding it—I either shut myself off from those who loved me or completely engrossed myself in one that I should not have cared for. I never fully allowed myself to acknowledge the pain I carried—the pain of the oppressed, the pain of the cast-off, the pain of knowing I deserved better.

I was on the ground, thrown forcefully by my guards. They didn't care if they hurt me. I was nothing to them, something easily disposed of and soon forgotten. Would James wonder what had happened to me? Damn. Why couldn't I force him from my mind?

The sounds that followed were not what I expected. The two men were arguing; one sounded scared, nervous. I couldn't make out the exact words as the pounding of my heart beat wildly against my ears.

Somehow amid their yelling I heard another vehicle approach, and it briefly made me wonder what had caused these men to be so scared. The only ones allowed to own vehicles these days were the chosen ones. Even the transports were driven by chosen ones.

I heard the crunch of dirt and rocks beneath shoes, then another exchange. Yet still I couldn't make out the words. My mind wouldn't focus on deciphering them. Perhaps this was its defense mechanism, its way of protecting itself from the truth. Another tool to avoid the darkness.

Something painful sliced through the air. My ears were ringing, burning. Again. Dear God, what was going on? Then silence. There was no sound now. This was worse than I could have imagined. Had I died? Was this what awaited those who died…nothing but the smell of the bag and a sharp ringing in the ears?

No. Someone was pulling me up, leaning me against the car. I didn't fight him. It meant I was still alive, for which I was thankful. I was surprised at how thankful I was.

The hands were gentle this time, like they were afraid I would break. Didn't they know I was already broken beyond repair? I felt someone begin to unbind my hands, sliding slowly up my arms once my hands were free. I shivered. Strangely, not out of repulsion. The hands were near my head now. I could feel the air dance around my face—the bag had been removed from my head. I kept my eyes shut. I was afraid to open them.

It was then I heard his voice.

"Tess," he whispered.

My eyes shot open.

James.

Chapter 32

The pain was bursting now. I could feel angry tears threaten
to spill from my eyes. My legs felt weak. I couldn't stand, so I
crumbled slowly to the floor, sliding against the cold walls of
the car. I clawed my fingers into the dirt; I needed something
to stabilize me.

James knelt before me. Why was he here? Was he choosing
to run, too?

Or was he simply doing his job?

"Tess, I can't explain right now. I know you have questions,
but we need to move." His voice was tense. I closed my eyes
again, hoping to banish the image of James in this place.

"We can't leave yet. You know there is something we
have to do first." This was a voice I couldn't label, but one that
wasn't utterly new to me, either.

James cleared his throat. The familiar, too human sound
caused my eyes to flutter open. His hands were shaking; he
looked almost ill. My eyes traveled to his partner. I stared in
disbelief at one of the "doctors" from my inspection.

"Don't be alarmed. This is my creator, Kendall."

Kendall held out his hand. He seemed thrilled, eager. "Pleasure to meet you, Tess. Well, I guess we have already met, sorta," he said with a small laugh.

"No," I managed to say. It was all I could say. *No.*

"We really do mean to help you. I know it seems a bit far-fetched, all things considered, but I'm a natural just like you. I wouldn't, couldn't possibly hurt one of my own kind. Now before we go, we have to do something first. It might sting a little," Kendall said as he crouched down beside me. He moved to my skirt and proceeded to slide it up my leg.

It all happened so fast. My hand sprung from the dirt, clutched the fingers together, and flew at his face. I felt no pain, though I was sure it would come later. But my heart sang with approval. Kendall whimpered five feet away from me. I shot James an icy look. Would I be brave enough to hit him, too?

Yes. I would.

He held his hands out in front of him, echoing a moment earlier in our relationship. Only this time I wasn't afraid of him—he was afraid of me. I was glad.

"Tess, they placed a tracking device in you. They did it to all the naturals."

"No. Impossible. I would remember something like that," I said, shaking my head. Was there any memory I could trust? Anything not touched by the council?

"You were a child, girl. Your momma probably told you it was just a shot," Kendall grunted, holding his bloody nose.

Yes. My mom. I remembered she was half drunk when we stumbled to the tents that served as our medical station at the time. Everything was still chaotic in those days. The first chosen ones had been created, but the council was still working on building the compounds for each sector. I'd tried to grab her hand as the doctor stuck the needle into my thigh, but she pulled it away.

"If we don't get the tracker out, they will be able to find you. I can't take them all on my own. And we need time to plan. If we don't do this now then there is no hope," James continued. His voice conveyed every ounce of despair he could portray. I wanted to believe him. I wanted to believe he wasn't the monster who beat George to an inch of his life. My mind frantically searched for a counterargument but could find none.

We stared at each other, only the sound of our breathing breaking the silence. It came out ragged but strangely in tune with each other, as if that was always how it was meant to be. I gritted my teeth. I was dead anyway.

"Fine," I spat, "tell me how to do it."

"Tess, I don't think you should," James pleaded.

I shook my head furiously. This was something I had to do myself.

Kendall was before us, holding a hand over his nose. I guess I packed a good punch. He proceeded to give something to James, silver flashing against the darkness of the sky.

James's eyes met mine once more, and his hand slowly reached for the hem of my skirt. He cautiously lifted it up, pausing above my knee. He cleared his throat, and I felt my cheeks burn hot. "The tracking device is in the thigh. I'll have to lift this a bit higher."

I nodded weakly, felt my mouth go dry. I nodded to Kendall. "Tell him to turn around. I think he's seen enough of me."

"Don't be foolish. I need him to guide you." James's voice

carried a new edge, a rawness I was unaccustomed to.

"Then he can guide me with his back turned. If he's such a humanitarian, I am sure this isn't the first one he's removed. He should be able to do it easily."

Kendall didn't wait for James to tell him to turn around. Wimp.

"That's enough! We have to get moving."

The sound of a new voice made all of us freeze. Henry was standing behind Kendall, and Robert followed closely on his heels.

I began to laugh. It was all so surreal. James. Henry. Robert. Doctor from hell. Talking about breaking me free, about removing tracking devices. It was all some nightmare, a dream I would soon wake from. It was freaking hilarious. The four men stared at me in shock. This made me laugh even harder.

Henry roughly and without hesitation lifted my skirt so my thigh was revealed. He paused for a second. For that one brief second his face showed weakness. I wasn't laughing anymore.

"Wait. I can do this myself," I growled, snatching the knife from James.

I clamped a hand over my bare skin, holding my thigh against the dirt. I bit my lip as I held on tightly to the knife, took a deep breath, and ripped open my skin. Then all I could feel was pain. I was ripping myself apart. It was as if someone had shot liquid ice through my veins, freezing my very soul. My breath stuck in my throat and sat there burning. It took everything in me not to scream.

"It's lodged in there pretty well," replied James, his voice monotonous.

The ice was ablaze now. I probed the opening the knife had created, every movement shooting scalding heat down my legs. The heat seeped through my vertebrae, making my head feel dizzy. I wasn't sure how much more I could take; it was unbearable. Would it never end? A muffled scream escaped my lips. I tried to clamp my mouth shut. Still, noise escaped it.

Then the physical pain eased, but it was replaced with something else. Something worse. The emptiness that haunted my very being had never been more present. I would never return to the compound. That identity, however flawed it had been, was forever gone for me. Would I miss it? Perhaps. It was the one thing that had always been constant. In that world, I always knew my place, always knew what role was assigned to me. I was in a new world now. I could no longer run from coming to terms with who I really was, not the person I'd murdered and buried long ago. I was scared as hell.

I vaguely felt James put pressure on the wound, attempting to stop the blood that oozed down my leg, ounces of my prescribed persona mixing with the dirt. Abandoned. Ripped from me.

I was so tired. So very tired. James quickly moved in front of me, but I couldn't keep my eyes open even to look at his face. I felt his arms wrap around me and lift me from the ground. I didn't fight the darkness, not anymore. My life would never be the same and the uncertainty of what I now faced left me petrified.

Maybe if I were lucky, I would sleep forever.

The room was dark. How long had I been out? Hours? Days? My eyes were crusted over and I felt the sleep dust off into my cramped fingers as I attempted to free my eyes. I slowly sat up, my head feeling light as I stretched my arms in front of me, my elbows popping loudly in the much too quiet room. Tomb-like. Was it night? Next to me on a nightstand was a glass of water. I reached for it, consuming it faster than I'd thought possible.

I took note of my surroundings. I was in a bed, a rather large bed. The room was much too vast, filled with furniture from a time not so long ago. Everything was covered in dust, signaling the house hadn't been used for some time. The room made me feel small, weak. Too much space. I tried to listen for noise but was only greeted with an eerie silence. I didn't like the quiet so much anymore.

I knew I could open the door, explore, find answers, but I wasn't ready. I lay back down on the bed and proceeded to curl myself into a ball. The bedspread smelled of mold and neglect.

I still felt a hole inside of me. I held my wrist up into the sliver of light that peeped into the room. My numbers were still etched there. Good. I rubbed them gently, caressing them, possessing them. They were mine.

I wasn't ready for answers. I closed my eyes and let myself once again drift to sleep.

When I awoke my stomach was writhing with hunger. Next to my water now stood a jar of peanut butter. I undid the top and stuck my finger into the gooey contents. I hadn't tasted peanut butter since before the compounds were inhabited. It was sweet and thick, and I instantly wished I had something else to drink.

Where the hell was I? I needed answers.

Robert. Things were too complicated with James and Henry, and I didn't have time to sort through it at the moment. Robert was my best chance for getting the information I needed. There was a time I had trusted him. Could I trust him again?

If Robert had ever thought about running, why didn't he run with Emma?

Did he do it for me?

Why?

How did he know I was going to be taken?

And James. He could never go back to his life.

Guilt. Damn, what a powerful emotion. But at least I felt something besides empty.

I was in a tattered nightgown—plaid, glaringly not part of the council-approved wardrobe. Someone had changed me. I shivered. The thought of a stranger's hands on me made me want to stop my journey before it began. Who ever decided to place such fragile souls in such utterly destructible bodies?

I spotted a robe lying across a chair and slipped it over me. I clutched it tightly as I pushed open the door. If the room looked neglected, the house was completely abandoned. Pictures hung crookedly off the walls. The paint was peeling. I even thought I saw something scurry off into the corner when I opened the door.

Was this a house from before? A relic from the time when we knew what it meant to be free? It looked abandoned, forgotten. Yet it was still standing.

I was still standing.

Chapter 33

I hadn't gotten more than a few steps down the hallway when a noise rushed into my ears. I turned to see James sitting in a broken wood chair not five feet from the room where I had slept. His clothes were rumpled, his hair tossed about, his eyes heavy. I never imagined he could look this way.

"Robert?" It was all I could bring myself to say.

He quietly told me Robert was in the barn. Those were all the words we could share with each other.

The brightness of the sun stunned my eyes into submission; I held my hand in front of me to ensure I wasn't going to run into anything. The ground was hilly, making my already weak legs impossible to coordinate. Finally, my eyes began to adjust and I noticed the abandoned barn. How long had it been since I had seen one of these? Had I ever actually seen a barn? Or was it something that I'd only glimpsed in the days of television and movies?

The doors moaned loudly as Robert pushed them open. Even inside the barn, I could feel how cold it had gotten. We must have been somewhere north. I suddenly felt embarrassed, like a child who got caught sneaking out. Except what I had done, what I had caused, was so much worse. And the results had affected not only me.

"I'm sure you need some answers," he said, concern on his face.

"I don't know what to ask," I finally managed, my voice cracking. And it was true. Where would I possibly begin?

"Do you love him?" Robert asked.

His question took the breath right out of me. I felt my cheeks burn and my eyes once again found the floor. "I…I don't know what I feel," I stammered. "How bad is it?"

"It isn't good. It's complicated."

"How complicated?"

"We're not sure if we're still being tracked. I took care of the snatchers but by now the compound will know you're missing, and so the chosen ones will know you're missing. A girl gone right before deportation doesn't look so innocent. It looks planned. Not only that, it looks planned by someone on the inside."

Too many questions were screaming to be answered inside my mind. But I could only focus on one, because it was about him, about James. Later I would ponder how Robert rid us of the snatchers. Later I would wonder how many girls went missing without anyone truly questioning our leaders. But first I needed to know about him.

"You mean they could suspect that James helped?"

"We're not sure. Of course, he will be the first one questioned.

Your relationship, from what I understand, wasn't exactly secret."

No, it wasn't, though no one really knew the truth behind it. The world thought I was merely a plaything to James. They didn't know about dancing or reading *Jane Eyre*.

"But he seems to have figured out a decent cover story," Robert said, breaking my train of thought.

I nodded for him to continue.

"James is supposed to be traveling to the compound he was assigned to in sector seven. They won't expect him there for another few days. So Kendall and I got a few members of the council to vouch for him, saying they called him in for questioning regarding your disappearance. He will help us get you out, then return."

"Wait. What? Hold on. Members of the council are on our side? And James—he isn't running with us?" I asked as the panic began to take complete control.

"We have several members placed in the upper ranks of the council."

"Members? *We*?"

Robert nodded, taking a seat in an old wooden chair. "The resistance. Did you think that everyone was just sitting back, content with what the chosen ones were doing? There has been a system in place for quite some time."

"Like a resistance movement?" I asked.

"Yes."

"And you're a part of it?"

"Yes."

"And the doctor, the one who saw me at my inspection, is he a part of it?"

Robert hesitated before answering. "Yes. Kendall is a part of it. I think he may have been one of the first members."

His hesitation unnerved me—there was something he was holding back, but a more urgent question forced itself out. "How long have *you* been a part of the movement?"

Robert's eyes narrowed as if he were seeing something I couldn't. "For a long time. Long before I came to your compound."

"Did Emma know?"

"Yes."

I inhaled deeply. How much had been kept from me and for how long? "And Henry is a part of it as well?"

"And Henry."

"And Julia?" I asked, afraid of the answer.

"And Julia," he repeated, a sad note lingering in his voice. "But don't think that everyone in the resistance approved of her actions. She had help getting into Templeton from a rather extreme sect. Most of us would never condone her need to kill those younglings. I thought at first she did it on her own, but when she spoke the words…" He stopped.

"You mean the quote from *Frankenstein*?"

Robert nodded. "Yes, it's a sign. Lets us know who's part of the movement."

James's creator must have been the one to give him the book, to point him in the self-reflective direction he sought. Maybe Kendall wasn't bad at all. Maybe he was a revolutionary. Maybe he even created James merely for helping him with his own war.

"We have pockets all over the sectors. Gathering Intel about the council and chosen ones." Robert must have guessed my next question because he shortly followed with more. "There are whole populations of naturals who don't live in compounds."

"How is that possible? We had no choice. It was compulsory.

Are you talking about Isolationists?"

"Mostly," he said. "But not everyone who escaped to the Middlelands is on our side. Some people don't like to follow any rules. You of all people should know that," he replied with a small smile.

I kicked at the floor. "Why would the chosen ones just allow this to happen?"

"They can't stop them if they don't know where to find them."

"And *you* know where to find them? The Middlelands is a wasteland."

He laughed. "Is it? Have you ever been? Well, I certainly hope not, since that's where we're going to spend the rest of our natural lives. We're going outside the grid, Tess. In the places between the East and the West."

"What sort of people would chose to live as fugitives?"

"The same people who long ago figured out that the balance of power had been destroyed. People who predicted that one day the protection promised by the chosen ones would no longer hold true. People who knew one day deportation wouldn't mean a better life, it would mean—"

"Death," I replied, finishing his sentence. It had meant my death.

"These people, Tess, most of them left their homes and hid before things became too serious. They raised what was left of their families in hiding because they sensed that something wasn't right. Others have been brought there because, well, because it was where they belonged." The way he spoke these words caused a chill to run up my spine.

"These groups, they will just let us come and live with them?"

Robert nodded.

"It seems dangerous, letting new people in. I mean, if I had a place that was secret, safe, I wouldn't be so quick just to let anyone in. I would worry if I could trust them." The words were tumbling out of my mouth quickly. I only briefly cringed at how easy it was for me to dismiss the world as liars and cheats.

"They don't let just anyone in. They only let people in when they have good reason."

"Good reason? What possible reason could they have for wanting us in their community?" I was no one. I had no parents. My once best friend was connected to a murderer. My sister hated me. And I was quite sure that whatever I had with James was near destroyed.

"I don't know if I should be the one to tell you that," Robert said softly.

"Please, Robert. I certainly can't talk to that man, doctor or no doctor, not after my inspection. I don't even want to be in the same room with him."

"And James?"

My heart fluttered at his name but something inside of me silenced its call. "No," I said, shaking my head. "I can't talk to him. Not yet. There are too many things I need to figure out."

"Very well," he replied, and I saw something change in his eyes, a look I had never seen. It was a mixture of rage and desperation only being held together by the thinnest string of control. "They will let us in, Tess, because you are different. You're important to them. You're important to them for the same reason you are a threat to the chosen ones. The same reason the resistance craves your company is the very reason your name was on that deportation list."

I swallowed. It was all becoming clearer—it had something to do with my inspection. It was only after it that things became so chaotic, that my name was put on the deportation list. "Tell me," I begged.

He took a deep breath. "When you went in for your inspection they discovered something." Robert seemed to be struggling. I wasn't sure which emotion was causing the difficulty, the anger or the desperation—I could hear both in his voice. He closed his eyes for the briefest of seconds as if he were trying to shut some unnatural image out of his mind. When he opened his eyes, they were soft, almost kind.

"Tess," he continued, "you're not like the other girls, women, at the compound. When you decide to settle down and have children, you will not die. Your children will see the world and get to live in it."

"What are you talking about?"

"What happened to Emma will never happen to you," he replied, his voice cracking.

My hands were shaking. How could I believe what he was saying?

"There has to be some mistake. That's impossible."

"No, Tess. It's true. Kendall says it is very rare, but sometimes when a girl comes in for an inspection they discover that her body has somehow changed, evolved. It has learned to protect itself from what's killing the mothers. He and his kind are instructed to report any cases to the council."

I could feel my lungs shutting down, the air trapping itself in my throat. "No. If that were true then how come we haven't heard of anyone else finding this out?"

"Well, of course you wouldn't. Don't you see? When they report a girl's name, the council takes care of it. That was why you were on the deportation list."

"But other women were on that list!"

"They picked people at random to make your death look less planned. What does the council care if a bunch of naturals die? They can just make new humans and train them to be whatever they want them to be."

"So you're saying those women and children are going to be killed because of *me*? Because I'm some sort of freak?" I could hear how wild my voice had become but had no desire to control it.

Robert slowly stood up and took a step closer to me. "Tess, you have done many things wrong. *Many.* I won't sugarcoat it for you, but this, what the council is doing, that is not your fault."

"And yet here I am," I said, throwing my hands in the air and taking a step away from him. "In a barn, sitting here talking to you. And where are the others on that list? Are they dead yet? Why do I get saved and they don't?"

"We can't save the world just yet," he said with a small smile.

"Then why bother saving me?"

"Because those people in the Middlelands, those people who are risking their lives by joining the resistance, need hope. You're that hope, Tess. Hope that it isn't the end of a people. You're one in a thousand. Hell, maybe one in a million."

"Don't! Don't you label me with some damn ideology for a people I don't even know!"

"Tess."

"What about you, Robert? Why are you here? James could have done this with the help of Kendall. Why would you just leave? Didn't the resistance need you at the compound?

And what about Louisa?" I was yelling now and didn't care who heard me.

Robert ran a hand through his well-kept hair. He was slow to answer me. I slammed my hand against the wall of the barn. He jumped.

"And don't give me some crap about because it was what Emma wanted. Emma would have wanted you to stay and protect Louisa."

"We're in a war. The sooner you figure that out the better. The council has to use science and test tubes to create life, but for you it comes naturally. What we need now more than anything in the world is hope.

"I have people watching over Louisa. When the time is right, we'll go get her—I swear it. Everything sort of happened very quickly. When we get to where we're going, we'll have to convince them she is worth allowing in, too."

I began to tremble; shaking so hard I felt like everything inside of me would fall onto the floor for the world to see, for the world to judge. "I didn't ask for this," I whispered, more to myself than to him.

Robert took my hands in his, and the shaking of my body ceased as if his very touch controlled it. He stared at me for a long, quiet moment before speaking. "I know none of this makes much sense, but I promise it will one day. I can't even quite explain it all myself just yet. But we're both here, for better or worse. This is our life now. Together. I'm your family."

The word *together* caused my eyes to find his. How much had he given up in the name of this alliance? How hard must it have been to watch over the disgruntled sister of his lost love? How difficult must it have been for him to know that I, a girl he probably found to be both selfish and silly, got to live while the woman he loved laid dead in a grave he would never again visit. For the first time in my life I felt sorry for Robert.

I gave his hand a small squeeze.

"Please, tell me more. I'm ready. I promise no more outbursts." It was time I was the one willing to sacrifice, even if it meant my sanity. For once I would comfort someone else.

I barely heard the words that came out of his mouth. I was able to acknowledge them, nod when I was supposed to, frown when it was called for, but I never truly mingled with them. There was too much inside of me to truly accept what he was saying. I was feeling too much emotion all at once, and it made me feel antsy and useless. It took every ounce of willpower to sit still in the chair as he told me the story. My story. Our story.

Kendall had become a part of the resistance soon after he began creating. Robert had come to know him quite well through communication that was passed along the lines. As a result of some discrepancy with the council, Kendall was placed in the inspection center, a demotion. The alliance had Kendall spying on the center and using his creations to gather information. His creations like James.

James had come to Kendall with a problem. He had met a girl, a girl to whom he felt an unnatural attachment. Kendall, later asked to spy on me by Robert, was thrilled that the girl ended up being me. It made it all much easier. The fact that it was visions of me that first alerted James to his gift caused Kendall some excitement. Anything that James told Kendall about our relationship or secret meetings was then told to Robert.

Kendall alerted Robert and James that my name had come up for inspection. When the test revealed its surprising results, Kendall approached James and Robert together. Soon after, word trickled down that my name had been put on a deportation list, but the council planned to wait for me to leave the compound on my own, and then planned for me to be dragged off by chosen ones. Soon medical tests would follow, ultimately ending with my death. The council would then report that I had run off in the middle of the night and they had found me dead. Tragic.

James had tried to tell me this the night of our last meeting.

James and Kendall followed the snatchers once they took me, until they were far enough out of range of backup. Robert had taken care of the snatchers.

Now we were to wait. In a few days' time, Robert and I would travel to an extraction point where members of the resistance would come and get us.

I'm not sure how the conversation ended, or even if I had said anything remotely comprehensible to Robert before I left. But somehow I ended up back inside the ghost of a house, leaning against the wall, trying to catch my breath. It refused to come, just lay bundled, curled upon itself in my throat. I knew James was in the hallway with me, even without seeing him. The thought of James seemed to release the tension inside of me. My breath wildly clawed its way up my throat and freed itself from my tortuous body.

James took a step out of the darkness and was now only a few feet from me. How tired he looked. Without a second thought, I pried myself from the wall, rushed toward him, and threw my arms around his neck. He quickly wrapped his arms around my waist, crushing me against him. I didn't care, just buried my head into his chest. One of his hands slid up my back into my hair. I pulled away slightly and found his eyes; they were filled with anxiety and longing. I promised myself that I would forever rid his eyes of their nervousness. I would convince him that the only place either of us belonged was with each other. The whole world could go straight to hell and it wouldn't matter, not as long as I was with him. He wouldn't be able to leave me. Wherever I went, he would have to go, too. I knew now I couldn't go through life on my own, and I didn't want anyone but him.

Everything in my world had changed. I needed him. And I would convince them to allow me to keep him.

I was going to make him run, too.

Chapter 34

"Good morning, Kendall," I managed, fully aware of how shrill my voice sounded. I self-consciously placed my hand against my cheek, hoping it wasn't as flushed as it felt. I pulled the blanket that had fallen on the floor quickly back over me.

Kendall looked from me to James and then back to me again. "I certainly hope I'm not interrupting," he said, an oddly paternal tone to his voice.

"Of course not," I replied, trying to muster a smile. "We were just talking," I said as I pulled away from James. We had been making out. We hadn't talked about anything that had happened, or anything I'd learned from Robert. I think we both just needed to feel normal for a while. James and I moved to opposite ends of the lumpy, greenish couch, both pretending to stare at the snow continuing to fall through the hole that had been blasted out of the living room by some bomb.

Apparently, they had abandoned the transport after driving several hours through the destruction and rubble of towns and cities that once were. Then continued on foot for another several hours, taking turns carrying me and stumbled upon this house, which, for the most part, was still left standing. Most likely because it was nestled within the forest, away from major neighborhoods.

"I could leave," Kendall suggested.

"No need," James finally spoke up. "It's not a conversation we can't continue later," he said, throwing me a look that made my legs feel weak.

Kendall kept staring at the two of us while he and James talked and I pretended to listen. It was odd to watch their relationship play out. On the surface there didn't seem to be much affection, but every so often Kendall's eyes would light up if James said something profound or witty. I watched James in these moments as well, and he seemed like he really wanted to make this man happy. It was the closest he would ever come to having a father figure, and I would do my best to respect that.

When Kendall finally left us alone, we didn't keep kissing. A comfortable quiet settled over us as we cuddled under the blanket in the living room. I focused on the way his fingers seemed to softly move up and down my arm of their own accord. I glanced out at the giant hole blasted in the wall; the snow was really coming down. I jumped up and grabbed James's hand, attempting to pull him up with me.

"What is it?"

"It's snowing, and we're sitting inside. I want to go outside and play," I said.

James only hesitated for a moment. "You need a coat first."

"No. I want to feel it on my skin," I replied, tugging him

toward the door.

"I don't think that's such a good idea. You'll get sick," he replied sternly.

"Oh, live a little. When will we ever have the opportunity to do this again?"

We wouldn't. In a matter of days my new home would be the Middlelands. A home I wasn't sure included him, despite how much I wanted it to. For just a few days I needed to forget the hole in the wall of the living room; I wanted to be normal.

I didn't wait for James to approve. Instead, I pulled him along with me. I was almost running, unable to stop from laughing as I did so. I could feel the hesitation stiffen his arm, but he didn't pull against my grasp, either.

When we got outside, the air sucked the breath from my lungs. It was biting, almost painful, and I was immediately enamored with it. It caused all of my senses to become alert at once, proving I was alive. I had survived.

My skin began to burn from the rawness of the wind, and yet all I could do was smile. It filled me with such an inner sense of pure joy and unfamiliar peace. I closed my eyes and lifted my face up, letting the snow fall where it may. I squeezed James's hand to make sure he was still with me. He squeezed my hand back.

I opened my eyes to find James staring at me intently, dangerously, a look that would have frightened me to my core in the early days of our relationship. I shivered, and not from the cold. His face was so serious, it was as if he were contemplating all the world's problems at once.

I tugged on his hand. "Why so serious? You're supposed to be having fun, James. Snow means fun. Don't make me show you," I said, reaching down to grab a handful and raising my arm to aim it at him.

James cracked a smile. "You're not planning on throwing that at me, are you? I *am* a chosen one. My reflexes might just be a little faster than yours. You sure you're serious about taking me on?"

I lowered my arm and took a step closer to him. "I'll take you on," I whispered as I lifted my chin, leaning toward him. Before his lips could meet mine, I smashed the snow into his face. Too stunned to move, he watched me run as fast as I could from him, laughing the entire time.

This was the life I should have had.

I didn't get very far. He was fast. Very, very fast. I was in his arms before I knew it.

I could feel my face burn from a mixture of the temperature and his presence. "I thought I was going to lose you. You're the only thing that makes me feel human," he whispered.

Something new stirred inside me, something blazing. I didn't feel one ounce of coldness now. James reached out his hands and began to rub them up and down my arms, and my skin flushed in response. The snow continued to dance around us, dusting our hair and shoulders. In a quick succession of movements, his hands were on my cheeks, and he had pulled me so my body was against his. He hesitated for the briefest of moments, checking something in my eyes. Whatever he saw must have given him confidence, because before I could think out the repercussions of this kiss, his mouth was on mine.

His lips were hungry and mine were just as ravaged by neglect. All the fears and mistrust were gone. It was now just two people who desired each other without any second-guessing. The kiss embraced this freedom.

I knew Kendall had told him about me, about my freak status. I wouldn't die if we were to…

It was like nothing I could have imagined. He was everywhere and yet not nearly close enough. I reached my hands up to his hair, curling my fingers around it, pulling him closer. I heard a grunt escape his lips before they were back on mine. I couldn't breathe and I didn't care.

I was sweating. It was too hot. Was this normal? I needed to pull away, but the urge to continue was so hypnotizing. I felt waves of heat envelop my body, almost suffocating me. I pulled away, wildly gasping for air. James's hands were on my face, yet he sat very still, statue-like. I looked up at him and his eyes were unfocused, as if he was seeing something in the distance. His body stiffened and his nose began to bleed.

His eyes closed and a look of pure horror washed over his face. His hands became iron shackles against my face. I tried to say his name but could only cry out in pain. He was going to crush my skull.

Without warning he crumpled to the ground, dragging me with him. He began to shake.

Oh, God! What was happening?

"Somebody help!" I screamed, hoping there was anyone around to hear. The sound of my shrill voice seemed to cause a change. Once I yelled those words, James's body went limp. I scrambled to his side, the snow whipping me in the face. I tried to shake him awake, tears streaming down my cheeks. I couldn't lose him. I needed him to survive. I didn't want to survive without him. I cradled his head in my lap as I continued to scream for someone to save him, to save both of us.

Chapter 35

The ticking of the clock was echoing in my ears. I sat in my room, alone in the dark. I drew my legs against my chest and hugged them into place.

Kendall had said James would be all right, but he still hadn't woken up. Only now did I feel embarrassed about describing in graphic detail what had happened. At the time, I would have easily told Kendall everything if it meant he could help James. I was willing to do anything. I would have told him every secret I had left.

I had worried it was the sickness that took Frank. A sickness I still didn't understand.

Kendall surmised that James must have had some sort of vision. Our closeness must have triggered him, and James being too weak with his gift, he was unable to handle it. It had been the first time he had a vision while awake. It must have worn him out.

I shivered when I thought about the look of horror that swept over his face. What had he seen? He was so frightened.

And would it always be like this? Could we ever just be normal together?

The door to my room creaked open, and Henry's head popped around it. "Can I come in?"

"People usually knock before asking that," I replied sourly.

"I heard about what happened," he said, ignoring my comment and taking a seat on the edge of the bed.

"If you're here to comfort me, please don't."

"I'm not. I'm here to tell you how foolish that was, Tess."

Of course he was.

"Is that so?"

"Tess, I don't particularly enjoy the role of the bad guy, but someone has to be the responsible one, and since neither you nor James, nor Kendall for that matter, seem to want to, I will."

"Lucky you," I mumbled.

He sighed. "Yes, lucky me."

It was silent for a long moment before he spoke again. "This can't go on. In two days you will have to say good-bye."

"I know," I spat at him.

"I don't think you do. You and he are not made for this."

"What are you talking about?" I asked as my foot began to tap furiously against the bed.

"Romeo and Juliet are fictional, Tess. Their story could never happen in a world like ours. Besides, even in their world, they both end up dead." His voice was barely above a whisper, but in it I could still hear pain.

"But couldn't he come with us?" I asked weakly. Maybe in the Middlelands we could be the Romeo and Juliet who lived.

"The only reason they are allowing us in is because of your situation."

I rolled my eyes. "My *situation*. Well, if I'm so special shouldn't they let me have what I want?"

"It doesn't work like that. He would have no place there, no home. He would be giving up everything he knew, everything he felt comfortable with. When someone loves you, Tess, it is unfair to ask too much of them, because often they won't be able to say no. Trust me. I speak from experience," he replied, his voice cracking.

"Maybe he wants to go," I offered.

"He'll go if you ask him, but is it fair to?"

"So I'm just supposed to give up the one thing I want in life? I'm sure that sounds real easy to you. I mean, you let your girlfriend die for some cause without a second thought."

"Don't try and make sense of my relationship with Julia. You're not like me. Could you survive if something happened to him? What if the sector is raided and we're all caught? He would be *tortured*, Tess. His punishment would be worse than ours. Could you survive that? And even if you could, you wouldn't want to." His hands clutched against the side of his head.

A low ragged sob finally broke free from my throat, and I turned my back toward Henry. I was ashamed to have him see me like this.

I felt his hand gently touch my back. "I am sorry. I really am. But for better or worse, his life was meant to be different than ours. He could have everything that we can't. Would you ask him to turn his back on that to live a life filled with uncertainty?"

Henry's words stung because they were filled with a truth I could no longer deny. I loved James. I loved him more than I thought my poor, inexperienced heart was capable of. I would not, could not, banish him to the life that slowly destroyed my own sense of being. He had already done so much for me. He had saved my life twice, and beyond that, he'd made me realize that I had a heart and soul that still lived inside me. He showed me that love existed in a world full of darkness, something I long thought was impossible. I couldn't ask him for more.

A low knock on the door interrupted my agonizing thoughts. As if on cue, James's voice broke through my moment of grief.

"May I come in?"

I quickly wiped the tears off my face and managed to mumble that he could.

James looked from me to Henry and then back to me again. His face scrunched up as if he saw something unpleasant, something disturbing. The look only lasted a moment, though, before his face relaxed into a look of curiosity. "Am I interrupting?"

I shook my head, still unable to manage a coherent sentence. The weight of the good-bye was crushing down forcibly upon my chest. Two days. I had two days.

Henry said nothing to James or me but quickly stood up and rushed out of the room, closing the door behind him. I didn't know how to explain the scene to James, and I didn't really want to.

James hovered near the end of the bed, looking hesitant. "Are you crying?"

"It's nothing. I'm just tired. It's been a long day." I reached my hand toward him greedily. I needed him near me now more than ever. The touch of his skin to mine, something that had once frightened me, was the only thing that could sustain me now. He was sitting by my side on the bed in an instant. He placed his hands on my shoulders and turned me so I was facing him.

"What is it?"

The way his eyes looked into mine caused my stomach to tighten and my breathing to quicken. God, this was going to hurt. But it didn't have to happen now. No, not now.

"I've just been worried about you," I replied. Not a total lie.

He stroked my face. "Oh, Tess, no need. I'm just fine. I have a slight headache, that's all."

"I was so scared. It all happened so fast," I whispered as the horrifying images replayed before my eyes.

He chuckled. "Yeah, that was some kiss."

His attempt at humor didn't distract me. "What happened?"

James sighed. "Not sure, really. I think that when we kissed I just got overwhelmed."

"You had a vision?"

He nodded, his face smooth, but his jaw was clearly clenched.

"You've have had visions before, though. Why did you react like that?"

James offered a small shrug, clearly trying to pass off the event like nothing of importance. "I have never had one while I was conscious before. I guess my body wasn't completely ready for it."

I knew I was most afraid of the answer to the next question, but I had to ask. "What did you see?"

James shook his head, instantly looking anywhere in the room but at my face.

"You saw something about me?"

"Isn't it always about you?" he replied bitterly.

"Tell me."

"I can't."

"Yes, you can. Haven't we learned about keeping secrets? I don't do well with that!"

"Please, just drop it."

"I most certainly will not," I replied angrily. I could feel my face flushing. I would no longer allow myself to be kept in the dark about important things in my life.

Now he was angry, too. "I can't tell you, Tess! Don't you think I would if I could? Do you think I like living alone with these things? I can't tell anyone anymore. If I tell you what I saw, I risk something changing. If something changes, even the smallest thing, I might not be in the right place to stop it. So I'm left alone with these images attacking my mind. It's maddening. And knowing all the time that I need to keep seeing them, wishing my mind would show me more, so I could prevent it."

I could barely keep up, he was talking so fast.

"I told Kendall and Robert about your deportation, about how the council wasn't going to wait. And things changed. Suddenly, parts of my vision went black; I couldn't see anymore. We almost didn't make it before those snatchers…before they had their fun," he hissed.

His hands were on my face now, his eyes not wavering from mine. "So I have to live with this on my own, Tess. It's the only way I can assure I will be in the right place at the right time to stop it."

His fingers moved down my neck so they rested over my heart. I could feel the goose bumps across the trail his hand made. "I can't lose you."

I closed my eyes, my head dizzy from the combination of his touch and his words.

"I'm sorry," I breathed.

He pulled me closer so he was cradling me against his chest.

He kissed the top of my head. "No need to apologize."

"So if you were to see this image again would it help you?" I asked, hoping my voice didn't sound as shaky to him as it did to me.

"Maybe."

I pulled away slightly so my face was in front of his. "Should we try again?" I couldn't help but blush at the possibility of living another kiss like that, or the shudder that ran through my body at the thought of his violent reaction.

I could see the anxiety on his face but also something else—desire. "Maybe the vision won't be as strong this time. Maybe since I know what to expect I won't see anything…and if I do maybe my body will be prepared for it."

I nodded. "Maybe." It was the only word I could manage to mumble.

I titled my chin up toward him, and before I could think another thought his lips were on mine. My body instantly heated up just like before. His hands knotted into my hair as I crushed myself against him. The kiss was filled with desperation. I knew I had very little of these moments left with him, and maybe his vision made him realize he had very little of these moments left with me.

"Did you see anything?" I panted.

"No."

I didn't care and neither did he. This kiss was more than just an experiment. I found his lips again, wrapped my arms around his back, clutching him to me as tightly as possible. His lips moved down my neck. Suddenly, I was on my back, James on top of me. I reached up into his hair and grabbed it, forcing his lips onto mine again. I needed more. One of his hands was under my back as the other moved down toward my waist, leaving a blazing trail of heat as he did. I felt my back arch on its own, my chest now against his. I wondered if this was going to stop. I wondered if I wanted it to.

My body was burning; I felt the sweat drip down my neck. It was happening again. I trembled with anticipation, waiting for the dreadful moment when he would pull away, and I would watch the scene of horror once again pass across his eyes. But he didn't stop. He didn't pull away. The kiss only deepened. I didn't know how long I could stand the heat. I felt the cotton of my top begin to stick to my back. I knew we were racing toward the line that once was crossed couldn't be uncrossed. Was I ready for that? Did it matter? I didn't have time to feel ready. I only had two days.

I knew I wouldn't die if the worst happened. I could feel my lips begin to still themselves, and my hands fell limply to my sides. His lips moved back to my neck, his hand holding tightly onto my waist.

I wasn't ready.

My first kiss had only been weeks ago. I wasn't ready for what came next. I had barely made sense of my own feelings, my new situation in life. I didn't need a new complication. And would this, this embrace of closeness, forever tie me to James? Tie me in a way that would make our parting much more difficult, if that were even possible? We hadn't thought of protection. We hadn't even discussed it. Yet, here it could be happening. Everything was happening so fast in my life.

"Stop," I whispered.

He froze the second the word escaped my lips, the sound of our ragged breathing mingling with the silence of the room. I made an attempt to scoot away, but he was too heavy. I needed to be far from him, doubting my own self-control.

He quickly lifted himself off of me and muttered, "Sorry."

I tried to read the emotion on his face. Did he look angry? Hurt? No, he was relieved. I wondered if he had been feeling the same way as me, unsure and not ready. I wondered if my self-control somehow was better than his, or if he was merely trying to give me what he thought I wanted. I briefly remembered the way his lips had moved and knew he had wanted it, too.

"Some kiss," I joked.

James chuckled weakly. "Yeah."

"I'm sorry. I shouldn't have let it get so out of control," I replied quietly.

"You? It's my fault. You have always made it clear your thoughts on this sort of thing," he replied.

"I think a lot of things I felt before have changed, James. I just didn't feel—"

"—ready," he finished.

I offered a small smile in response.

He tucked a strand of hair behind my ear. "It's fine. We have time." The word *time* sounded stale, unreal, and I knew we both understood it to be a lie. We both knew what we had just given up. This was something we would never share. I wondered if later in life I would regret it. In this moment it seemed like the right choice to stop. I couldn't imagine remembering our time together connected to only feelings of desolation and loss. I'd rather not have that experience at all than to see it so tainted.

"I should probably go, let you rest," he said, patting my hand gently as he moved to get off the bed.

I locked my hand around his. "Wait. Maybe you could stay. I mean...just sleep."

He raised an eyebrow in response.

I forced a grin. "We're two rational people. We can handle it."

His face lit up in a relaxed smile. "I guess we have handled worse."

I moved to the other side of the bed and patted the spot next to me. After a brief moment of hesitation, he pulled back the covers and lay down. Both of us lay on our backs, not touching, staring at the ceiling.

It was most certainly awkward. I couldn't help but laugh. It was the most normal I'd felt in days. I had come to almost cherish these moments of teenage instability. They made the rest of my life seem like some bad dream. Just thinking about the situation made me laugh harder. James began to laugh, too, and it made me happy to know I didn't have to explain what was so funny to him. He already understood.

Chapter 36

I kept having the same nightmare. I knew the memory was haunting me for a reason, but I couldn't figure out why.

I was six the first time I saw the mangled body of a rejected chosen one. I didn't understand a lot of things back then. Now, at sixteen, some things had become quite a bit clearer. Others I still didn't understand.

My father bringing in the body of the chosen one is near the top of the list.

I shouldn't have seen it, but without a proper education us children had a lot of free time. The schools had been closed a few months prior. There were plenty of excuses thrown around to appease the parents at the time. Some claimed that education would no longer be needed once the compounds were completed. We wouldn't work. We would have no need for reading and writing. We would want for nothing. Besides, books were filled with stories of emotions and selfish personal wants. These were the very things that had brought our society near extinction.

Some people claimed our local sector couldn't afford to search for and hire a new teacher. Our previous one had disappeared without warning six months prior. We had a war going on, and securing a new teacher just didn't seem all that important.

Those who wanted to educate their children would have to find the time to do it on their own. The council would provide simple guidebooks for these parents.

My father worked ridiculous hours for the council, so I never expected him to become my teacher. My mother mostly kept to her liquor, so she wasn't much help. Emma, God bless her, meant well when she tried to teach little Louisa and me, but since she found it damn near impossible to raise her voice, she couldn't really keep us in check.

I didn't mind not going to school. I had friends to play with all day. Our house was a pretty popular destination for the sector kids, since we were one of the few with a working television, thanks to my dad's job with the council. The sector had a large screen television brought out for council announcements, but a personal television set was a rarity. There's no doubt that most of my friends only liked me for the TV, but at the age of six, I didn't realize.

It's funny the things the council could supply us with in such desperate times. Electricity. Televisions. But I was beginning to suspect it had only been because it suited their purposes. How much did they keep from us in order to create a people so frenzied with poverty they would allow their government to do anything it wanted?

One day I woke up anxious and exhilarated. They were scheduled to replay the very first public showing of the chosen ones' power. For some reason I felt compelled to watch it every single time it aired. Mom had been having a good few weeks, so it seemed safe to invite my friends over to watch as well.

But whatever had kept my mom sober for that brief amount of time had crumbled. When I trotted into the kitchen that morning, I saw my older sister holding back her hair as she threw up into the sink. Louisa sat crying in the corner. She always cried when our mother got like this.

My older sister looked back at me when she heard me enter. Sympathy was written all over her face. She always tried to hold us all together.

I used to wish she were my mother.

I wanted to cry, but even then I saw that it would be pointless. I left without a word, slamming the door to the room I shared with my sisters. Even though our house was still small, and there were weeks we went without things like sugar and eggs, at least we had a house.

There was no way to get word to my friends in time before they all started showing up. The phone lines had been down for weeks.

I hid underneath my bed as Emma answered the door time and time again, telling each friend that I had come down with the flu and we couldn't watch TV that day. I wish I had thanked her for it before she died. I never told her how much it meant to me that she saved me.

After the last friend left, she knocked quietly on the door. "Tessie? Mama, Louisa, and I are going to take a walk and get some fresh air. I think it's just the thing to get us all feeling right this morning. You want to come?"

Yes, I wanted to go. If it could be just her and me I would go anywhere.

I didn't answer.

"Please, Tessie."

"Please, Tessie," I heard little Louisa begin to chant. The girl just wanted to be loved. She didn't care by whom.

After a while my older sister gave up. I didn't blame her—at the moment my mother was the bigger crisis. I stayed hidden under my bed while they were gone. There wasn't really anything else to do.

I'm not sure how much time passed before I heard the front door open. I scrunched farther under the bed—I wasn't ready to see the paleness of my mother's face, or the way Louisa clutched onto her, forever hoping her love was enough to make Mom quit drinking. Louisa didn't understand what was going on, not at all. All she knew was sometimes Momma didn't want her at all.

Much to my surprise, I heard my father's voice travel through the house. "Anyone home? Girls?"

I should have answered. Especially when he called out again I should have, but I stayed silent. I wanted to remain in my own little world for as long as possible.

"What the hell we doing, Charlie?"

My father wasn't alone. The voice sounded faintly familiar, but I couldn't identify whom it came from.

"Just help me bring him into the bathroom. He's losing a lot of blood."

Was that my father's voice? It sounded so unlike him that I had to question it.

After a moment of silence, I heard a strange shuffle as both men let out muffled groans.

I crawled a little closer to the light that attempted to reach me under the bed.

I could hear the bathroom door swing with force against the

wall, followed by something crashing to the floor. I would have sworn my mother was home, but I knew she wasn't. These noises made up my mother's symphony.

I slowly pulled myself onto my feet. Something inside of me was forcing my legs to walk toward that bathroom. It was the same part that always had to watch the television anytime they talked about chosen ones. An odd obsession I just didn't understand at the time.

I just needed to know.

I always needed to know.

I pressed myself against the wall near the bathroom door so no one would see me.

"This is bad, Charlie. This is really bad," the other man called out.

"What was I supposed to do, just let him die? They were going to kill him. We're not murderers, Jacobson."

Jacobson let out a short, bitter laugh. "Yeah. How much longer we gonna be able to claim that?"

My father heaved a sigh.

"We won't get away with this," Jacobson charged.

"You don't know that. We can ask for their help. I think we've proven what side we're really on."

"I don't think anyone is going to be able to help cover this up."

"Well, maybe I just don't give a damn anymore," my father snarled.

The sound of running water made my eavesdropping near impossible.

"Help…lift…up," said my father.

I could tell by their heavy breathing and grunts that this task was easier said than done. I figured the two of them would be distracted by the task, and it would be safe for me to take a peek.

I wasn't ready.

I couldn't see much over my father and his friend, who sat on their knees tending to the chosen one in the tub. I could see the top of a head—a damp, bloodied head of sandy blond hair. One of the thing's hands was clutching onto the edge of the bathtub, and I noticed the water faucet was turned to cold. I remembered my father doing this when Louisa had one of her spells. It had been important to get her fever down.

The chosen one wasn't making much noise, but I could tell he was in pain by the tension in the hand that gripped the tub. I could see one of his eyes widen as he spotted me over my father's shoulder. The chosen one lifted his head to get a better view, and when he did I swear I saw a look of disappointment cross his face.

Whatever he had been searching for, it certainly wasn't me.

As he looked, I saw the perfection of his features. Even bloodied I saw beauty. I couldn't make out his whole face, just a chin and the outline of his cheek. But it was a beautiful outline. His eyes were just as they appeared on television—icy blue.

There was a chosen one in my house.

A noise issued from my lips. I'm still not sure if it was of excitement or fear—maybe both. My father turned on me with such quickness that it made me a little dizzy.

If he was surprised to see me, he didn't show it. Even in the biggest of crises, my father kept his mask firmly in place.

His voice was calm when he spoke. "Tess, can you get me some ice?"

I didn't hesitate a second before running into the kitchen. By the time I got back to the bathroom with the bucket of ice, my father had pulled closed the shower curtain, blocking my line of sight.

I handed my father the ice with a frown. He actually laughed at me.

"I take it you got something you want to ask me?"

Jacobson kept his eyes on the floor as my father crouched in front of me, waiting for my question.

"I got lots of things to ask you," I replied.

I didn't know how to hold my tongue.

My father laughed again.

"You won't tell the other girls about this, will you?"

I shook my head. Of course I wouldn't.

"Go to your room. I'll be there in a bit."

It was a while before my father came into my room. Maybe hours, I'm not quite sure. I sat on my bed waiting patiently. Every once in a while I would get up and run my hands across the spines of the few books that graced my and my sisters' bookshelf. More and more books made it onto the banned booklist every day, and our bookshelf was getting emptier and emptier.

I could barely read, but I still loved the things. I loved the way they felt in my hands. I loved the way they smelled.

By the time my dad came into the room, I could hear my mother and sisters in the kitchen. My father shut the door behind him and took a seat on the bed. Much to my dismay, he didn't mention what I'd seen in the bathroom. Not once.

He pretended as if it had never happened.

"Tess."

"Yes, Daddy."

"Every night after dinner you will spend two hours studying with me."

"What?"

"You can't afford to go through life without an education. You will work on your reading with me every night. If I can't be here, you will sit still and listen to your sister. Do you understand me?"

I didn't. "But I don't want—"

"I don't remember asking you what you wanted, little girl. You will work on your reading. You will be read to every night. You will remember the stories you hear. You will commit them to memory, and you will learn from them. Do you hear?"

I looked up at my father, unsettled by the mystery man before me. "But I thought the books were bad."

"Anything is bad in the wrong hands, Tess. But you're a smart girl. You gotta be ready for what's coming."

"What's coming, Daddy?"

This question stopped him. For a few moments he was unable to speak. Whatever he was thinking of saying never made it to his lips.

"Just do what you're told."

I nodded.

"Open your hands."

My father placed a book into my open palms, a book I remembered having to remove from our bookshelf sometime back. I remembered it only because I'd liked the title. It was called *A Tale of Two Cities*.

I looked up at my father. I knew this wasn't allowed. But he made no explanation for the book. He didn't explain why it was so important to educate me and not Louisa. He didn't give any reasons for how he had kept this book. One thing was certain—my father had secrets.

His secrets became my own. I began to sound out the words

on the first page. It was the best of times. It was the worst of times.

James, surprisingly, was a very heavy sleeper. He barely budged as I crawled out of bed and headed to the kitchen. Robert had been smart enough to bring a supply of food and water for our journey; I didn't think anyone would mind too much if I had a snack. We were down to having only one hot meal a day. I was used to three square meals in the compound. The whole run-for-my-life thing was going to take some adjusting.

And the toughest part of the journey hadn't even started yet.

We were to hike a good twenty miles over the next couple days to meet the group who would take us to our new home. That was only the first leg of the trip.

"It's not nice to steal from the group's stash, Tess."

I nearly jumped out of my skin. "Jesus."

"Nope. My name is Henry, remember?" he asked with a grin.

"Shut up," I replied, taking a seat across from him at the kitchen table. I still wasn't sure where we stood. I wasn't even sure I knew him at all.

"Can't sleep?" he asked.

I shook my head.

"Want to go take a walk? Explore like the old days?" He raised an eyebrow.

I nodded. Despite everything that now stood between us, I didn't hesitate. I wanted to see more of the world that had existed before me. "Here. Wear this," he said, standing and walking over to me, placing his jacket on my shoulders. I was suddenly very much aware of the fact that I was standing in my pajamas, and he was fully clothed.

Henry laughed good-naturedly at my discomfort and headed out the door.

It took a solid hour of walking before we found what once was called civilization. I don't know what I expected to find in the darkness of this forgotten city, but I certainly didn't find hope. We were both quiet as Henry aimed his flashlight on various symbols of the destruction that had ravaged this place: overturned cars, windows smashed out of buildings, light posts bent in half. I thought I even saw human bones, but Henry moved the beam so quickly that I couldn't be sure.

We walked for hours. The more we explored, the more I realized this was only the beginning. Leaving the compound didn't mean a better life; it just meant a different one. Every world I stepped foot in seemed decided for me.

Henry sighed as we reached the house. "Tess?"

"Hmm?"

He shoved his hands in his pockets. He seemed unsure. This was the Henry I knew from my childhood. "You could be happy, you know."

"What?"

He took a step toward me. "Just because he can't go with you doesn't mean you'll be sad forever. I can see you happy. You could have a family. Or you don't have to have one. But you have the ability to choose. We could make a life somewhere out there, Tess."

"We?" I asked, my throat suddenly dry.

Henry was even closer to me now. I recognized the look in his eyes. There was a lot I didn't know about life, but I knew what it meant to want. I took a small step away from him. "Good night, Henry."

"Wait."

I stopped, my back toward him. "Did you know my father was a part of your little resistance group?"

"Tess."

I turned around to face him. "He brought a chosen one home once. Do you know anything about that? I think he meant to save him. I keep dreaming about it. I know it's important, but I don't know why."

Henry looked down at his feet. "I can't tell you everything."

I clenched my jaw. "Of course you can't. Just another person who needs to keep me in the dark. You know what kind of life I want, Henry? One where everyone doesn't treat me like I'm weak, like I couldn't understand. One where the people I care about most let me see who they are."

And with that I left him standing in the dark.

Chapter 37

I watched as James was flipped into the air, landing painfully on his back. I watched as the man he was fighting wiped the sweat from his brow. Could I call them men when they moved like something unknown to me, something so alien? I didn't know men could fight in such a way.

With a growl, James pulled himself to his feet. His arm whipped back and pushed through the air, making contact with the attacker.

Somehow they had found us.

We had begun our long trek to the extraction point. We never saw them coming.

Henry lay on the ground. Not moving. He was no match against a chosen one. No natural was. I didn't know if he was dead.

I saw the other one staring—he was coming for me. I turned my attention back to James. He and the chosen one were moving too fast for me to see who was winning.

My heart was pounding.

The other was coming for me.

Kendall grabbed my arm and pulled me away. My feet dragged across the dirt. I couldn't leave James.

"Go, Tess. Run!" James yelled.

Kendall tugged again on my arm, and I ran. I ran as fast as I could. I had no idea where Robert was. The three chosen ones were everywhere at once. We hadn't been prepared.

Kendall dragged me deeper into the unknown, closer to the line that separated West from Middlelands. I pushed with all the strength I could muster.

I wanted to live. This would be the start of my rebellion.

Suddenly, Kendall stopped. We were both panting, gasping with the need for life. "We have to keep running. We're just naturals, Kendall, we won't be able to beat them. Running and hiding is our only option."

It was the truth. I didn't know where Robert was, and Henry was already down. I knew James could fight, but was his training enough to beat three older, wiser chosen ones?

Kendall, whose face was covered in sweat, gave a small shake of his head. I grunted and stalked over to him, grabbing his arm. I used all my strength to pull him along with me, but he fought me every step of the way. I felt angry tears threaten to spill from my eyes. Too many people had risked so much for me to live; I wasn't going to die like this.

I had to see what else life had to offer.

"Please, Kendall! We can make it. We'll find a place to hide, and we'll wait for James to come for us. He can save us. But we have to move!" I could hear how frantic my own voice sounded.

"I can't," Kendall whispered.

I let go of his arm and backed away. "Then I'm sorry, but I'm going to run. I won't die for you." I would have to find a way to explain it to James later.

"But you *are* going to die, Tess." And there it was—the same look Henry had given me when we discussed the chosen ones outside the compound. Kendall's eyes were filled with a sort of wild desperation that echoed the darkest thoughts of my mind. He would do anything to get what he wanted—and I stood in his way.

I went still. "What are you talking about?" I asked, slowly moving away from him, unable to deny the feeling of dread that had settled over me.

Kendall started to walk toward me. "I used to believe so much in the cause. I helped men like your father build up their resistance group. I gave them information from the inside. I even helped them sneak out chosen ones. You'd be surprised how many chosen ones the resistance movement has tucked away. But what I didn't understand was that I was trading one life of servitude for another. The resistance movement will ask for you to give them everything, Tess. *Everything.* At least the council offered me power, wealth, any material thing I wanted."

I scanned the horizon, looking for the best escape route.

"You won't get away. You can't beat them. We had the element of surprise."

"I am not dying today," I said through my teeth.

"Do you know why I was demoted by the council? It's not like they caught me passing information or anything; no, it was over James. His scar."

"What are you talking about?" I asked. The longer I kept him talking, the more time I was giving James. If he wasn't already captured. Or dead.

"When the chosen ones first wake up, they're not exactly the most agile things. I guess that's to be expected for someone who spends the first half of his life sleeping. James took a nasty spill one day during combat practice. He was rushed to me so I could fix him. It would be a quick procedure, but he didn't want me to fix the imperfection. He begged me to let him keep it. I think he liked being different. And I couldn't say no to him. I've made a lot of chosen ones, but James is special."

"And so you let him keep the scar, and they punished you for it? Why wouldn't they just force you to fix it?" I asked. I looked around me for some kind of weapon, but Kendall had chosen wisely. We were in an open space.

Prey.

"Come now, Tess. You know how the council works—they let you believe you have a choice," he replied with a bitter grin. "That small action, and I am demoted to the inspection center. But I've found my way back in."

Something inside me knew, knew without him having to say it.

He had betrayed us.

"Why?"

"Because the council promised me they wouldn't hurt James. They promised me they would elevate me. You have no idea what it's like having them look down on you, making you feel like you're nothing every single day. I helped *create* life!"

"But you're like me. You're a natural."

He laughed, running his hands through his thinning hair. "Chosen ones and naturals are just titles. The only difference between the two is power. I understand that now. I need that power. They knew when they saw how much I cared about him how to get to me. They came to me, questioned me. About you. About James. They knew you two weren't right. They offered to change his placement, offered him a position on one of the subcommittees. They would reinstate me, too, I just had to go through with the plan. Wait till we got close to meeting those weirdos from the Middlelands, kill you, and force Robert to tell us everything he knows."

I didn't feel fear. I felt pain. I felt pain for James.

"But he trusts you!"

"He'll never know." Kendall pulled something silver from his jacket.

A knife.

I backed away from him. "Don't pretend you're doing this for James. If you cared for him, if you loved him, you wouldn't do this. We're the same, he and I."

"No you're not. We are nothing like him," he said to himself as he stared at the knife. He was a man without hope, a man with no options. As he began to stalk toward me, I thought about how he was no different than Henry. How easily we kill for some cause.

He didn't get very far.

It was Robert.

He sprang from behind and snapped Kendall's neck as if it was nothing. Kendall crumpled to the ground without a sound, without a last word. Only silence. I didn't cry out—I was frozen. For one moment the world had gone completely still.

I saw something move from the corner of my eye. The other chosen one had found us. Robert could easily take out an old man like Kendall, but he couldn't beat a chosen one—it was impossible. Robert grabbed the knife that lay by Kendall's forgotten body. I still didn't move when he stood in front of me. I vaguely saw the knife rise into the air again and again. The gray sky became forever dyed by red.

The chosen one lay next to the creator.

"We can't tell James," I whispered.

Chapter 38

Someday both of us would have to deal with the events of the day. Someday James would have to come to terms with the fact that his creator was dead. I had made Robert promise to keep Kendall's deception a secret. I couldn't destroy Kendall. It would only destroy James.

I felt the pain James was feeling, as if I was connected to him, as if we were one. I knew he felt guilty, as though he had made a choice—me over Kendall. I knew that the guilt was nothing compared to what he would have felt if he knew the choice Kendall had made.

I had no time to comfort him. As we walked in silence toward the extraction point, I wanted to tell him it got easier. To tell him I no longer mourned my father. But it would be a lie. And since I couldn't lie to James, I said nothing.

Robert half carried a badly injured Henry. Later, I would have to find the time to thank God that he lived.

A chorus of unfamiliar clicks echoed in my ear. James

grabbed me and pushed me behind him as three men appeared from the tree line. The men were oddly dressed, but not so differently than us to appear completely absurd. They wore cotton or wool pants similar to the uniforms worn by the men of the compound. Their shirts were all varieties of plaid, their faces covered in beards. They looked like some reckless, wandering lumberjacks.

And they were holding guns.

The treaty didn't apply to these men. They were Isolationists.

"The deal was we would take one chosen one," the tallest of the three said, pointing his rifle directly at our group.

Despite his cryptic words, a surge of hope went through me. They were going to allow me to keep James. He could escape with me.

Robert nodded. "Deal's a deal. I'm sorry, James."

James heaved a heavy sigh. "Figured it would go something like this."

He began to pull away from me. "Wait. But he's the only one. I don't understand," I said.

"Robert's a chosen one, Tess," James replied quietly.

"No. No, he's not. He's…"

But as I looked for him I noticed his ice-blue eyes, the same eyes that haunted my dreams.

It wasn't possible.

But I could see it on his face. He was. I remembered the ease with which he'd killed Kendall and the chosen one, the fact that the earlier models hadn't had the same mismatched flaw as the newer models. The mysterious circumstances under which he'd appeared at our compound. And James had known the whole time. There were too many questions buzzing in my head.

And then I knew why I kept having the same dream over and over again. "You were the chosen one my father and Jacobson brought home?"

Robert nodded. "Your father saved my life. He connected me with the resistance network. They forged papers for me, so I could protect your family in the compound when the time was right."

"My father wrote of you. He showed you pictures of Emma, and you wanted to meet her…"

I should have felt thankful, but it was just another betrayal. Another secret kept from me. How blind had I been? He wasn't as beautiful as James, but then again, the earlier models weren't.

"It wasn't my secret to tell, Tess," James replied quietly. He grabbed my hand and pulled me to the side.

"Then you can go with me. I choose him," I called to the men who still held their guns on us.

"No," James replied, pulsing with emotion, "he knows these people. Or at least knows a lot more about them than I do. Robert will keep you safe."

"No. My father saved him and he got Emma. I don't owe him anything. What will *you* do? Go back?"

"Yes. I'll fight them from the inside."

I remembered Kendall's words. Would fighting for a cause be enough for James? Wasn't there more to life?

It was time to say good-bye.

I thought that when this moment came I would want to shut down, feel nothing. Yet I wanted to feel everything. Would this be the last time I saw James? The thought was unbearable. There were no words.

I ran my hands across his face, trying to memorize every inch of its glory. I brushed my lips over his scar. He sighed. I pressed my forehead against his. His hands clutched feverishly to my jacket.

"Tess."

"Don't. Don't say those words. I'll die if I hear them." I knew to anyone else it would sound melodramatic, but I knew a part of me would die the minute he said good-bye.

"I'll find you," he whispered to me. "When it's safe, when I can figure out something, something these people need."

"Don't make promises."

"I'll find you."

"You can't. I don't want you to. I don't want you to give up anything else. You have to go. Get your life back."

"I'll find you."

"Don't."

His lips pressed against mine.

"Tess, we have to go," Robert said from somewhere distant.

We were running out of time.

"Don't forget who you are," I whispered urgently.

I took a step from him.

"Tess."

"Go," I commanded.

"Tess."

He pulled a book from his jacket and shoved it into my hands. I looked down at the title, *Frankenstein*. "I want you to have this."

"I love you," I admitted.

"I love you, too."

He took a step away from me.

"Wait. I want you to have something," I said, pulling out my father's letters. "I want you to see me, too."

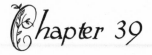

Chapter 39

I had no idea what was next. I didn't know if we would make it. I didn't know what sort of life awaited me. The thought of so much change terrorized me. But there was also something else—hope.

I was on a journey. I didn't know where it would take me or who I would become. All I knew was I could become someone.

And it was sublime.

Acknowledgments

First, I'd like to thank two of Entangled Publishing's finest: Heather Howland and Stacy Abrams. Heather—your encouragement and honesty gave me the push I needed when I felt like giving up. I will never be able to thank you enough for believing in me and my work. Stacy—thank you for being so patient and understanding with me on my first venture into the publishing world. Your insight changed the story in such utterly marvelous ways.

To my friends—the past year of my life hasn't been the easiest, but your continued excitement and interest in my work made each and every day better.

To my work family—thank you for making me laugh every single day.

Erin—you are the single greatest friend a girl could ask for. No one has listened to me talk more about my ambition to become a published writer. I wouldn't have stayed sane through this without you.

To my parents—I could not ask for better or more supportive parents. Every success I find in life is a result of my upbringing. Every struggle I face I will overcome with your guidance…GO BEARS!!

A DENAZEN NOVEL

TOUCH

"Memorable characters, heart pounding action, sizzling hot romance — TOUGH has it all!"

Jennifer L. Armentrout, author of HALF-BLOOD

JUS ACCARDO

OUCH

Jus Accardo

When a strange boy tumbles down a river embankment and lands at her feet, seventeen-year-old adrenaline junkie Deznee Cross snatches the opportunity to piss off her father by bringing the mysterious hottie with ice blue eyes home.

Except there's something off with Kale. He wears her shoes in the shower, is overly fascinated with things like DVDs and vases, and acts like she'll turn to dust if he touches her. It's not until Dez's father shows up, wielding a gun and knowing more about Kale than he should, that Dez realizes there's more to this boy—and her father's "law firm"—than she realized.

Kale has been a prisoner of Denazen Corporation—an organization devoted to collecting "special" kids known as Sixes and using them as weapons—his entire life. And, oh yeah, his touch? It kills. The two team up with a group of rogue Sixes hellbent on taking down Denazen before they're caught and her father discovers the biggest secret of all. A secret Dez has spent her life keeping safe.

A secret Kale will kill to protect.

Available online and in stores everywhere...

Keep reading for sample chapters of
TOUCH
book one in the Denazen series
by Jus Accardo

When a strange boy tumbles down a river embankment and lands at her feet, seventeen-year-old adrenaline junkie Deznee Cross snatches the opportunity to piss off her father by bringing the mysterious hottie with ice blue eyes home.

Except there's something off with Kale. He wears her shoes in the shower, is overly fascinated with things like DVDs and vases, and acts like she'll turn to dust if he touches her. It's not until Dez's father shows up, wielding a gun and knowing more about Kale than he should, that Dez realizes there's more to this boy—and her father's "law firm"—than she realized.

Kale has been a prisoner of Denazen Corporation—an organization devoted to collecting "special" kids known as Sixes and using them as weapons—his entire life. And, oh yeah, his touch? It kills. The two team up with a group of rogue Sixes hellbent on taking down Denazen before they're caught and her father discovers the biggest secret of all. A secret Dez has spent her life keeping safe.

A secret Kale will kill to protect.

1

I couldn't see them, but I knew they were there, waiting at the bottom. Bloodthirsty little shits—they were probably *praying* for this to go badly. "What do you think—about a fifteen-foot drop?"

"Easily," Brandt said. He grabbed my arm as a blast of wind whipped around us. Once I was steady on my skateboard, he tipped back his beer and downed what was left.

Together, we peered over the edge of the barn roof. The party was in full swing below us. Fifteen of our closest—and craziest—friends.

Brandt sighed. "Can you really do this?"

I handed him my own empty bottle. "They don't call me Queen of Crazy Shit for nothing." Gilman was poised on his skateboard to my left. Even in the dark, I could see the moonlight glisten off the sweat beading his brow. Pansy. "You ready?"

He swallowed and nodded.

Brandt laughed and tossed the bottles toward the woods. There were several seconds of silence, then a muted crash, followed by hoots and hysterical laughter from our friends below. Only drunk people would find shattering bottles an epic source of amusement.

"I dunno about this, Dez," he said. "You can't see anything down there. How do you know where you're gonna land?"

"It'll be fine. I've done this, like, a million times."

Brandt's words were clipped. "Into a pool. From a ten-foot-high garage roof. This is at least fifteen feet. Last thing I want to do is drag your ass all the way home."

I ignored him—the usual response to my cousin's chiding—and bent my knees. Turning back to Gilman, I smiled. "Ready, *Mr. Badass*?"

Someone below turned up one of the car stereos. A thumping techno beat drifted up. Hands on the sill behind me, drunken shouts of encouragement rising from below, I let go.

Hair lashed like a thousand tiny whips all along my face. The rough and rumbling texture of the barn roof beneath my board. Then nothing.

Flying. It was like flying.

For a few blissful moments, I was weightless. A feather suspended in midair right before it fluttered gracefully to the ground. Adrenalin surged through my system, driving my buzz higher.

The crappy thing about adrenalin highs, though? They never last long enough.

Mine lasted what felt like five seconds—the time it took to go from the barn roof to the not-so-cushy pile of hay below.

I landed with a jar—nothing serious—a bruised tailbone and some black and blues, maybe. Hardly the worst I'd ever walked away with. Stretching out the kink in my back, I brushed the hay from my jeans. A quick inspection revealed a smudge above my right knee and a few splotches of mud up the left side. All things the washing machine could fix.

Somewhere behind me, a loud wail filled the air. Gilman.

Never mix tequila and peach schnapps with warm Bud Light. It makes you do stupid things. Things like staying too long at a party you were told not to go to or making out in the bushes with someone like Mark Geller.

Things like skateboarding off the roof of a rickety barn...

Well, that's not entirely true. I tended to do these things without the buzz. Except kissing Mark Geller. That was *all* alcohol.

"You okay?" Brandt called from the rooftop.

I gave him a thumbs-up and went to check on Gilman. He was surrounded by a gaggle of girls, which made me wonder if he wasn't faking it—at least a little. A scrawny guy like Gilman didn't warrant much in the way of female attention, so I'd bet all ten toes he'd run his mouth tonight to attract some.

"You are one crazy ass, Chica," he mumbled, climbing to his feet.

I pointed to the pile of hay I'd landed in—several yards farther than where he'd crashed. "*I'm* crazy? At least I aimed for the hay."

"Wooooo!" came Brandt's distinctive cry. A moment later, he was running around the side of the barn, fist pumping. He stopped at my side and stuck his tongue out at Gilman, who smiled and flipped him off. He punched me in the arm. "That's my girl!"

"A girl who needs to bail. Ten minutes of kissy face in the bushes and Mark Geller thinks we're soul mates. *So* don't need a stalker."

Brandt frowned. "But the party's just getting started. You don't want to miss the Jell-O shots!"

Jell-O shots? Those were my favorite. Maybe it was worth…no. "I'm willing to risk it."

"Fine, then I'll walk with ya."

"No way," I told him. "You're waiting for Her Hotness to show, remember?" He'd been trying to hook up with Cara Finley for two weeks now. She'd finally agreed to meet him at the party tonight, and I wasn't ruining his chances by having him bail to play guard dog.

He glanced over his shoulder. In the field under the moonlight, people were beginning to dance. "You sure you're okay to go alone?"

"Of course." I gestured to my feet. "No license needed to drive these babies."

He was hesitant, but in the end, Cara won out. We said good-bye, and I started into the dark.

Home was only a few minutes away—through the field, across a narrow stream, and over a small hill. I knew these woods so well, I could find home with my eyes closed. In fact, I practically had on more than one occasion.

Pulling my cell from my back pocket, I groaned. One a.m. If luck was with me, I'd have enough time to stumble home and tuck myself in before Dad got there. I hadn't meant to stay so late this time. Or drink so much. I'd only agreed to go as moral support for Brandt, but when Gilman started running his mouth… Well, I'd had no choice but stay and put up so he'd *shut* up. I had a rep to worry about, after all.

By the time I hit the halfway point between the field and the house—a shallow, muddy stream I used to play in as a child—I had to stop for a minute. Thumping beats and distant laughter echoed from the party, and for a moment I regretted not taking Brandt up on his offer to walk home with me. Apparently, that last beer had been a mistake.

I stumbled to the water's edge and forced the humid air in and out of my lungs. Locking my jaw and holding my breath, I mentally repeated, *I will not throw up*.

After a few minutes, the nausea passed. Thank God. No way did I want to walk home smelling like puke. I shuffled back from the water, ready to make my way home, when I heard a commotion and froze.

Crap. The music had been too loud and someone must have called the cops. Perfect. Another middle-of-the-night call from the local PD wasn't something Dad would be happy about. On second thought, bring on the cops. The look on his face would be so worth the aggravation.

I held my breath and listened. Not sounds coming from the party—men yelling.

Heavy footsteps stomping and thrashing through the brush.

The yelling came again—this time closer.

I crammed the cell back into my pocket, about to begin what was sure to be a messy climb up the embankment, when movement in the brush behind me caught my attention. I whirled in time to see someone stumble down the hill and land a few feet from the stream.

"Jesus!" I jumped back and tripped over an exposed root, landing on my butt in the mud. The guy didn't move as I fumbled upright and took several wobbly steps forward. He'd landed at an odd angle, feet bare and covered in several nasty looking slices. I squinted in the dark and saw he was bleeding through his thin white T-shirt in several places as well as from a small gash on the side of his head. The guy looked like he'd gone ten rounds with a weed whacker.

Somewhere between eighteen and nineteen, he didn't look familiar. No way he went to my high school. I knew pretty much everyone. He couldn't have been at the party—he was cute. I would have remembered. I doubted he was even local. His hair was too long, and he was missing the signature Parkview T-shirt tan. Plus, even in the dark it was easy to make out well-defined arms and broad shoulders. This guy obviously hit the gym—something the local boys could've used.

I bent down to check the gash on the side of his head, but he jerked away and staggered to his feet as the yelling came again.

"Your shoes!" he growled, pointing to my feet. His voice was deep and sent tiny shivers dancing up and down my spine. "Give me your shoes!"

Buzzed or not, I was still pretty sharp. Whoever those guys yelling in the woods were, they were after him. Drug deal gone south? Maybe he'd gotten caught playing naked footsie with someone else's girlfriend?

"Why—?"

"Now!" he hissed.

I wouldn't have even considered giving up my favorite pair of red Vans if he hadn't looked so seriously freaked. He was being chased. He thought having my shoes would somehow help? Fine. Maybe as a weapon? Rocks would have worked better in my opinion, but to each his own.

Against my better judgment, I took several steps back and, without turning away from him, pulled them off. Stepping up, I tossed him the sneakers—and teetered forward. Instead of trying to catch me, he took a wide step back, allowing me to fall into the mud.

My frickin' hero!

I struggled upright and flicked a glob of mud from my jeans as he bent down to snatch the shoes—without moving his gaze from mine. His eyes were beautiful—ice blue and intense—and I found it hard to look away. He set the sneakers on the ground and poised his right foot over the first one. A giggle rose in my throat. No way he'd be jamming his bigass feet into them.

He proved me wrong. Cramming his toes in, heels poking obscenely over the edges, he wobbled with an odd sort of grace to the embankment and wedged himself between a partially uprooted tree and a hollowed-out log. He teetered slightly as he walked, and I remembered the nasty gashes on his foot. Great. Now on top of *borrowing* my kicks, he was going to bleed all over them.

My gaze dropped to the spot he'd been standing. It was dark and the moon had tucked itself behind the clouds so I couldn't see very well, but something about the ground didn't look quite right. The color seemed off—darker than it should be.

I squinted, bending to brush my fingers along the dark spot, but more rustling in the woods had my gaze swinging hard left, heartbeat kicking into high gear. The next thing I knew, a group of four men exploded from the brush and came storming down the embankment like ravers on crack. Dressed in dark blue, skintight body suits that covered them from fingertips to toes, little was left to the imagination. Mimes. They reminded me of mimes.

Mimes with what looked a lot like Tasers.

"You!" The one in the front called out as he skidded to a stop. Looking at the ground, he surveyed the trail leading to the shallow water. "Has anyone been past here?"

From the corner of my eye I saw the boy, face pale, watching us. All the men would have had to do was turn to the right and they'd surely see him.

"Some punk came barreling through a few minutes ago." I stomped my sock-clad foot. Mud sloshed through the material and oozed between my toes. Ick! "Stole my damn shoes!"

"Which way did he go?"

Was he serious? I was about to make a joke about not being allowed to talk to strangers, but the look on his face made me think twice. Mr. Mime didn't seem like he was rocking a sense of humor. I threw my hands up in surrender and pointed in the direction opposite the one I planned on going.

Without another word, the men split into two groups. Half of them heading the way I'd directed, the other half taking off opposite. Huh. Guess they didn't trust a semi-drunk chick with a nose ring and no shoes.

I waited till they were out of sight before making my way over to where the boy crouched, still hidden behind the brush. "They're gone. I think it's safe to come out and play now."

He held my gaze and maneuvered out of the hiding spot. When he made no move to remove my sneakers, I nodded to his feet. "Planning to give my kicks back anytime soon?"

He shook his head and folded his arms. "I can't give them back to you."

"Why the hell not? Because seriously, dude, red is *not* your color."

He looked at the ground for a moment, then let his gaze wander over the path he'd traveled earlier. "I'm hungry." He was staring again. "Do you have any food?"

He gets my shoes then asks for food? The guy had some

serious nerve.

The gash on his head still oozed a little and the faint bluish-purple of a bruise was beginning to surface across his left cheek, but it was the haunted look in his eyes that stood out above everything else like a flashing neon sign. He kept flicking his fingers, one at a time. Pointer, middle, ring, and pinky—over and over.

An owl hooted and I remembered the time. Dad would be home soon. This might work to my advantage. I knew bringing the guy home would royally piss him off. He'd have puppies if he found a stranger in the house. Hell, he might even have a llama.

But while the thought of pushing Dad closer to the edge gave me warm tingles, it wasn't my only motivation. I kind of wanted a little more time with the guy. Those arms... Those *eyes*. We were all alone out in the middle of the woods. If he'd wanted to go serial killer on me, he would have made a move by now. I didn't believe he was dangerous. "My house isn't far from here—Dad went to the grocery store the other day. Lots of junk food if that's your thing."

The look in his eyes made me think he didn't trust me—which I didn't get. I'd given him my *shoes* for crap's sake. "I don't know who your friends were, but they might double back. You'll be safe at my place for a while. Maybe they'll give up."

He looked downstream and shook his head. "They are not the type of men who give up."

2

It was a straight path through the woods and across to Kinder
Street. The small cul-de-sac bordered the Parkview Nature
Preserve and was home to five houses, all painfully similar
except for their color. As we walked, I tried to get the guy to
talk a few times, but all I got were simple, one-word answers
that told me jack-shit. Eventually, I gave up and settled on
counting the heavy fall of my shoes—still on his feet—as they
clomped against the earth.

By the time the house came into view, I was dying of
curiosity.

"So, ready to fill me in yet? Who were those guys in the
fruity leotards?" I fought with the front door lock. Damn thing
always stuck. "Did you piss off a herd of male ballet dancers?"

Silence.

The door finally gave way and I stepped aside, waving him
in. He didn't move. "Well?"

"You first."

Alrighty then. Someone had a serious case of paranoia.

I stepped in and waited. It took a few moments, but finally, he crossed the threshold.

"Can you at least tell me your name?"

He wandered the room, running his fingertips along the edge of the couch and over some of Mom's old knickknacks. "Sue calls me Kale," he mumbled after a minute of hesitation. He picked up a small crystal horse, held it to his ear, then shook it several times before setting it back down and continuing on.

"Kale what?"

The question halted his inspection and earned me a funny look. In his hand was the tile ashtray Mom made at an arts and crafts fair the week before I was born. It was cheesy and cheap looking, but I was still afraid he might drop it.

"As in your last name?"

"I don't need one," he said, and returned to his surveillance. It was like he was searching for something. Picking apart each item in the room as if it might contain the clues to a mass murder—or maybe he was looking for a breath mint.

"How very Hollywood of you." I hefted the laundry basket off the floor, set it on the couch, and rummaged through it till I found a pair of Dad's sweatpants and an old T-shirt. "Here. The bathroom is upstairs—second door on the right. There should be clean towels in the closet on the first shelf if you want a shower. Take your time." *Please* take your time.

This would be the perfect payback for the ass-chewing Dad gave me for sneaking out last week. That, and it didn't hurt that Kale was a total hottie.

He made no move to take the clothes from me.

"Look, no worries, all right? Dad isn't due home for awhile and you're covered in mud and gunk." I set the clothes down on the seat in front of him and took a step back to grab a pair of my jeans from the basket.

Without taking his eyes from me, he gathered the clothes in his arms and stared. His expression was so intense I had to remind myself to keep breathing. Something about the way he watched me caused my stomach to do little flips. The eyes. Had to be. Crystalline blue and unflinching. The kind of stare that could make a girl go gaga. The kind of stare that could make *this* girl go gaga—and that was saying a lot. I wasn't easily impressed by a pretty face.

He seemed to accept this because he gave a quick nod and slowly backed out of the room and up the stairs. A few minutes later the shower hissed to life.

While I waited, I changed out of my muddy clothes and started a pot of coffee. Even if Dad didn't find a strange guy in the house when he got home, he'd be pissed about the coffee. I couldn't count the times he'd told me the El Injerto was strictly *hands off*. He even tried to hide it—as if *that* would have worked. If he wanted me to leave his coffee alone, he should go back to drinking the Kopi Luwak. No way—no matter how much I loved coffee—would I drink anything made from a bean some tree rat crapped out.

I'd almost finished folding the laundry when Kale came down the stairs.

"Much better. You look almost human." The pants were a little baggy—Kale was a few inches shorter than Dad's six three—and the shirt was a bit too big, but at least he was clean. He still had his feet crammed into my favorite red Vans. They were soaked. Had he worn them in the *shower*?

"Your name?" he asked once he'd reached the bottom, the sneakers sloshing and spitting with each step. He *had* worn them in the shower!

"Deznee, but everyone calls me Dez." I pointed to the soggy Vans. "Um, you ever gonna take my sneakers off?"

"No," he said. "I cut myself."

Maybe something wasn't screwed on right. There was a mental facility in the next town—it wasn't unheard of for patients to get out once in a while. Leave it to me to find the hottest guy in existence and have him be a total whack job. "Oh. Well, that explains it all then, doesn't it…?"

He nodded and began wandering the room again. Stopping in front of one of mom's old vases—an ugly blue thing I kept only because it was one of the few things still in the house that belonged to her—he picked it up. "Where are the plants?"

"Plants?"

He looked underneath and inside, before turning it over and shaking it as though something might come tumbling out. "This should have plants in it, right?"

I stepped forward and rescued the vase. He jerked away. "Easy there." I carefully placed the blue monstrosity back on the table and stepped back. He was staring again. "You didn't think I was going to hit you or something, did you?"

In eighth grade I'd had a classmate who we later found out was being abused at home. I remembered him being skittish— always twitching and avoiding physical contact. His eyes were a lot like Kale's, constantly darting and bobbing back and forth as though attack was imminent.

I expected him to avoid the question, or deny it—something evasive. That's what abused kids did, right? Instead, he laughed. A sharp, frigid sound that made my stomach tighten and the hairs on the back of my neck stand straight up.

It also made my blood pump faster.

He crossed his arms and stood straighter. "You couldn't hit

me."

"You'd be surprised," I countered, slightly offended. Three summers in a row at the local community center's self-defense classes. No one was hitting *this* chick.

A slow, devastating smile spread across his lips. That smile had probably ruined a lot of girls. Dark, shaggy hair, tucked behind each ear, still dripped from the shower, ice blue eyes following every move I made.

"You couldn't hit me," he repeated. "Trust me."

He turned away and wandered to the other side of the room, picking up things as he went. Everything received a quizzical, and almost critical, once-over. The trio of *Popular Science* magazines sitting on the coffee table, the vacuum I'd left leaning against one wall, even the TV remote sticking between two cushions on the couch. He stopped at a wall shelf full of DVDs, pulling one out and examining it. "Is this your family?" He brought the box closer and narrowed his eyes, turning it over in his hands several times.

"You're asking me if"—I stood on my tiptoes and looked at the box in his hands. Uma Thurman glared at me from the cover, wearing her iconic yellow motorcycle suit—"Uma Thurman is a *relative*?" Maybe he wasn't loony. Maybe he had been at the party. I'd missed the Jell-O shots, but obviously he hadn't.

"Why do you have their photograph if they're not your family?"

"Seriously, what rock did you crawl out from under?" Pointing to a small collection of frames on the mantle, I said, "Those are pictures of my family." Well, except my mom. Dad didn't keep any pictures of her in the house. I nodded to the DVDs and said, "Those are actors. In movies."

"This place is very strange," he said, picking up the first picture. Me and my first bike—a powder-pink Huffy with glitter and white streamers. "Is this you?"

I nodded, cringing. Pink sneakers, Hello Kitty sweatshirt, and pink ribbons tied to the end of each braid. Dad used it on a daily basis to point out how far I'd fallen. I'd gone from fresh-faced blonde with perky pigtails—his sunshine smile girl—to pierced nose and eyebrow with wild blonde hair highlighted by several chunky black streaks. I liked to think if my mom were alive, she'd be proud of the woman I'd become. Strong and independent—I didn't put up with anyone's crap. Including Dad's. That's how I imagined her when she was alive. An older, more beautiful version of me.

I looked at the scene in Kale's hands again. I hated that picture—the bike was the last gift Dad ever bought me. The day he gave it to me—the same day the picture was taken—had been a turning point in our lives. The very next day my relationship with Dad started to crumble. He started working longer hours at the law firm and everything changed.

Kale set the picture down and moved on to the next. His hand stopped mid-reach and his face paled. The muscles in his jaw twitched. "This was a setup," he said quietly, hand falling slack against his side.

"Huh?" I followed his gaze to the picture in question. Dad and me at last year's Community Day—neither of us smiling. As I recall, we weren't happy about taking the picture. We were less happy about being forced to stand so close to each other.

"Why not let them take me at the water's edge? Why lead me here?"

"Let who take you?"

"The men from the complex. The men from Denazen."

I blinked, sure I'd heard him wrong. "Denazen? As in the law firm?"

He turned back to the picture on the mantle. "This is *his* home, isn't it?"

"Do you know my dad?" This was priceless. Score another point for my megalomaniacal Dad. One of his cases, no doubt. Maybe some poor chump he'd sent to the happy house, because that's clearly where he belonged.

"That man is the devil," Kale replied, lips pulled back in a snarl. His voice changed from surprised to deadly in a single beat of my heart and, crazy or not, I found it kind of hot.

"My father's a shit, but the Devil? A little harsh, don't ya think?"

Kale scrutinized me for a moment, taking several additional steps back and inching his way closer to the door. "I won't let them use me anymore."

"Use you for what?" Something told me he wasn't talking about coffee runs and collations. Acid churned in my stomach.

His eyes narrowed and radiating such hatred, I actually flinched. "If you try to stop me from leaving, I'll kill you."

"Okay, okay." I held out my hands in what I hoped was a show of surrender. Something in his eyes made me believe he meant it. Instead of being freaked out—like the tiny voice of reason at the back of my brain screamed I should be—I was intrigued. That was Dad. Making friends and influencing people to threaten murder. Glad it wasn't only me. "Why don't you start by telling me who you think my dad is?"

"That man is the Devil of Denazen."

"Yeah. Devil. Caught that before. But my dad's just a lawyer. I know that in itself makes him kind of a dick, but—"

"No. That man is a killer."

My jaw dropped. Forget balls, this guy had boulders. "A killer?"

Arms rigid, Kale began flicking his fingers like he had by the stream. Pointer, middle, ring, and pinky. Again and again. Voice low, he said, "I watched him give the order to *retire* a small child three days ago. That is not what a lawyer does, correct?"

Retire? What the hell was that supposed to mean? I was about to fire off another set of questions, but there was a noise outside. A car. In the driveway.

Dad's car.

Kale must have heard it too, because his eyes went wide. He vaulted over the couch and landed beside me as Dad's keys jingled in the lock on the front door and the knob turned. Typical. The damn thing never stuck for *him*.

He stepped into the house and closed the door behind him. Eyes focused on mine, he said, "Deznee, step away from the boy." No emotion, no surprise. Only the cold, flat tone he used when speaking to me about everything ranging from toast to suspension from school.

I used to be sad about it—the fact that his career seemed to have sucked away his soul—but I was over it. Nowadays, it was easier to be mad. Trying to get a reaction from him—any reaction—was my sole purpose in life.

Kale stepped closer. At first, an insane part of my brain interpreted this to mean he was protecting me from Dad. It made sense somehow. According to him, Dad was the enemy, and I, the one who helped him back by the stream—the one who gave him my shoes and lied to those men—was a friend.

But then Kale spoke; his menacing words were delivered in a cold, harsh tone that obliterated the crazy theory.

"If you do not move aside and let me leave, I will kill her."
Some friend.

Despite Kale's threat, Dad remained in the doorway, blocking his path. "Deznee, I'm going to say this one last time. Step away from the boy."

Everything Kale said about my dad rushed bounced in my head like a bad trip, churning in my stomach like sour milk.

"What the hell is going on?" I demanded, glaring at Dad. "Do you know him?"

Dad finally made a move. Not the kind of move you'd expect from a father fearing for his teenaged daughter's life, but a simple, bold step forward. One that screamed *I dare you.*

He was playing chicken with Kale.

And he lost.

Kale shook his head, and when he spoke, he sounded kind of sad. "You should know I don't bluff, Cross. You taught me that."

His hand shot out, lightning fast, and clamped down on my neck. Warm fingers brushed my skin and curled around my throat. They were long and calloused and wrapped more than halfway. He was going to snap my neck. Or choke me. In a panic, I tried to pry his fingers away, but it was no use. His grip was like a vice. This was it. I was a goner. All the stupid stuff I'd done and survived, and a random, almost-hookup was going to do me in. Where was the fair in that?

But Kale didn't crush my windpipe or try to choke me. He just turned toward me—staring. His face pale and eyes wide. Watching me as though I was a fascinating first-place science project, mouth hanging open like I'd presented the cure for Cancer.

On my neck, his fingers twitched, and then he let go. "How—?"

Movement by the door. Dad reached into his pocket—and out came a *gun*? Things had gone from really weird to *I-fell-down-the-rabbit-hole*-surreal. My dad didn't know how to shoot a gun! He lifted the barrel and aimed it at us, hand steady.

Then again, maybe he did.

"What the hell are you doing, Dad?"

He didn't move. "There's nothing to worry about. Stay calm."

Stay calm? Was he crazy? He was pointing a gun in my general direction! If anything about that situation said calm, I was missing something.

Thankfully, my normal catlike reflexes saved our asses. Yeah. More like dumb luck. Dad squeezed the trigger and I dropped to the floor, pulling a very surprised Kale with me. I nearly ripped his arm out of its socket in the process, but it didn't seem to bother him. He wasn't concerned about the gun either, his attention still fixated on me. We hit the ground as a small projectile embedded itself into the wall behind us with a dull thud. A dart. A tranq gun? Somehow this didn't make me feel any better. I could console myself with the fact that the dart hit the wall closer to Kale than me, indicating I hadn't been the target, but still. Bullets or not, a gun was a gun. And guns freaked me the hell out.

"Move!" I hauled Kale to his feet and shoved him through the door and into the kitchen. He stumbled forward but managed to keep himself upright. Impressive considering he still had on my ill-fitting, soggy sneakers.

"Deznee!" Dad bellowed from the living room. Heavy footsteps pounded against the hardwood as he chased after us. No way was I stopping.

Dad had a specific tone he used when mad at me—which

was like, ninety-eight percent of the time—and it never fazed me. In fact, I found it kind of funny. But tonight was different. Something in his voice told me I'd gone above and beyond and it scared me a little.

Something shattered—probably the half-full glass of Coke I'd left on the coffee table last night while watching "SNL" reruns. "Get back here! You have no idea what you're doing!"

What else was new? Truthfully, even if the gun hadn't freaked me out, it was obvious Kale, despite the badass vibe, was afraid of my dad. He'd been through something brutal—and Dad had somehow played a part in it. I wasn't sure why this guy's past was so important, but I needed to find out.

I propelled him out the back door and into the cool night air. We didn't stop—even when we came to the property line. And even as we put distance between Dad and us at a breakneck speed, I could still hear my father's angry words echoing in the cold night, "This isn't one of your goddamn games!"

"We're almost there," I said. We'd stopped running a few minutes ago so we could catch our breath. Kale hadn't spoken since he'd threatened to kill me, only continued to stare as though I'd grown a second—and third—head. I was full of questions, but they could wait for now.

We finally reached the mustard-yellow Cape Cod on the other side of the railroad tracks and followed a small stone path around the back, to a set of bilko doors that had been spray painted black. Written across the front in bulbous white graffiti was *Curd's Castle*. I kicked the hatch twice, then waited. Several moments later, with an ear-piercing clatter, the doors opened, and a spiky, blond- and purple-streaked head popped out. Curd. With a nod and a too-eager smile, he waved us inside as if we were expected.

We descended the dark cement staircase and stepped into a dimly lit room. It was surprisingly clean—none of the typical staples you'd expect to see when walking into a seventeen-year-old guy's room were visible. No half-eaten plates of food or empty soda cans. No scattered piles of video games or magazines. There weren't even any posters of skanky women in obscene poses on the wall. Not that Curd wasn't a dog. The place may have looked clean, but it smelled of sex and pot.

Kurt Curday—Curd to his adoring public—was the go-to guy for all your partying needs. Kegs, pot, X, Curd could get it all. A big name on the raver scene and fellow senior-to-be, Curd was one of the organizers of Sumrun. The party, one of the biggest raves in four counties, was a week away, so Curd was a busy guy.

"Dez, baby, I'd be much happier to see you if you weren't towing along a little pet." He ran a finger up my arm, then curled a lock of my hair around his thumb, "But hey, I'm up for whatever."

"This isn't a social call, Curd." I glanced at Kale. He stood stiffly by the door, eyes fixed on Curd's finger running along my skin. His gaze lifted to mine, and I felt a shiver skitter up my spine. Shaking it off, I shuffled away from Curd and into the room. "I got into some trouble with my dad again. I need a place to lay low. You were the closest."

He shot me a disappointed frown and flopped onto the futon, kicking his heels onto a small, rickety table. "Not to worry, baby. What'd ya get caught doing this time?"

I forced a sly smile and shrugged. "Oh, you know, the usual." I hitched my thumb back at Kale. "What Dad is thrilled to find a half-naked guy in his daughter's bedroom?" I hoped that would explain the clothing Kale wore—clothing that obviously wasn't his.

"Such a little hellcat." He blew me an exaggerated kiss. A grin that told me he was picturing himself in Kale's place slipped across his face. "Tell me again why we haven't hooked up yet?"

I sank into the chair across from him. "I don't like dealers?"

"Oh yeah, that's right. How could I forget?" He nodded in Kale's direction. "Who's the mute?"

"Curd, Kale." I waved in Kale's direction. "Kale, Curd."

"I touched you," Kale interjected after a moment of silence.

Curd snickered. "If you were in *her* bed, I certainly hope you weren't touching yourself." He turned to me, right eyebrow cocked. "Is he *special*?"

I glared at him.

He shrugged. "You guys thirsty? I'll go find some soda — or something a little harder?"

I sighed and said, "Soda's fine."

Kale watched Curd disappear up the narrow staircase leading to the first floor and took a step forward. He repeated his previous statement. "I touched you."

"Yes," was all I could manage. His blue eyes pinned me to the chair. A mishmash of emotion raged inside my head. I was torn between checking the exits for men in weird suits and checking out Kale. And then I remembered Dad and the gun...

"You're still alive."

"Should I not be?" There was that look again. Like he was standing in the presence of some mythical creature and had been granted a year's supply of wishes. It made me uncomfortable. It's not like I wasn't used to being stared at, and to be fair, I'd done my fair share of staring tonight, but this was different. Intense in a way I'd never felt before.

He took another step forward, head tilted to the side. "That's never happened. Ever." He reached for me, hesitating for a moment before pulling his hand back. "Can...can I touch you again?"

I probably should have been weirded out by a question like that. Any other day, I would have been, but Kale's eyes sparkled with wonder and curiosity. Gone was the cold expression he'd worn back at my house. His voice was soft, but there was a fierce longing in it that made my mouth go dry. I pushed my discomfort aside, nodded, and stood.

For a big guy, he moved surprisingly fast, darting around the coffee table to stand in front of me. Close. Breathing-the-same-air kind of close. I expected him to grab my wrist, or maybe my arm, but instead he brought his right hand up to cup the side of my face.

"You're so warm," he said in awe as his thumb traced whisper light under my eye—like wiping away tears. "So soft. I've never felt anything like it."

Neither had I. His thumb, barely skating across my skin, left a trail of warm tingles in its wake that spread throughout my entire body. His breath, puffing out softly across my nose and forehead, was warm and sweet, almost dizzying.

A loud clanking rang from upstairs—Curd must have dropped something—snapping me out of it. I cleared my throat. "Um, thanks?"

"You helped me escape Cross," he said, stepping back. "I tried to kill you, and you helped me escape. Why?"

I shrugged. "My dad's a dick. Pissing him off is a hobby. 'Sides, you didn't really *try* to kill me. You were scared."

"I don't get scared."

"Everyone gets scared."

Now wasn't the time to argue. I needed answers. Things started churning in the back of my brain. Strange, late-night phone calls. Oddly timed trips to the office. All things that, had I been paying attention, might have popped up as red flags. "You said my dad was a killer. That's some kind of euphemism, right?"

"I'm one of his weapons."

"Weapons?"

"He uses me."

The way he said it gave me chills. The creepy kind, this time. "To what? Like, spy on the other side's clients?" Even though I knew it was likely crap now, my subconscious was desperate to hang onto the belief that Dad was a lawyer.

"No."

I folded my arms, getting irritated. "Then give me a hint here. What is it you do for Dad?"

Taking two steps forward, blue eyes bright, he spoke softly. "I kill for him."

I blinked and tried to visualize Dad as the big bad. Couldn't do it. Or wouldn't. Sure, he was a tool and we hadn't really talked in years, but a killer? No way.

Turning his palms upward, Kale raised both hands and flexed his fingers. "They bring death to anything I touch."

I remembered the ground he walked across at the stream had looked wrong. Discolored.

I passed it off on the beer at the time, but…

He jerked away each time I got close enough to touch him…

He wouldn't take my shoes off…

The air caught in my lungs and the room began to shrink. "Your skin…?"

I would've called bullshit, but I of all people knew first hand crazy shit was possible. Plus, there'd been rumors floating through the raver scene for years now, ever since a local boy was arrested during Sumrun seven years ago. Rumor had it, the guy shorted out the electricity with a single touch of his fingers after being chased to the party by police. After they took him away, no one ever saw him again.

"Is deadly to anything living. Except you. How am I able to touch you? Everyone else would have died a horrible death."

I took a step back. It was hard to concentrate with him staring like that. "Let's focus here for a sec. You're trying to tell me that my dad uses you as a weapon? A weapon against what exactly?"

His face fell. "Not what, who."

"Who?" I really didn't want to hear his answer. Either my mysterious hottie was crazy or Dad was… Well, either way his answer was bound to throw another bird at my building.

"People. He uses me to punish people."

"My dad has you touch people? To *kill* them?"

"That is correct." The shame in his voice was like a vacuum, stealing all the air from the room. Eyes rising to meet mine, he reached out and ran his finger along the line of my chin and to my cheek, letting his touch linger for a few moments. I found myself wanting to take it all away. The heavy, sad look in his eyes. The pain in his voice. I could do it, maybe. Tell him something about myself that might make him feel less alone. Less isolated. A secret I've never spoken aloud before.

I opened my mouth, but when the words came out they weren't what I'd expected. "You're wrong. My dad's a *lawyer*." The walls that had been in place for as far back as I could remember stood strong.

"A lawyer kills people?"

"Are you serious?" This so wasn't happening. Dad wasn't part of some super-secret conspiracy theory. He was a stick-up-the-ass control freak workaholic. With weird hours. And, for some reason, a gun. Not a killer.

Kale's face remained blank.

"Of course they don't kill people! They put the bad guys away, get rid of 'em so they can't hurt anyone." Not the most accurate description, but the simplest I could come up with.

"No, that's definitely not what your father does. That's what *I* do. The Denazen Corporation uses me to punish those who have done wrong. I'm a Six. Does that make *me* a lawyer?"

Ugh. So much for simple. "What the hell is a Six?"

"It's what we're called."

O-kaay. "And punish those who've done wrong? Who says what's right and wrong?"

"Denazen, of course." He frowned and turned away. "And I belong to them."

"Where the hell are your parents?"

Voice barely a whisper, he said, "I don't have any parents."

"You're a human being, not a weapon. You don't *belong* to anyone," I hissed. "And of course you have parents, even if you don't know where they are."

Fuming, I ripped the little leather cardholder from my back pocket and tugged out a picture. My mom. I'd found it years ago in Dad's bottom desk drawer. I'd only known who she was because of her name written on the back in scrawling blue ink. Dad refused to talk about her—he told me her name, gave me a brief, watery description—and that was it. As I got older, I'd started looking more and more like the woman in the picture, which was probably why he hated me. I'd catch him watching me once in awhile. Like he might have been imagining it was her sitting there, and not me. Like he wished it was her instead of me. It made sense. It was my fault he'd lost her, after all. She'd died having me. Sometimes I hated myself, too.

"My mom is gone—that doesn't mean I don't have one." I shook the photo at him.

Kale closed the gap between us and took the picture from my hands. He purposefully let his fingers brush my wrist, giving a quick smile. "This is your mother?"

I nodded.

"You don't visit her?"

"I can't *visit* her, she's dead."

"She's not dead. She lives at the complex with me." He wandered away, picture still in his hands, and picked up a pair of Curd's worn boots. Leaning back against the wall, he kicked off my Vans and slipped on the boots. The sneakers fell to the floor with a heavy thud.

The world stopped. The air, the four walls, everything, it all fell away. "What?"

He held up the picture. "This is Sue."

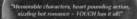

GRAVITY

Melissa West

In the future, only one rule will matter:
Don't. Ever. Peek.

Seventeen-year-old Ari Alexander just broke that rule and saw the last
person she expected hovering above her bed—arrogant Jackson Locke,
the most popular boy in her school. She expects instant execution or
some kind of freak alien punishment, but instead, Jackson issues a
challenge: help him, or everyone on Earth will die.

Ari knows she should report him, but everything about Jackson makes
her question what she's been taught about his kind. And against her
instincts, she's falling for him.

But Ari isn't just any girl, and Jackson wants more than
her attention. She's a military legacy who's been
trained by her father and exposed to war
strategies and societal information no
one can know—especially an alien
spy, like Jackson. Giving
Jackson the information he
needs will betray her
father and her country,
but keeping silent
will start a war.

Gravity
drops
10.09.2012

Death doesn't fall
in love. Usually.

Coming to a bookstore near you

08.07.2012

inbetween

a kissed by death
book 1

tara fuller

Pretty Amy

a novel by Lisa Burstein

Sometimes date is a four-letter word...

Amy is fine living in the shadows of beautiful Lila and uber–cool Cassie, because at least she's somewhat beautiful and uber–cool by association. But when their dates stand them up for prom, and the girls take matters into their own hands—earning them a night in jail outfitted in satin, stilettos, and Spanx—Amy discovers even a prom spent in handcuffs might be better than the humiliating "rehabilitation techniques" now filling up her summer. Even worse, with Lila and Cassie parentally banned, Amy feels like she has nothing—like she is nothing.

Navigating unlikely alliances with her new coworker, two very different boys, and possibly even her parents, Amy struggles to decide if it's worth being a best friend when it makes you a public enemy. Bringing readers along on an often hilarious and heartwarming journey, Amy finds that maybe getting a life only happens once you think your life is over.

Coming to a bookstore near you

05.15.2012

Pretty Amy

a novel by Lisa Burstein

Keepers of Life
BOOK ONE

"Reading Shea Berkley is like
watching magic unfold before your
eyes. I could not get enough of this
delicious tale."
– Dacynda Jones, author of
First Grave on the Right

THE MARKED
SON
SHEA BERKLEY

THE LOST
PRINCE
SHEA BERKLEY

THE BASTARD
KING
SHEA BERKLEY

THE KEEPERS OF LIFE SERIES
BY SHEA BERKLEY

Seventeen-year-old Dylan Kennedy
always knew something was different about
him, but until his mother abandoned him in
the middle of Oregon with grandparents he's
never met, he had no idea what.
When Dylan sees a girl in the woods behind
his grandparents' farm, he knows he's seen
her before...in his dreams. He's felt her fear.
Heard her insistence that only he can save
her world from an evil lord who uses magic
and fear to feed his greed for power.
Unable to shake the unearthly pull to Kera,
Dylan takes her hand. Either he's completely
insane or he's about to have the adventure
of his life, because where they're going is full
of creatures he's only read about in horror
stories. Worse, the human blood in his veins
has Dylan marked for death...

AVAILABLE ONLINE AND IN STORES EVERYWHERE...

HE'S SAVED HER.

HE'S LOVED HER.

HE'S KILLED FOR HER.

HUSHED
KELLEY YORK

Eighteen-year-old Archer couldn't protect his best friend, Vivian, from what happened when they were kids, so he's never stopped trying to protect her from everything else. It doesn't matter that Vivian only uses him when hopping from one toxic relationship to another—Archer is always there, waiting to be noticed.

Then along comes Evan, the only person who's ever cared about Archer without a single string attached. The harder he falls for Evan, the more Archer sees Vivian for the manipulative hot-mess she really is.

But Viv has her hooks in deep, and when she finds out about the murders Archer's committed and his relationship with Evan, she threatens to turn him in if she doesn't get what she wants... And what she wants is Evan's death, and for Archer to forfeit his last chance at redemption.

HUSHED

AVAILABLE ONLINE AND IN STORES EVERYWHERE

flawed

kate avelynn

he'll never let her forget her half of the pact...

Sarah O'Brien is only alive because of the pact she and her brother made twelve years ago—James will protect her from their violent father if she promises to never leave him. For years, she's watched James destroy his life to save hers. If all he asks for in return is her affection, she'll give it freely.

Until, with a tiny kiss and a broken mind, he asks for more than she can give.

Sam Donavon has been James's best friend—and the boy Sarah's had a crush on—for as long as she can remember. As their forbidden relationship deepens, Sarah knows she's in trouble. Quiet, serious Sam has decided he's going to save her. Neither of them realize James is far more unstable than her father ever was, or that he's not about to let Sarah forget her half of the pact...

Coming to a bookstore near you

07.10.2012

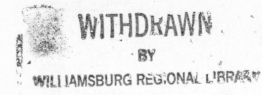